Sunset House

Ellie Jordan, Ghost Trapper,

Book Eighteen

by

J. L. Bryan

Published March 2023

JLBryanbooks.com

Acknowledgments

Thanks to my wife Christina for her support and my son Johnny for always doing his homework and his chores.

I appreciate everyone who helped with this book, including beta reader Robert Duperre (check out his books!). Thanks also to copy editor Lori Whitwam and proofreaders Thelia Kelly, Andrea van der Westhuizen, and Barb Ferrante. Thanks to my cover artist Claudia from PhatPuppy Art, and her daughter Catie, who does the lettering on the covers.

Thanks also to the book bloggers who have supported the series, including Heather from Bewitched Bookworms; Michelle from Much Loved Books; Shirley from Creative Deeds; Kelly from Reading the Paranormal; Lili from Lili Lost in a Book; Kelsey from Kelsey's Cluttered Bookshelf; and Ali from My Guilty Obsession.

Most of all, thanks to the readers who have supported this series!

Also by J. L. Bryan:

The Ellie Jordan, Ghost Trapper series
Ellie Jordan, Ghost Trapper
Cold Shadows
The Crawling Darkness
Terminal
House of Whispers
Maze of Souls
Lullaby
The Keeper
The Tower
The Monster Museum
Fire Devil
The Necromancer's Library
The Trailwalker
Midnight Movie
The Lodge
Cabinet Jack
Fallen Wishes
Sunset House
The Funtime Show

Urban Fantasy/Horror
The Unseen
Inferno Park

Time Travel/Dystopian
Nomad

For my parents

Coming soon...

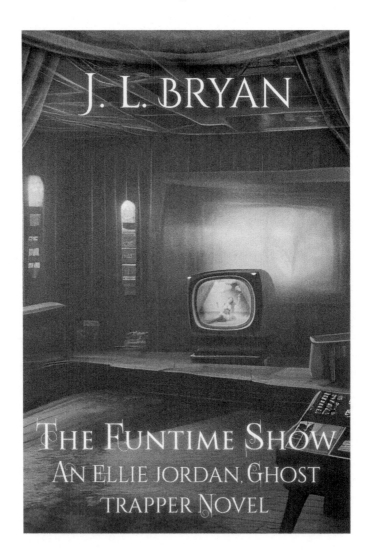

Chapter One

The morning started off more than promising.

At sunrise, I hopped into the ancient black Camaro I'd inherited from my father. I seemed to catch every green light in Savannah between my apartment and Duck Donuts, arriving just as the shop opened for the day. I picked up three wickedly appealing doughnuts and three iced coffees—plain with a little cream for me, mocha for my boyfriend Michael, and salted caramel latte for his younger sister Melissa.

An upbeat song thumped on the radio, and I turned up the volume. It was "Slow Down" by Selena Gomez. Ironically, the fast beat encouraged me to press the accelerator a little harder.

Another point in the "promising morning" column was the cooling clouds blanketing the sky, breaking up the summer's long, blistering heatwave. It had even rained a couple of times in the past week. It was

August, following a painfully hot, dry July, but Labor Day and autumn were finally in sight.

"Good luck, Melissa," I said to my reflection in the rearview mirror. "I know you'll do great. It'll be so... great." I sighed, feeling stupid for rehearsing what I'd say to her. Melissa's attitude toward me was by turns hot and cold, reflecting her mixed feelings about my relationship with her brother. My work meant constant danger for those around me, and she and Michael had both suffered for it, had taken turns being possessed by an entity intent on tormenting me. We'd won that battle, but the war for my place in their tiny, two-person family continued.

"I know you'll do great, Melissa," I repeated. "Or 'well'? I know you'll do well." Too bland? "You'll kill it up there, Melissa!" Too violent?

I parked at their building, a nineteenth-century Queen Anne house divided into apartments long ago. As I left my car, I looked up at the turret window where Michael's bed was located behind a drawn curtain.

Melissa was crossing the front porch toward the small parking area, the hard plastic wheels of her rolling suitcase clanking over the floorboards. She grunted as she lifted the suitcase to carry it down the front steps.

"Hey, Melissa!" I greeted her as brightly as I could manage, which was apparently a notch too loud, because she looked up at me, startled, and nearly tripped over the last step, almost suffering a nasty fall because of me. I ran to help her, though I couldn't do much with a three-coffee to-go caddy in one hand and a box of ultra-premium doughnuts in the other. "Sorry!"

She recovered nimbly, not surprising for someone

with years of soccer games and dance lessons behind her.

"I got you an iced salted caramel." I held out the coffee caddy. "And a blueberry lemonade doughnut, to celebrate your first day as a Blue Devil. I always see the blueberry lemonade on the menu, and it always sounds good, but I never actually get it—"

"My hands are full." She rolled on past me, her voice unusually thick, her green eyes a little damp and swollen. She'd pulled her blonde hair back in a loose, careless ponytail, and her shoulders slumped morosely under her soccer jersey.

"Oh, right, sorry. I'll set these on the porch."

Michael emerged from the door to the first-floor hallway where the big house's various staircases and apartment entrances converged. He was hung like a summer clearance rack, sporting a selection of small luggage, handbags, and a mesh laundry bag full of towels and sheets. He wore a pensive frown, an unusual look for him, until he saw me and smiled, putting up a positive front.

"Good morning," I said, then kissed him. "I brought you coffee for the big road trip. And a maple bacon doughnut. You can thank me when you come back from North Carolina."

"Thanks," he said, trying but failing to put more cheer into it. "I'll grab it in a second."

"Can I help carry anything?" I set the coffee and doughnuts on the railing and took the laundry bag from him. Dropping my voice, I asked, "Is Melissa okay?"

"She's been eager to leave all summer, but now she's suddenly afraid to go." Michael started down the stairs.

"You mean she's feeling several months' worth of delayed and deferred fear and anxiety, all at once."

"Way to totally just psychoanalyze me," Melissa grumbled, returning empty-handed from the parking area.

"Sorry," I told her yet again. My social skills were really in peak form today. "But fear is totally normal when you're facing a major life change. You're going to do so well at Duke."

"Yeah, you'll totally kill it!" Michael said, and she smiled. Drat, missed opportunity.

"I know you'll be fine," I said. "Everyone who's ever met you knows it, probably."

"It's just so far away." Melissa looked up at the third-floor windows to the apartment where she and her brother had lived since their mother's death. "I'm leaving everything behind."

"Doesn't feel that way to me." Michael trudged past her, loaded down with her belongings.

"You went to college here in town, Ellie," she said. "Why didn't I do that? It would be cheaper."

"Because you were lucky enough to get a scholarship," I said. "It's smart to take advantage of that."

"It doesn't cover everything, though. I'll still graduate with debt—"

"Which you'll pay off with help from your degree," Michael said, before turning the corner to the house's driveway. "Because you'll pick something smart that earns you a good living."

"No pressure, though," Melissa grumbled. "I'll just start by digging a big, dark hole of debt and jumping in. That's what I feel like I'm doing right now, actually, jumping into a dark hole." She looked up at her own bedroom window again.

"That's not what you're doing at all," I said. "Listen, after my parents died, I had to go live with my cousins in Virginia. I didn't really know them well. New school, new everything. I thought I'd never fit in, never find my, uh, tribe, as some people like to say."

"But you finally did?" Melissa asked, with a sort of fragile hope in her voice.

"Well…" I looked back on my later high school years, living in the shadow of my ebullient cousin Alison, who moved like a glowing lamp of bottomless glee through what felt to me like a bleak adolescent nightmare of an existence. I'd kept away from other kids, a weird loner reading arcane books and hanging around cemeteries in the dark hours of the morning, trying to understand how the dead behaved and why they haunted the living. "Not really, but I'm a bad example."

"Great." Melissa sighed and shook her head.

"That's because I *chose* to keep to myself," I said. "I didn't want to put down any roots because I wanted to move back here to Savannah. You'll make different choices, because you're going somewhere you chose. It's the power of making your own choice that matters. You'll belong there, you'll put down all kinds of new roots, and branch out into an exciting new life, and… sprout new twigs and leaves, I guess…"

"And acorns," Michael added, rejoining us. "Or cashews, because you're totally nuts."

"Shut up!" Melissa scowled.

"With that attitude, you can drive yourself to North Carolina," Michael said.

"I *am* driving. The whole way." She drew car keys from her pocket and jingled them like Christmas bells.

"That was not part of the deal."

"You said I needed to practice, Mikey."

"I didn't say I wanted to be in the car when it happened." He shook his head and returned inside.

They loaded Melissa's possessions into her car, a 1980s Pontiac with a sharply sloping hatchback. Michael had rescued it from a junkyard and repaired it by hand, as he often did with antiquated bits of machinery. He'd done the same with his own blazing-red 1949 Chevy truck.

"I'm jealous of this car," I told Melissa as she climbed into the driver's seat. The sunroof was open, letting the breeze of the relatively cool summer day pass through.

"Don't worry, I've drilled her in every aspect of maintaining this beast." Michael slid into the shotgun seat and patted the dashboard affectionately.

"Drilled and drilled." Melissa rolled her eyes. "I got it all the first time."

"There's nothing to worry about," I said. "You're starting a great adventure, Melissa. And you *are* going to kill it."

"That's what I keep hearing," she said.

I walked around behind the car, aiming for the passenger side so I could say goodbye to Michael, but maybe Melissa didn't realize that, or she was just anxious to get going on her life-changing road trip.

Either way, I tried not to take it personally as she drove away, hoping it wasn't me that she was so eager to flee from.

"Oh, wait!" I yelled after them. "Your doughnuts!"

I sprinted to the porch and back, sloshing cold coffee and whipped cream everywhere as I waved my caffeinated, sugary offerings at them.

They turned out of sight a few blocks away and apparently hadn't noticed me trying to stop them, because they didn't circle back. They headed out of town, stranding me at their empty home with too much coffee and too many doughnuts for one person.

Chapter Two

After they left, I needed to go meet Stacey at our office. A potential client was expecting us to visit that morning, and the location was a bit of a drive from Savannah, out in a remote, rural part of south Georgia.

My encounter with Michael and Melissa, and the sight of them driving off without a backward glance at me—even when I had free doughnuts—had left me feeling extra alone. I really could identify with Melissa's fear of the huge change in her young life, though surely her situation would turn out far more positive than mine had.

Maybe that was why I drove out of the way to visit the suburban neighborhood where I'd grown up. I had memories of it being a reasonably happy place, with kids occasionally bicycling or skateboarding in the street, a place were people hung bright, blinking, fabulously tacky decorations during the holidays.

In more recent years, it had taken a turn for the worse, the decay seeming to spread from the empty lot where my house burned down to the houses beside it, which had fallen into disrepair and neglect, turning the whole neighborhood gloomy.

The last time I'd visited, months earlier, some construction company had cleared out my family's old lot, preparing to build something new there. I hadn't checked on it recently, but now I found myself in the mood to have a look, to go kicking at the loose stones of my past.

What I found was not at all what I expected.

For as long as I could remember, the front of the neighborhood had been marked with a tall, gradually decaying wooden sign installed when the neighborhood was built back in the 1970s. A jaunty sailboat design had adorned the words *Riverside Point*, an utter scam of a neighborhood name since the river was nowhere nearby.

Now that sign was gone, along with the entire neighborhood.

The earth was churned up everywhere, construction equipment rolling behind temporary orange-mesh fencing. The original streets remained, so far, but that was about it.

I pulled into the neighborhood and immediately had to stop at a row of traffic cones blocking the street. A muscular, dark-skinned man with a gray beard and yellow hard hat approached, so I lowered my car window.

"Can I help you?" he asked.

"I, uh..." I really didn't have an answer. I doubted

he could help me. "I used to live here."

"Oh, yeah?" He was being polite, but I could sense the impatience behind it. He kept watching me, waiting for me to say more, to get to whatever annoying point I'd come to make while interrupting his work.

Alongside the main road, where Mrs. Hernandez's house and giant azaleas had once stood, a huge sign presented an artist's conception of a three-level community loaded with cutesy wooden benches and stacked-stone walls. Shoppers browsed at boutiques and dined at cafes on the bottom level, while happy-looking couples stood on plant-filled apartment balconies above, beaming in awe at the incredibly convenient stores below.

Coming soon, the sign read, **Ocean Bluff Terrace, an exciting new mixed-use village! The finest in retail living!**

"Ocean Bluff?" I said. "That's even more of a lie than Riverside Point. We are miles from the ocean."

"True," the construction guy said, still acting polite, "but I can't let you park here, ma'am."

"Sure. Of course. It's just a shock. I came here expecting a glimpse at the old neighborhood, and I know it was in bad shape, but I had no idea all *this* was happening." I shook my head, trying to reconcile a hundred competing childhood memories of walking my dog, trick-or-treating, and playing hide-and-seek with the neighbor kids against the empty wasteland laid bare in front of me.

His expression softened. "I see how it would be a surprise. But I saw it before the tear-down, and honestly, I think this is going to be a step up. It'll be a good place."

I nodded. "I hope so."

"Sorry about your old house, though," he said.

"Well, the house was already gone."

He nodded. "I felt the same when I visited my grandparents' old place, found it blown over by a storm. Guess it's why they say you can't go home again."

"That's true." I watched bulldozers clear away the stand of trees where a few middle-schoolers had once built a treehouse. I'd been nine at the time, too young to qualify for entry to their club.

"I'm going to need you to leave the area," the construction guy added. "For everyone's safety."

"Right. Sorry." I smiled up at him and noticed him eyeballing my surplus of coffee and doughnuts. "Would you, uh, like an iced mocha or salted caramel?"

"Salted caramel," he said, but I noticed his eyes still lingered on the Duck Donut bag.

"Maple bacon or—" I reached into the bag.

"Maple bacon." The guy did not care about the other options. He gave me a huge smile as I forked over the coffee and doughnut. "Thanks. You made my day, kid."

"Glad I could make somebody's." I gave him a sort of awkward wave and then put my car in reverse, rolling slowly past the Ocean Bluff Terrace sign to the neighborhood.

A New Home is Coming for You! the sign proclaimed.

"Sounds vaguely threatening," I muttered as I hit the road. My phone rang. Stacey was calling, no doubt already waiting at work because I was running late.

Chapter Three

"Ooh, Duck Donuts?" Stacey leaned into my Camaro's passenger-side window after I'd pulled into the back of the workshop through the garage door. Stacey had also parked her green Escape in there, and the two cars together barely fit.

She'd already pulled the van out and had it waiting by the curb, too, which was something of a subtle comment on how late I was.

"You can have the blueberry lemonade doughnut," I said.

"Iced coffee, too?" Stacey grabbed Michael's abandoned mocha, still full to the brim. I'd already drained mine. "Ellie, I don't say this enough, but I love you." She took a sip, then made a sour face.

"There might be some ice melt by now," I said. "Sorry."

"It's okay." Stacey gave me a weak smile. "Even a melty mocha is better than no mocha. Usually."

I left my car and we climbed into the van. "How far are we traveling, again?"

"Fifty miles, but half of it's highway," Stacey said. "A little place called Burdener's Hill, way out in farming country. Maybe it'll be pretty!"

"Or maybe it'll be rundown and bleak," I said.

The interstate wasn't far from our location in the industrial area around Telfair Road. Once there, we made good time, enjoying the crisp bite of our van's recently repaired air conditioning.

We eventually turned off onto a country highway, taking us through many fields and stands of pine trees, and an occasional small town just big enough for a gas station, a barber shop, and maybe a feed store. A couple of rickety roadside stands offered fresh cucumbers, melons, and boiled peanuts.

A rail line ran parallel to the road, but we didn't see any trains coming. Weeds between the rails suggested they didn't get much use anymore, but the line didn't look totally abandoned.

A pasture of cows regarded us indifferently, jaws working like sullen, bored kids chewing bubble gum.

The town of Burdener's Hill did indeed have a bit of a sloping grade, though it wouldn't have counted as a hill up near the Appalachians. For the coastal plain region, though, it was pretty significant.

The rail line running parallel to us crossed another line, definitely abandoned, at a derelict brick depot at the foot of the hill, which sat alongside other old, disused buildings that might have been warehouses. The hill appeared to be the town's main street, though easily half of the businesses were shuttered relics, including a brick building labeled Morgan's Groceries and another labeled Hillside Hardware. Topsy's Diner had some signs of life, with an OPEN sign inside the glass door and shadows moving behind the dim windows.

At the crest of the town's hill, just beyond the tiny town hall with two columns and a churchyard full of headstones, towered a three-story, charcoal-colored Victorian house, the sharp peaks of its roofline soaring into the cloudy gray sky. Its high windows cast an imperial stare down along the mostly empty main street.

"Looks like that big house is our destination," Stacey said, checking the map on her phone.

"The lady did say you can't miss it." I drove us up the town's main street and parked outside the low, wrought-iron fence enclosing the mansion's lawn, home to wide-spreading magnolias and ancient oaks with twisting, gnarled limbs.

We parked on the brick driveway and walked up a long, shallow wooden ramp to the front porch. Heavy drapes darkened every window, concealing everything inside the house.

We rang the doorbell. About half a minute later, the door creaked inward toward a dim interior. A piano played in a soft minor key somewhere inside.

The elderly man inside glared at us. Half his face had the melted, shriveled look of bad burn scars, leaving one side of his mouth in a permanent angry-looking sneer. An eyepatch covered one eye. His appearance caught me off-guard, but I tried not to visibly react.

"What is it?" he asked, sounding grouchy. "Who are you?"

"Um, sorry to disturb you, sir," I said, consciously keeping my voice steady. "I'm Ellie Jordan, here for an appointment with Arden Stroup. Do we have the wrong address?" I double-checked the gray metal house numbers nailed beside the door, but they matched what the woman had told me.

"What do you want with Arden?" He narrowed his eyes suspiciously.

"She contacted us, actually—"

"Karl! Are you trying to scare these poor girls?" Another elderly man emerged from the depths of the house, turning up the lights in the front room. He looked to be somewhere in his seventies, but chunkier than the other guy and with a big smile rather than a scowl. He wore a cap with a bear mascot over his thin wisps of white hair. He looked Stacey and me over as he clapped Karl on the back. "They're probably just selling candy bars for their softball team."

"We're actually a tiny bit older than that," Stacey said. The man in the bear-mascot hat grinned and reached a trembling hand toward her, offering a handshake. Stacey took it gently, like she didn't want to break it.

"I'm sorry, you young folks all look the same these days. Hard to tell a middle schooler from a college kid, you know? I'm Joe Granberry, but everyone calls me Coach Joe. Led Mortimer County High to three straight triple-A football championships, '82 to '84. Ever heard of those games?"

"Congratulations!" Stacey said.

"And this poor slob trying to give you nightmares

is Karl Moller, my roommate."

"Only until one of us dies," Karl said, half a smile curling up the non-burned side of his mouth. He wore a frayed, checkered workshirt over old jeans. Coach Joe wore the kind of light khaki shorts that my own high school coaches had commonly worn, though some puffy extra padding indicated an adult diaper underneath.

"There he goes again." Coach Joe shook his head. "Allow me to invite y'all in, since Karl lacks any basic courtesy."

"They're here to see Arden," Karl told him as Stacey and I stepped into the foyer area, dominated by a grand, dark staircase that curved away to the second floor, the handrail spiraling up like a polished black tentacle where it ended by the bottom step.

On the wall, an array of framed photographs showed small groups of people at holidays and birthdays. The faces changed over the years, but in every group, the majority of people were in their elder years. Arden hadn't explained on the phone that she lived in a group retirement home, but that was what it looked like. A framed cross-stitch featured a cutesy, brightly colored cottage over the words:

The Sunshine House
Where Memories are Made

"Ar-den!" Coach Joe shouted toward the back of the house through cupped hands, like he was calling a struggling player off one of the ball fields he'd once ruled.

The piano music faltered, then gradually picked up

again as an elderly woman shuffled out from the back of the house, holding her back stiffly upright, as if walking was difficult but she wasn't going to dignify the pain by acknowledging it. She had a short crop of steel-gray hair and wore a plain beige blouse with brown slacks. Somewhere behind her, a frail female voice accompanied the piano, almost too soft to hear, and finally I recognized the song as "All I Have to Do Is Dream," the golden oldie made famous by the Everly Brothers.

"Arden, did you order a couple of girls?" Coach Joe asked, pointing at us.

Ignoring him, Arden continued toward us. "I'm Arden Stroup."

"Hello, Ms. Stroup, I'm Ellie Jordan. We spoke on the phone. This is my associate, Stacey Tolbert—"

"Arden," she said, her tone sharp. "Only salespeople call me Ms. Stroup."

"Okay, Arden," I replied, in a conciliatory tone, "It's so nice to meet you. Maybe you'd like to show us where you're having difficulties."

"Difficulties?" Arden snorted. "This goes way beyond 'difficulties,' kiddo. Come on up."

With her obvious difficulty walking, I wondered how she would manage the long, curving staircase. She didn't go anywhere near them, but instead took us down a side hall to an unusually wide door.

"Would you like some company there, Arden?" Coach Joe asked, trailing after us as if our arrival was the most interesting event of the week.

"Go back to the recital, Joe, or Georgette will wonder why so many are walking out." Arden opened the door and ushered Stacey and me into what looked like an empty coat closet with scuffed wood paneling, a threadbare carpet, and a round cut-glass light fixture overhead. She stepped in with us, closed the door, and pressed a single unmarked button set in an ornate brass plate.

The tiny room lurched, rattled, and began to rise.

"It's so nice they have an elevator," Stacey said. "Luxurious."

"Don't be fooled," Arden said. "This place might look frou-frou on the outside, but it's hardly the Waldorf. Not unless the Waldorf has palmetto bugs as big as your middle finger."

The elevator clunked to a stop, and we stepped out into a second-floor hallway. The upstairs was similar to the downstairs—a lot of dark wood, heavy curtains, and a smattering of antique lamps and potted plants. Arden led us down the hall to her room.

Arden's room was spacious, with more frills than I was expecting—lacy doilies on the end table, lots of ruffled throw pillows on the bed, cosmetics and costume jewelry crowding a light-studded vanity table.

"Georgette lived here first, but her old roommate died." Arden eased the door closed, revealing the other side of the room, which seemed to square better with Arden's personality—sharp hospital corners on the perfectly made bed, a plain brown bedspread, nothing on top of her dresser or even casually tossed into her armchair. The few pictures on her wall were in a straight row, including a faded black and white image of a woman and a few children on a farm, in front of a house that looked cobbled together from scrap and held together by hope and prayers. Another image, in color but decades old, showed Arden and a few other women in dark military dress.

"Whoa, you were in the Navy?" Stacey asked.

"A lifetime ago," Arden replied. "Not everything in the past was bad. But some of it needs to stay there. Don't you agree?" She looked at me with bottle-green eyes that reminded me of sharp glass.

"Yes," I said, sensing we were getting closer to talking about her problems. "Is there something from the past that isn't staying there?"

"Do you really know how to deal with them?" Arden asked, in by far the quietest voice I'd heard her employ yet. "When dead folks, you know, come back up from below?"

"We've dealt with a number of them." I nudged aside a heavy drapery from a window, revealing a view of the church and its grassy graveyard full of round shrubs. "What kind of entity are you seeing?"

"It's my daddy," she said, her voice almost a whisper, like she didn't want any risk of being overheard. "He's dead. Supposed to be dead. Instead, he's taken to coming up from his grave to harass me at night."

"When did he die?" I pulled out my little pocket notebook.

"I couldn't give you an exact date without looking it up. My memory's not as good as it used to be. It happened while I was in the service, so we're talking about decades ago."

"Do you mind if I ask how he died?"

"I wasn't around him near the end, so I can't say for sure, but you don't need to be Columbo to solve that mystery. What killed him was the Early Times and the Kentucky Gentleman. They found a stomach tumor during the autopsy. His liver wasn't doing so hot, neither."

"When did you start having your current trouble?"

"In the past few months, about the time I sold his land. I didn't really want to, but I needed a place to stay, with my knee and hip like they are. A place like this one, I mean. And I have a little retirement saved up, from my last job at Courtland Debt Collections—I was the top performer in my region five years running, they gave me a certificate—but I didn't want to spend that. So finally I sold my daddy's land, where I hadn't set foot in years anyway. That's when I think he started to bother me."

"In what way did he do that?"

"First, just being on my mind a lot, like he wasn't going to let me forget about him, like I tried to do all those years. After I left home, I always tried to pretend he didn't exist. Like I came from nowhere. After I moved in here, I started to feel him around. Then I saw him. Or his ghost, it had to be."

"Where did you see him?" I asked.

Arden raised a trembling, wrinkled hand and extended her index finger to a closed door next to the one where we'd entered.

"The closet," she whispered.

A rapping sounded on the other side of the door, and we all jumped.

Chapter Four

"Arden?" a voice asked through the closed door. It took a moment to realize the voice came from the door on the right, where we'd entered, and not the closet door on the left. "It's Chelsea. Mind if I come in?"

Arden sighed like this was a big imposition. "Keep it snappy. We're busy."

"I understand." The door opened. The woman who stepped in wasn't another retiree. She was in her mid to late thirties, wearing a faded, flower-patterned top over worn slacks, her black hair cut into a short, practical style. She smiled at Stacey and me, but her eyes were wary. She wore a name badge identifying her as Chelsea Bridger, managing director of The Sunshine House. "I didn't get a chance to meet your guests. We usually like visitors to sign in, just so we know who's supposed to be here and who isn't—"

"I feel like I'm paying an awful lot not to be able to have visitors come and go as I please," Arden said. "America's still a free country, isn't it?"

"Well…yes, of course, but—"

"We'll be happy to sign in," I told the lady.

"Thank you." Chelsea passed me a clipboard.

"You can tell she owns the place," Arden muttered. "Won't let you forget it."

"The bank owns more of it than I do." Chelsea kept a tight, professional smile as she accepted the clipboard back. "Are you family?"

"They ain't my family," Arden said. "My family's all dead, other than a couple of no-account cousins you wouldn't trust to hold your purse. They're ghost hunters, and they're here to get rid of my daddy's ghost."

Chelsea's jaw dropped as she processed this information.

"Well," Chelsea finally said, easing the door shut to make the conversation more private. "That is certainly something. Arden, when I suggested getting help with your unhappy visions of your father, I was thinking more along the lines of a qualified counselor."

"I looked at that list you gave me. Buncha shrinks. I ain't stupid, Chelsea. And I ain't crazy. And I never had trouble with Daddy's ghost until I sold his land so I could afford this place. In my book, maybe you ought to be glad I'm dealing with it instead of waiting for you to shake off your do-goodin' tra-dee-la-la attitude and wake up to cold, hard reality for maybe the first time in your life."

Chelsea looked stunned. So did Stacey. So did I, probably. I made a mental note to try to stay on Arden's good side, lest she come after me with her double-barreled verbal shotgun, apparently still loaded and ready after her years of working as a collection agent.

"We don't mean to cause any conflict," I told Chelsea. "I'm sure we can help Arden without disturbing the other residents."

"Help her how?" Chelsea frowned, clearly prepared to dislike any answer I might give.

"Typically our process is to observe the entity and try to determine its identity and motivations. All of that can help us remove it. In this case, Arden has already identified the entity she believes is bothering her—"

"Oh, he's bothering me, all right," Arden said. "Belief's got nothing to do with it. We ain't talking about Santa Claus here, ladies."

"—and that will help us speed things along. I'd recommend we set up a couple of cameras and microphones around her closet to record any activity, and at the same time we can start working on a solution. Arden, do you own any items that were of significance to your father?"

"Not a one," she said. "Would have sold 'em if I had 'em."

"Do you know where we might find anything like that?"

"You could go out to the farm, if they ain't tore it all down yet." She looked toward the black-and-white photo of the ramshackle house and the woman with her children. Something like wistfulness stirred on her face, but she clamped down on it and hid it away. "Momma helped Daddy build the place, not that he ever credited her for it. It went to seed after she died. He didn't keep it up too good."

"Can you give us any idea of what he held most precious in life?" I asked.

"Other than bottom-shelf bourbon? I suppose he loved my momma some, almost as much as Early Times. You could go find anything of hers. I should have done that myself before I sold the place, but I just couldn't stand the idea of going back to that house, even for an hour. If you do find things of my momma's, though, well, I suppose wouldn't mind having one or two for myself."

"Of course," I said. "Just give us the address—"

"I think we're getting way, way ahead of ourselves here," Chelsea said. "Let's go back to these microphones and cameras."

"Arden said she's seen the entity in the closet." I opened the door, revealing a short, wide walk-in. One side was packed with sequined gowns and dresses, more than one feather boa, some rhinestone-studded cowboy shirts, and a colorful selection of wigs, while the other leaned toward simple beige and gray shirts and slacks. "We'd place a thermal camera, microphone, and EMF meter in here to record any evidence of activity, and then maybe a camera recording the exterior of the closet—"

"I can't allow that," Chelsea said. "For one thing, Arden has a roommate, Georgette, with whom she shares the closet."

"As if Georgette ever shied away from a camera or a microphone," Arden said. "Shoot, she'll probably sing and dance around for 'em."

"And what did you say about significant objects?" Chelsea sounded suspicious. "Are you looking for things like jewelry?"

"We're looking for sentimental value, so we can use it as bait to draw the entity's interest," I said. "Sometimes we can trap the entity and transfer it to a more appropriate location. Graveyards in ghost towns work best."

"This is actually a real thing?" Chelsea asked.

"The basic trap design has been used for more than a hundred years. They work often enough that they're worth trying. If not, things can get more complicated, but there are other ways to make troublesome spirits move on."

"And how much does it typically cost when things get more complicated?" Chelsea asked, her suspicion plainly growing deeper.

"We don't anticipate charging much for this," I said.

"I can pay," Arden said. "I'm no charity case. Though really, it's *her* who ought to pay, if you ask me." Arden pointed at Chelsea.

"Excuse me?" Chelsea asked.

"It's your house," Arden said. "If I see bugs, you pay the exterminator. If the pipes clog, you pay the plumber. It ought to be included."

"You want me to pay them to trap your father's ghost, who you think is haunting your closet?" Chelsea asked. "That's what we're dealing with this morning? I'm lucky Pablo is here to actually run the place right now."

"Regardless, it'll probably be the most nominal of fees," I said. "We have a sliding scale, and obviously we're not out to gouge the elderly out of their retirement savings—"

"I ain't elderly," Arden said. "I figure I'll live to be a hundred and fifty. That makes me middle-aged."

"If anybody did live that long, it would be you," Chelsea said.

"What's that supposed to mean?" Arden squinted at her, looking ready to bite some heads off.

"That you're energetic."

"You mean annoying. You think I'm a hassle. You can't wait for me to kick the bucket."

"Now you're putting words in my mouth, Arden."

"Only after I read 'em on your face."

Chelsea closed her eyes, took a very deep breath, and released it. Then she opened her eyes and smiled pleasantly. "I believe we should ask these nice ladies to leave for the day so we can discuss this privately. We can contact them later with our decision."

"You're saying 'our' decision, but I'm hearing 'your' decision," Arden said.

"Don't you think everyone in the house deserves a say on something intrusive like this?" Chelsea asked. "This is a community, Arden."

"A community with dead folks in the closets," Arden muttered. "That's a little more community than I was hoping for."

"All right. I have to go prepare lunch. We're having chef salad, Arden. You always like that."

"Only if the tomatoes are fresh," she said. "Which, last time, they weren't. I wasn't all that impressed with the cucumbers, either."

"I'll double check." Chelsea looked at us like we were some kind of major threat to her residents. "Ladies, can I show you out?"

"But they ain't done nothing yet," Arden said. "I need this dealt with, Chelsea."

"We will discuss it," Chelsea said, calmly and

kindly but very firmly, like a kindergarten teacher dealing with a stubborn child.

"If your old farm's nearby, we could check it out," I said, while also easing toward the door, since it seemed pretty clear that our presence wasn't altogether welcome. It seemed best to minimize conflict. Arden gave me an address, and I scribbled it down as I left the room.

"It was so nice to meet you, Arden!" Stacey said, waving as she followed me out.

Chelsea stepped out of the room and closed the door behind her. "Would the two of you please come to my office?" she asked in a low, angry voice, without a trace of kindergarten-teacher kindness.

"Of course," I said, still going for a light mood, but as we followed her up the hall, past the balustrade overlooking the sweeping curve of the front stairs, Stacey and I shared a worried look. This morning wasn't going well at all.

Chapter Five

"Have a seat." Chelsea waved us into a small, windowless office packed to the ceiling with shelves of paperwork held in a chaotic mosaic of color-coded file folders.

An open doorway behind her desk looked into a small, cluttered living room with dirty sneakers and a baseball glove in one corner and a *National Geographic Kids* abandoned on the floor among some LEGO bricks. She hurried to close that door, as if eager to hide her private life and private self from us.

Stacey and I wriggled into two small, low-back, barely utilitarian plastic chairs on the visitor side of the desk while Chelsea took a matching chair on her own side. She sipped a mug of green tea that had already been sitting there and probably wasn't very hot anymore, and she looked us over quietly.

I took the opportunity to look her over, too, learning what I could from her office, including her framed degree in healthcare administration, an Employee of the Year award from a past retirement home employer, and family pictures. The pictures mostly featured a young boy who strongly resembled her and a much older man, maybe Chelsea's father, who looked quite frail in some of the pictures, though in other, more faded pictures, he was younger, stronger, and clearly enjoyed baseball.

Chelsea cleared her throat. "Are you kidding me with this stuff?" she finally asked.

"No, ma'am. We are private investigators." I handed her a business card.

"You came all the way from Savannah?"

"Arden contacted us," I said. "Well, she contacted an old friend of hers who'd previously been helped by Calvin Eckhart, who founded our agency. And that person referred her to us."

"Hm." Chelsea set down our card and typed at her desktop. "Okay. The internet has heard of you."

"Does it say anything about me?" Stacey asked.

Chelsea sighed. "I'm going to be honest. I believe Arden's first step really should be to consult with a mental health professional, and not rushing into…this. I have to look out for these residents. They're my responsibility. And scammers love to target the elderly."

"I understand," I said. "Is Arden known to have any mental health problems?"

"Not unless bull-headedness counts. I know she seems lucid. But I promise you, I've seen it before. Mentally, they go in bits and pieces at first, but then it picks up speed, like a sled going down an icy hill. I don't think Arden is at that point, but it's my place to look out for her and advocate for her."

"I'm obviously in favor of Arden getting any mental healthcare she needs," I said. "But believing in ghosts is not, by itself, a sign of mental illness."

"No, but repeatedly seeing one could be."

"All I can do is look for evidence. And to be honest, more than half the time, our investigation indicates there's no haunting at all, but some other cause. It's a squirrel in the attic, a woodpecker, something like that."

"I would certainly hope that's the case here," Chelsea said. "Maybe you could tell Arden everything's fine."

"We'll tell her whatever the truth happens to be."

"Hm." Chelsea didn't look satisfied. "Well, I have your card, so if we ever need your services, we'll be in touch."

"Okay." That sounded like a blow-off to me, and we couldn't exactly refuse to leave. I got to my feet, though I felt reluctant to go.

Chelsea escorted us to the front door. The piano music had stopped, replaced by a couple of chatting voices. One sounded like Coach Joe. "…so if not for his own kindness, Waylon Jennings would have been on that plane instead of the Big Bopper."

"But would anybody even remember the Big Bopper if he hadn't died in that crash?" asked another man's voice, one I didn't recognize. "I don't mean to be cruel, but 'Chantilly Lace' only gets you so far."

"He wrote 'White Lightning' for George Jones," said a woman with a whispery, smoky voice, possibly the one who'd been singing. "That was a big hit."

"But how well remembered is that song today?" the unknown man said.

"I could play it for you right now," she said.

"The gauntlet has been thrown!" Coach Joe boomed, and soon the piano began playing at a much faster tempo than before.

As we reached the foyer, a man in a bright blue polo shirt emerged from the back of the house. He looked younger than me, maybe Stacey's age, early twenties, with short black hair and a thin mustache that was unevenly trimmed, like he was something of a newcomer in the world of mustache care and design.

"I'll be right back, Pablo," Chelsea told him.

Pablo nodded, taking a quick look at Stacey and me before returning to the back room.

Stacey and I stepped outside, and I turned back toward Chelsea.

"Thanks again for—" I began, but she'd already closed the door on us.

Chapter Six

"Seems like a bust to me," Stacey said as I returned my phone to the dashboard holder. "At least we'll be home by lunch. Didn't you mention having some buddy passes to your kickboxing place? Let's do that this afternoon. I feel like kicking things."

"I had a different idea." I typed in the address of Arden's childhood home, the abandoned farm she'd sold to pay for her retirement housing.

"Oh, that *is* a different idea," Stacey said.

"It's not far. Couldn't hurt to stop by."

"Yeah, but it sounds like we're not getting the case, right?"

"Arden still wants our help, and she said the old farmhouse is going to be demolished if it hasn't already been. If we wait for her and Chelsea to get back to us, we might have missed our window to go check out the house."

"Because the house won't *have* windows anymore. Or doors, or walls. Or stuff to find. Okay, let's do this."

We soon drove along an isolated vein of rural blacktop with occasional red dirt roads branching off to one side or the other. The clouds thickened overhead, and the weather app predicted heavy rain. I supposed we needed it, after the hot, dry summer, but it would have been nice if it had waited a couple more hours.

The GPS dropped us at the turn-off to an unmarked dirt road, then gave up without even bothering to wish us good luck.

We nosed down the single lane, flattening the tall mohawks of weeds that grew up between the tire ruts, and slowly passed through a thick stand of pine woods that isolated us from any sign of modern civilization.

"On the upside," Stacey said, her voice hushed as if to avoid disturbing any local spirits, "it doesn't look like many construction vehicles have been through here lately."

After a small pond and some empty pastureland marked off by barbed wire, the road ended at a patchwork wooden house with a rusty tin roof. Trees had grown up around the house like giant hands gripping it from below, the limbs obscuring much of the house from view.

"That's the one from Arden's picture," I said.

"Looks like it to me."

We stepped out onto the weedy remnants of a dirt driveway, then hesitated.

"I'm not really loving this house, Ellie," Stacey whispered.

The windows were boarded up with plywood, and

the stairs to the small front porch were rotten. The front door stood open a few inches, giving us a peek through the rusty outer screen door to the darkness inside.

"We should gear up first," I said, and she nodded fervently. We grabbed our backpacks and utility belts from the van.

"This is my one good suit." I replaced my coat with my leather jacket and backpack, but I still wore my white button-up shirt and black slacks. "I wish we'd brought a change of clothes."

"That's what you're worried about right now? As we're about to walk into the old, abandoned house? Old, abandoned houses have never been good for us." Stacey blinked and looked away. I wondered if she was thinking of her own brother, who'd died exploring a similar abandoned, overgrown haunted house back home.

"You want to wait out here?" I asked.

"No, I'm sticking with you."

"Thanks. Keep an eye out for the ghost of Arden's father. Too bad we didn't get his full name, that can be useful."

"We got basically nothing about him, except that his ghost is so awful his own daughter wants it removed."

"Chelsea interrupted our conversation with Arden at a bad time. Let's call Arden back, if we can get a signal out here." I pulled out my phone and dialed the cell number from which Arden had originally contacted me.

"You've reached my voice mail," Arden's voice answered. "If you are attempting to sell me an auto warranty, I no longer drive and would like you to hang up now. Thank you." Then it beeped.

I left her a quick message and hung up. "Well, that didn't get us far. Maybe she'll call back."

We spent a few minutes looking around the farmstead. There wasn't much left to see. The small barn had caved in and been overtaken by weeds. The rusty barbed-wire fence around the empty pasture had weathered over years of neglect, its supports leaning, decayed, or broken by falling limbs that had pressed the wires to the ground. It was a ghost farm, seeming to echo with memories of the animals and people who'd once lived there.

Overhead, the clouds knotted together, growing thicker and darker, blotting out the sun. The wind whipped up, and a hard rain began to fall.

"She's not calling back." I drew my flashlight and started toward the house. "Let's just go."

Signs stapled on the front of the house greeted us with simple, bold phrases like NO TRESPASSING, DO NOT ENTER, and CONDEMNED.

"I feel like those signs are trying to tell us something," Stacey whispered at my side. "Also, on top of the spooky factor, isn't this illegal trespassing? Arden doesn't own it anymore."

"Let's hope nobody sees us. Or at least nobody with strong feelings about private property rights."

"Or ghosts with a strong sense of territory. Maybe Arden's father is too busy haunting her closet to hang around here."

We climbed carefully over the decrepit steps to the porch, where the tall weeds grew up through the soft, creaky floorboards. A stiff wind nudged the front door open a little further, as though inviting us to enter, or daring us to. I pulled open the rusty outer screen door, and it nearly fell off its hinges.

Crossing the threshold, I clicked on my flashlight. A sagging armchair faced a blackened stone fireplace. Yellowed newspapers were scattered around a shelf that had fallen from the wall.

In the kitchen, a small round table and three mismatched chairs lay overturned on the dirty linoleum. The oven door had been left open so long that something had once nested in it, leaving dried-out pine straw and scattered black droppings.

Deeper in the house, the lone bathroom was in foul shape, the tub and sink stained, the mirror cracked. Rain rattled the roof, filling the house with a menacing racket, and drizzled in along dark stains that already marred the ceiling and walls.

"I hate it here," Stacey whispered.

One bedroom had three small beds that looked homemade from mismatched lumber. Poking around revealed a toddler-sized wooden pistol and a dirt-encrusted purple stuffed elephant about the size of a hamster.

"We should take these," I said. "Unzip your backpack."

"Next time, let's bring a trash bag or something," she whispered, making a sour face as I deposited the grimy toys into her pack.

At the back of the house, we cautiously opened a final door and stepped into a room that was noticeably colder, with a rank, sour smell. Rain poured in from the long-broken windows and drenched the foul remains of the carpet. A tree limb had grown in through one of the windows like a big crooked finger poking into the room. Rivulets of rain ran through its bark and dripped onto the floor.

A mattress with yellowed pillows and a lump of blanket lay in the middle of the floor. Cracked pieces of what had once been a beautiful cherrybark oak bedframe leaned against the wall in the corner, next to a small dresser. A closet door stood half-closed, concealing whatever might be inside.

"You check the dresser, I'll do the closet," I said.

"I won't argue with that division of labor." Stacey grabbed the knobs of a dresser drawer and grunted as it pulled open with a wooden rasp like it had been stuck.

As I approached the closet, there was a scratching noise somewhere behind the door.

Stacey and I looked at each other. We'd both heard it.

I braced myself for a nasty surprise as I reached for the closet door's round wooden knob. Arden had seen her father's ghost in her closet at the retirement home, so maybe he was really into closets and liked to hang around this one, too.

I opened the door. A bone-white face erupted from the darkness inside. Its solid black eyes bored into mine, approaching fast. A horrific shriek assaulted my ears.

"Ellie!" Stacey shouted, while I dodged aside, knocking over pieces of the old bed that had been leaning against the wall. The heavy posts and rails toppled to the floor one after the other like the falling trunks of dead trees, thudding into the rotten carpet and warped floorboards. Stumbling into them left me off-balance, sending me staggering and struggling to stay on my feet.

Stacey's flashlight beam followed the shape across the room. The shape landed on a windowsill and twisted its head back to look at us—a barn owl, the common ghost-faced inhabitant of farm buildings and church belfries.

With another shriek, it flew out the window, fleeing the scene.

"Aw, poor thing," Stacey said. "You scared it."

"The feeling was mutual." I pointed my flashlight into the closet.

On the closet floor, a shotgun leaned against the back wall, near a box of shells. A man's patched coat and a couple of moth-devoured cotton dresses hung from the rod above, maybe a married couple's church clothes from long ago. Everything was spattered with white owl droppings.

"Looks like it nested up here," I said, poking my gloved fingers through a pile of mush heaped atop a small, badly cracked leather box.

"Ew. You know how barn owls build their nests? They cough up pellets and squish them together."

"Great." I grimaced as I raised the box and shook a pancake of mashed owl pellets, full of rodent fur and bones, onto an empty part of the closet shelf. Maybe the owl could rebuild, if I hadn't scared it away from its home permanently. The shelf was just above the height of my head, so the creature, no bigger than a cat with wings, had been at eye level with me when it flew out, its eerie face giving the impression of a ghostly person.

I finally opened the gross box and looked inside, finding a simple silver ring, a couple of mismatched earrings, and some faded hand-written notes.

"This looks promising," I said. "But I may have to

burn these gloves."

"Add my backpack to the fire. I can smell those gross old toys even with the zipper closed."

"Any luck with the dresser?"

"I don't know. Do you think the ghost of Mr. Stroup will be drawn to his old socks and suspenders?"

The tree limb rustled, shaking more rain loose in the room.

A loud bang sounded near the front of the house.

"Be careful," I whispered, then started out of the bedroom with the flaking leather box in one hand, my flashlight opened to full flood mode in another.

We returned through the warren of rooms, the knocking sound seeming to grow louder as we approached the front door.

The door stood wide open like we'd left it. The screen door, barely clinging to its hinges after I'd opened it carelessly, was slamming in the wind, thrown repeatedly against the house by the rising rainstorm outside.

"Okay, also not a ghost," Stacey said. "But I still don't like this house. Can we go yet?"

"I think we've covered the whole place." I tucked the leather box against my stomach, protecting the fragile papers inside against the rain, and grimaced as owl pellet residue smeared all over the front of my jacket. "Yeah, let's go."

We darted through the downpour toward the van, but the yard was full of stones and deep puddles, not easy to run across.

We finally reached the van and clambered inside. When I started it up, the tires slipped, and the van refused to budge, stuck in mud that had been dry earth when we'd parked.

An indistinct, billowing shape moved in the house's front window. Maybe it was a remnant of a curtain flapping in the wind, or just my eyes playing tricks on me, helped along by the unsettling atmosphere of the house and by my encounter with the shrieking, otherworldly-looking owl, that legendary conductor of souls between the world of the living and the world of the dead. Maybe not.

Finally, I got the van moving, but slowly.

Rain had melted the dirt road into a soft, muddy creek, and the van didn't have four-wheel drive. It barely had two-wheel drive. I made my way back along the flooded track as quickly as I could manage. When we finally reached the paved road, I floored it for a while, pressing down on the accelerator with my muddy shoe.

Chapter Seven

Back at the office, we sealed the stolen belongings from the farmhouse inside our special safe for troubled items down in the basement. If Mr. Stroup's ghost came searching for his lost possessions, at least he'd come here and not to my home or Stacey's.

"Arden still hasn't called back." I checked my phone yet again, though I hadn't received any notifications. "Looks like we're off duty."

"I don't know if I'm up for kickboxing anymore," Stacey said. "I need more of a hot yoga to burn out some of my memories of that house. And the smell of owl barf. Want to come?"

"I'll probably just go home and have some quiet, ghost-free time to myself."

"Text me if you change your mind."

We split up, going our separate ways in our

separate cars.

I returned to my apartment, a studio with very old brick walls and plumbing to match. The building had originally been home to a glass-making shop, long since shuttered.

My black-and-white cat, Bandit, greeted me with a yawn. I gave him a pet and opened the door to my laughably small balcony, letting in the smell of the falling rain outside. Bandit strolled over to take in the view but hissed and drew back when a stray raindrop struck him.

After a long, hot shower aimed at scouring away the bad memories of the day, I made some tea and sat near the balcony.

I ended up staying home reading a mystery novel, listening to the rain, never calling Stacey to take her up on the very mildly tempting offer of hot yoga. I knew it might help clear away the shadows of the day, but to be fair, the opera singer murder mystery was fairly intriguing. Spoiler: the clown murdered the pirate king backstage with a dagger during the princess's big aria.

Two days later, I was at the office when I answered a call from Chelsea, owner of The Sunshine House. She sounded far from enthusiastic. "There have been some developments," she told me.

"Oh?" I had no idea what to expect.

"Normally, this kind of activity would be completely out of the question," Chelsea said. "However, Arden pressed the other residents about it, despite what I had to say. I was concerned she would scare some of the others, especially the more delicate ones like her roommate, Georgette."

"We never had any intention of trying to scare

anyone," I said.

"It's worse," Chelsea said. "They were *intrigued.*"

"Intrigued?"

"Yes. Apparently, our entertainment programs have been on the lackluster side, according to at least two of them. Arden led them to vote about it, and they all agreed to have you come back and…look for the ghost." It sounded like it pained her to say the last. "However, they do have a condition."

"What's that? I'm sure we can accommodate—"

"They want you to meet with them, all of the residents, to explain what you're doing and answer questions."

"That's completely fine." I relaxed a little.

"Then Spencer and Wallace, two of our gentleman residents, suggested that the event be made into something of a dinner party. A ghost-themed dinner party."

"Okay. A what?"

"Yes. That would be on a Saturday. You would come and explain yourselves to them. Please feel completely free to decline. I'll be happy to pass along your sincere regrets."

"No, we'll come," I said, and I could hear her exhausted sigh on the other end. It was clearly not the answer she'd been hoping for.

"All right. If you go through with this, everything must remain private. I don't want any of my residents showing up in any way in any media, including social media."

"We will keep everything confidential. Should we go ahead and plan to set up our observation that night, too?"

"Whatever gets this over with. Be here at five-thirty."

"Five-thirty for a dinner party?"

Chelsea let out another tired-sounding sigh. "Yes. Five-thirty for a dinner party. Don't be late or you'll miss the chicken Kiev entree. It's frozen. Store brand."

After she hung up, I called Stacey, who was out of the office. "Get out your favorite beaded sweater," I said. "We're going to a party at The Sunshine House."

Chapter Eight

The house, atop its little hill, was still well-lit by the sun when Stacey and I arrived on Saturday evening, though the town below was already in shadows for the evening. Beer signs glowed in the windows of the town's lone watering hole, the Horse and Bull, where a scattering of old cars and beaten-up trucks had parked outside. Topsy's Diner served an early-bird dinner customer or two, but otherwise the downtown looked dead.

Stacey looked overly smashing, I thought, for this casual dinner party at the retirement home, wearing a midnight purple dress that would have looked fine at an awards show or posh nightclub.

I'd personally gone for a light sundress so I could later add my jeans and jacket when we, hopefully, set up our observation for the night.

Chelsea looked beyond frustrated to see us when she opened the front door, dressed in a rumpled polo shirt with some kind of liquid spattered on it, her hair disheveled and sweaty. Arden stood at her side, wearing a freshly ironed checkered-beige pantsuit, a brown turtleneck, and a triumphant smile.

"Ellie and Stacey!" Arden gushed. "You look so lovely. Let's hope you don't give the men a heart attack."

"I don't think that's an appropriate joke, given that certain residents may have serious heart conditions," Chelsea said.

"Well, tell Coach Joe to lay off the pork rinds, then," Arden snapped back at her. Then to us, all gushing sweetness again, Arden said, "Come on, I'll introduce you to everyone."

"I'll check on the chicken," Chelsea grumbled, stalking out of the room.

We followed Arden past a dining room where grinning plastic jack o' lanterns, smiling green witches, and artistically folded orange paper napkins adorned the place settings. Halloween was a couple of months away, so I assumed the spooky décor was in honor of our visit.

"Here's everybody," Arden said as we emerged into a spacious sunroom that took up the entire western side of the house, comfortably furnished with sofas and armchairs. A row of tall, arched windows looked out toward the churchyard we'd seen from Arden's room upstairs. A woman in her seventies or eighties wearing a large, puffy blonde wig sat at an antique piano, rippling the keys softly and skillfully.

Four men played cards at a round table near the

middle of the room, and I recognized two of them as the guys who'd answered the door on our first visit.

"There they are!" Coach Joe proclaimed, rising to his feet and laying a hand on Stacey's bare shoulder. He wore a sports coat and tie, like he was planning to announce a game on TV later. Stacey gave the elderly man a half-hug, patting him on the back, and he looked utterly charmed.

"Good to see you again." Karl nodded at us from his seat.

"You know Karl and Joe, but you haven't met Spencer and Wallace," Arden said.

"It's a pleasure to meet you!" said a trim, smiling, sort of dashing man with smartly styled gray hair and a blue herringbone suit with a silk tie. He turned the wheelchair of an older, shaking man who was, if anything, even better dressed in a three-piece suit with a dove gray tie. "I'm Spencer Alcott, and this is my roommate—"

"Wallace McMurtry." The man in the wheelchair raised his trembling hand to shake ours. Despite his age, his baritone voice had a vibrant power, like his voice could have easily reached the back row of a theater, maybe even a stadium. "We look forward to learning more about why you're here."

"Thank you," I said. "I heard there might be chicken Kiev, too."

"It's frozen," Spencer said with an apologetic tone, and Wallace nodded ruefully. "But one or two little elves may have whipped up a special ghost-themed dessert in hopes of tying the dinner back together at the end. I hope you like stevia, because sugar's the devil around here, for some of us."

"Stevia's great," I said.

The piano music stopped. The woman who'd been playing it approached us, wearing quite a lot of make-up and colorful stage jewelry and a sequined gown that showed off her arms, which she'd kept visibly toned into her advanced age.

"Here's the last one you haven't met," Arden said. "My roommate, Georgette."

"Our resident songbird," Spencer said. "We're so lucky to have her. She'll be the featured star of our upcoming talent show, if only we can find enough participants to actually stage the show. Perhaps Arden will agree to perform a brief—"

"Nope," Arden said.

"Pleased to meet you, Georgette," I said.

"We've been enjoying your music," Stacey said. "We heard you singing the other day. It's great!"

"That is so kind of you to say," Georgette replied in a gentle, throaty voice. "Are y'all involved with any of those paranormal-investigator programs on television? Like *Nightmares in Nashville*?"

"No, ma'am," I said. "I promise we'll keep everything confidential."

"Well, that's too bad." She pursed her lips and looked disappointed. "I wish my son was here, because he always did like scary movies and Halloween. And he loves magic. He's coming to visit me soon."

"That's nice," I said.

"Dinner is now being served," announced the young man named Pablo, whom we'd only briefly met, as he emerged from the dining room. He had a wide, easygoing smile, and a compact, muscular build under his crisp blue polo shirt. He rolled Wallace's wheelchair into the dining room, putting him at the head of the table. Georgette followed, frail and bird-like in her movements, and Karl hobbled after her, leaning on his cane. Coach Joe went last, after waving Stacey and me into the room with a smile.

The eight of us gathered around the dining room table, where the centerpiece was a candelabra of bats holding electric red candles.

"Ooh, my plate is haunted!" Stacey said, picking up an orange napkin bundled into a ghost shape. Karl, across from her, smiled with the less-damaged half of his mouth.

"Spencer made the ghosts," Wallace told us, glancing to the somewhat younger man on his right. "He's the artistic one."

"I also convinced Chelsea to let me rummage through the Halloween decorations," Spencer said. "I hope this isn't all too silly for you. We just wanted to have a little fun."

"Oh, it's a lot of fun!" Stacey said.

"I'm having a good time, too," I assured them. I mean, it could have been worse.

Chelsea and Pablo brought out the food. Chelsea wore an apron embroidered with colorful kittens tangled in yarn, and the phrase JUST KITTEN' AROUND.

The first course was a slice of pear with a dollop of low-fat cottage cheese. Stacey sprinkled hers with salt and pepper and chowed down merrily.

The residents asked questions about our work. Wallace wanted to know about our backgrounds and about Calvin, the former Savannah homicide detective who'd trained us. It turned out Wallace was a retired

local real estate and tax attorney, and had also owned a
store selling antiques and books, which Spencer had
managed for many years.

The main course arrived, each of us allotted an
oven-warmed, very lightly seasoned chicken Kiev with
a side of asparagus. It was plain but edible.

"Should we get to it?" Karl asked, looking at me
with his good eye through his half-blackened glasses.
"We all know what we really want to talk about."

"Karl, not now," Chelsea said, coming to collect
our plates.

"I'll get the dessert!" Spencer rose to his feet,
taking Wallace's dinner dish and his own.

"You don't have to do that, Spencer," Chelsea said.

"Please. It keeps me young." Spencer followed
Chelsea to the kitchen.

"What were you going to say, Karl?" I asked.

"Well, you know. The Heusinkveld murders."

"Oh, no," Chelsea said as she returned with a
platter of small diet chocolate pudding cups. Spencer
opened one and topped it with a puffy white splurt of
whipped cream from a can, then used sugar tongs to
add a pair of chocolate chips, making a little ghost with
eyes.

"Who would like their pudding haunted?" Spencer
asked, and a few people raised their hands, including
Stacey.

"What murders?" I asked.

"It was just one murder." Chelsea dropped into a
spare dining chair placed back against the wall,
catching her breath. She did not seem thrilled to be
discussing this aspect of the house's history.

"Well, that's the official story," Karl said, leaning

toward Stacey and me a little. "Some people believe that Bartel Heusinkveld killed his mother *and* his brother."

"Who says that?" Arden snorted. "Tabloid reporters? Art Bell?"

"Just do a little research," Karl said. "Sure, Bartel was *convicted* of killing only his mother. But his brother died a few months before that, very suddenly and suspiciously. They said it was liver failure. Think about it. Follow the money. If Bartel killed his brother and his mother, and got away with it, then he'd inherit everything."

"I'm sorry, but I feel like I'm three steps behind here," I said. "What are the Heusinkveld murders?"

"Murder," Chelsea said, sounding resigned. "Singular."

"Well, everybody in town knows the story of this house," Georgette said.

"Or *thinks* they do," Karl said.

"There's not much to know," Coach Joe said. "It was open and shut."

"Or so they say," Karl added.

"We're not from town, so maybe someone could catch us up," I said.

"Oh, I will," Spencer said eagerly. "This fine house was constructed by the Heusinkveld family. Andries Heusinkveld was a grocer in the early days, when the town was a busy rail crossing. Through his wholesalers, he discovered he could make a profit packaging local produce to ship by rail to distant cities. He built the cannery near the depot and put people to work. Tomatoes, vegetables, jams and jellies, praline pecans, anything that could be grown here.

"Along came Rhea Loundes, a ragged gal from a rough family up on Possum Creek, dirt poor but heartbreakingly pretty. She won the heart of Andries's son and heir, Pieter Heusinkveld. Pieter and Rhea reigned as lord and lady of Burdener's Hill for years to come, but they say Pieter lacked his father's business sense and preferred carousing instead."

"They don't need the whole history of the town, Spencer," Arden said.

"Spencer is a natural performer who understands the need for a dramatic build," Wallace said.

"Exactly. I am setting the scene," Spencer replied, not even sparing a glance for his critic. He spoke with energy, his hands moving with his words as if to act them out. "However, bowing to audience pressure and skipping ahead to the final act, when Rhea began to grow older and more frail—we're in the 1960s here—"

"1968," Wallace said. "That's when she died."

"Backing up a little before that," Spencer said, while drawing two small counterclockwise circles in the air with his index fingers, so that I could almost see a bicycle pedaling backward. "By the time Rhea reached old age, the family's diminished fortunes made this house difficult to maintain, so her adult children decided to rent rooms in this house to other elderly citizens in need of a supportive place to live. That was the beginning of the transformation into the fine establishment you see here today. The family moved Rhea and her things up to the attic, giving her the privacy of her own floor while also providing a support staff to care for her, paid for by the residents' rent and fees. Maybe it would even make a profit."

"Don't bet on it." Chelsea stood and stretched.

"Pablo has the evening medication schedule. I'd better go check on Taggart before he rots his brain staring at YouTube."

"Did Tag like the new Hot Wheels I gave him?" Coach Joe said. "The red Corvette with the lightning streak? That was a lucky find on grocery store day."

"Well, Tag's getting a little past his Hot Wheels years," Chelsea said.

"Are you sure? How old is he?"

"He's eight now."

"That's prime matchbox-car age, or used to be." Coach Joe shook his head. "The problem with kids these days is all they want to do is push buttons on computers."

"I agree, which is why I need to go back upstairs." Chelsea cast another disapproving look at Stacey and me, the unwanted invaders in her domain, before she left.

"In my day, eight years old, you'd be out on your bike with the neighborhood kids, moving in little gangs, rasslin' up trouble," Coach Joe said.

Karl nodded. "If we had a little money, we'd go to a matinee at the Smith Theater."

"Oh, the Smith Theater!" Georgette touched her hand to her heart. "It was my favorite place in town."

"When I was a kid, they had live performances, not just movies," Spencer said. "The day the theater closed was like a funeral."

"So much of the town has gone," Wallace said. "Remember the Tomato Day parade?"

"I was Junior Tomato Princess when I was twelve," Georgette said. "They let me sing 'The Star-Spangled Banner.'"

"I'm sure it was a fantastic performance," Spencer told her.

"I remember that, Georgette," Coach Joe said. "I played right tackle on the varsity football team that year. We won the regional. But the past is the past, and that's where it stays."

"Getting back to the murders—" I began.

"Yes, let's!" Spencer said. "Where was I? They moved the old lady to the attic, but she was in a wheelchair, and the elevator doesn't run to the attic, so she was effectively a prisoner up there, in charge of nothing—"

"Her son Bartel pushed her wheelchair down the stairs and murdered her," Arden said, and Spencer sighed and shook his head, his narrative spoiled. Arden added, "The cops arrested him, he went to prison, the end. This has nothing to do with my problems."

"Or does it?" Karl looked at Stacey and me. "Could the murder in this house be related to what Arden is seeing?"

"I can tell you right now, my daddy had no association with the Heusinkvelds," Arden said.

"You never know," Karl said. "The strangest paths can cross over a long time in a small town."

"You said there was another death, Karl?" I asked.

"Rhea's older son, Gerrit, died of liver trouble a few months before," Wallace said.

"The later generations of Heusinkveld men had a reputation for excess," Spencer said in a whispery, gossipy tone, miming a drinking glass with one hand.

"Could have been murder," Karl said. "Like I said, if Bartel killed off his whole family and got away with it, he would have inherited the family fortune."

"What fortune?" Wallace trembled harder in his wheelchair and let out an amused laugh. "By the 1960s? With the cannery and store closed? Gerrit's poor widow inherited almost nothing but the house, with the renovation bills and a pack of elderly residents to care for, when she had previously expected to move into a Lincoln Park apartment in Chicago with her husband and child."

"Then what was the motive?" Karl asked.

"At trial, the prosecution proposed that Bartel wanted to reverse the transformation of the family home into a group home so that he could use the house for his own residence," Wallace said. "His older brother Gerrit had started the process to see that their mother was cared for while he took a promising job in Chicago."

"That's what I'm saying." Karl fitted his fingers together like pieces of a puzzle. "If Rhea died, there was nobody to take care of. When Gerrit moved off to Chicago with his wife and son, Bartel would get the big house for himself. He could just throw out the elderly residents if he wanted."

"Bartel tried to make his mother's death look like an accident," Karl said, "but everyone saw through that."

"Where exactly did it happen?" I asked.

"The attic stairs," Spencer said in a hushed voice, casting his gaze upward at the chandelier and coffered ceiling, and presumably the unseen attic above.

"Near Louise's old room." Georgette gave a small, amused smile. "Louise used to talk about her high school boyfriend all the time."

"And hardly ever mentioned her husband of forty

years." Spencer chuckled. "I miss her. She was a character."

Arden drummed her fingers impatiently. "I hope y'all are splitting the cost for these investigators, because they're here for my problem, and we ain't talked about it yet."

"It's getting late, anyway." Coach Joe yawned and stretched. "Sun'll be down in just an hour or two."

"We should probably go set up our equipment in Arden and Georgette's closet," I said, looking to Arden and Georgette. "If that's okay."

"Of course it is," Arden said. "You should have done it already, if you ask me."

Pablo returned with a clipboard and evening medication for those who needed it. Stacey and I got to work carrying in gear, glad for the wheelchair ramps and indoor elevator, setting up our observation for the night.

Chapter Nine

Stacey and I placed observation gear in and around Arden and Georgette's closet, enabling us to watch and listen through the night. We also set up a ghost trap in the middle of the closet, inside a tall structure of a pneumatic stamper that would slam the trap's lid shut if the sensors detected signs of an entity entering the trap, like a combined temperature drop and electromagnetic energy spike.

Arden observed all of this closely, with an attitude full of doubt. Georgette was still downstairs, playing the nostalgic song "'57 Chevrolet" on the piano.

"So, that's supposed to do it, huh?" Arden asked, squinting at the trap.

"Only if we can lure him inside." I unzipped my backpack and brought out the cracked, flaking leather box from her father's closet. I'd managed to brush away most of the owl residue before bringing it into the house.

Arden took a sharp breath.

"That was my daddy's," she whispered. "What was in there?"

I opened it and showed her. Arden touched each of the unmatched earrings like they were holy relics, then lifted out the simple silver ring. She winced as if something had bitten her, then closed her hand around it.

"This was my mother's wedding ring," she said.

"Anything we put in the trap might be lost," I said. "So, if there's anything you'd like to keep—"

"The ring," she said. "Maybe the notes. You can put the earrings in."

I nodded and carefully transferred those to the trap. We would leave the trap's candle unlit, because there were too many fire hazards in the closet. Georgette's old wigs and boas looked especially flammable.

Then I opened a tiny bottle of whiskey and set it inside the trap.

"Early Times." Arden nodded. "That'd get his attention, all right."

"Don't forget the grungy toys." Stacey grimaced as she brought out the filthy toy gun and stuffed elephant.

"Sniffles!" Arden placed the ring on her end table and reached for the elephant. It looked like she was going to embrace it before she realized how dirty it was. Instead, she picked it up with two fingers, touching it as little as possible, and placed it on the end table, too. "I named her after Momma. She always had the sniffles, was always sick. Died when I was nine. That's when the wheels started to come off."

"How do you mean?"

"We always struggled before, but Momma was the one thread holding us together. When she went, the thread broke. Or it was more like the dam broke. Daddy turned a whole new shade of hateful. My brother quit going to school at all, just went in the woods to hunt and drink. Ended up dead in a fishing boat accident when he was thirty-eight."

"I'm sorry to hear that," I said.

"It was a lifetime ago." Arden shrugged.

"What can you tell us about your father?" I asked. "To help prepare us if we encounter him?"

"Well, he was mean. Tongue like a snake, fists like a boxer, and nothing ever satisfied him. I tried to hold things together for him at first, but there was no money to fix the tractor, and there weren't any jobs in town. Daddy didn't want me leaving because there'd be nobody left to take care of him. Nobody left for him to beat up on, neither. The day I left, he cursed me to the devil and back, and he stumbled and fell off the porch chasing after me. I kept going all the way to the Navy recruiting office, because I wanted to get out and see the world. I felt bad leaving him alone, felt bad for a long time, and I never saw him again. He died a couple years later."

"I'm sorry," I said again. "That all sounds—"

"I didn't mean to say so much." Arden straightened up and wiped her bottle-green eyes. She gestured at the toy and ring. "All this just got me to thinking."

"I'm glad you did, because we can use all the insight you can give us. Ghosts are psychological beings, driven by emotional attachments and trauma."

"Just get him out of here so I don't have to see him

again."

"Are they filming yet?" Georgette shuffled into the room and checked her wig in the mirror. She applied a little blush.

"We'll be out of your way in just a minute," I said.

"You're only going to film the closet?" She blinked slowly, whisking her long false lashes.

"That's where the trouble is, Georgette," Arden said. "Remember?"

"I suppose." Georgette sank slowly onto her bed and looked at the framed pictures on the nightstand beside it. A poster advertised Georgette Chambers on a list of musical acts playing the Kentucky State Fair in Louisville in 1968. A faded, decades-old Polaroid showed a boy with thick round glasses on a red tricycle. Another more recent and far less washed-out photo showed a balding, longhaired, fiftyish man in similar glasses and a cheap, purple-ruffled tuxedo fanning some cards and pointing to them with an astonished smile, like he'd just amazed himself. "My son is coming to see me soon," Georgette said, following my gaze.

"That sounds nice," I said. "What's his name?"

"Dexter. Dex. He grew up so fast. Boy one day, man the next." She picked up a pair of two-pound pink dumbbells and began to pump them, working her arms.

"I hear that's what happens," Stacey said.

"If you'll excuse me, it's time for my evening bath," Arden said. "If I start now, I can shovel my way through Georgette's oils and soaps and reach the tub by midnight."

"Mind if I add this to the trap?" I held up the wooden gun toy.

"Go ahead." Arden waved it off.

"My son had a gun that fired paper caps," Georgette said. "They were loud and smelled just awful."

I added the toy to the trap and eased the closet door shut. "What did you say your father's name was, Arden?"

"Darryl."

"Okay. That can be good to know if I have to speak to him."

"What on Earth are you going to speak to him about?" Arden gathered up a beige nightgown and matching slippers.

"Knowing their names can help make them listen."

Arden snorted. "Can't nobody make Daddy listen, alive or dead." She walked to the bathroom and closed the door.

"Thanks again for letting us investigate the room, Georgette," I said while starting toward the door. "I know it means a lot to Arden."

"Well, just don't take any pictures of me without my makeup." Georgette looked at the camera, which faced away from her bed on its tripod, allowing her as much privacy as possible. "I like to maintain a certain image for the public."

"We won't get images of anything but the closet, I promise."

"I wonder what my son will make of all this." She sounded amused.

Stacey and I walked down the hall to an empty bedroom that had belonged to the apparently recently deceased Louise. It had a single bed, a wingback chair, and a dresser, but otherwise had been stripped of all personality, no pictures or personal decorations remaining. The carpet had the sharp, distinct tracks of a recent steam cleaning.

We'd set up a couple of monitors and a speaker on the dresser, turning the spare bedroom into a little nerve center that would keep us close to our client in case of an emergency.

"Kinda sad she's scared of her own father's ghost," Stacey whispered. "He must have been really mean."

"That's what I'm worried about. Someone like that doesn't usually become nicer as a ghost."

"I see you're settled in." Chelsea's voice was polite, with a layer of sarcasm under the surface. "Comfortable?"

"We appreciate you letting us borrow this room," I said.

"It's easier to humor them at this point. What time are you planning to leave? Eight-thirty?"

"That's not long from now," I said. "The sun will barely be down."

"Nine?"

"Still too early."

"We keep early hours."

"Arden says the apparition usually bothers her later than that," I said. "We'll need to stay past midnight."

"I'm not sure I feel safe allowing you around my residents that late. We're short-staffed, so I'm alone after Pablo leaves tonight."

"I thought the residents wanted us here," I said.

"That's not the point. Their safety is my responsibility."

"What would make you feel better?"

She appeared to think it over. I felt sorry for her;

she looked completely drained and clearly needed more help running the place.

"How long have you been short-staffed?" I asked.

"Ever since I took over the house last year," she said. "Night staff is the hardest to keep. Who wants to work those hours? Emmanuel and Veronica both quit soon after I got here. Both were experienced and worked hard, but they left without much warning. When I looked in their files, I saw they were pretty recent hires, more recent than Harold let on."

"Who's Harold?"

"Harold Heusinkveld," she said. "We bought the house when he retired. It's his grandmother whose death everyone was gossiping about like a local soap opera. After his father and grandmother died, and his uncle went to prison, he ended up living here with his mother and running this place until he retired."

"So, you're the first owner outside of the original family?" I asked.

"I am."

"How did you end up buying this place?"

"I used to be a community director for Serenity Care Villages, that big chain of senior homes," she said. "When it came time for my father to go into a group home, I couldn't see him in a place like that. It was impersonal, like a laboratory. Heartless. My husband and I searched around and found this place for sale. A family-style home with a lot of character, already converted for senior group living, right here in my dad's childhood hometown—he lived in Burdener's Hill until he was about ten. That's the kind of place where I wanted to work, and that's what I wanted for my father. So we sold my dad's home, and what remained after all his medical debt went toward a down payment on our future. New job for me, and I'd get to spend my dad's last years with him. Three generations of my family under one roof, together. But with separate apartments on different floors, which is also good."

"It sounds like a big leap," I said.

"Off a cliff and into a canyon," she said. "Now you're going to ask where my husband is."

"Where's your husband?"

"Clint is district manager for Everybody Apartments," she said. "Terrible corporate-chain place, building flimsy, roach-infested homes out of cardboard, basically. He decided he'd rather be with a skinny, horse-faced leasing agent in one of their locations than with his family. Never mind how he'd promised, repeatedly, to renovate this house with his own hands. So my son and I are still living in the resident manager's apartment here on the second floor, when we're supposed to be in the newly renovated attic by now, and converting this into more resident rooms. And we're supposed to be…doing all that together." She shook her head. "He left us in a lurch. Our old timeline is impossible now. I can barely keep things balanced day to day, especially with our problems keeping staff."

"Wow, that is tough," Stacey said.

"On top of all that, my father took a turn after moving here and died. I thought we'd have a few more years, but I was wrong. This place was supposed to knit my family together. And now…what family?" She shook her head. "And now I have to go make sure Taggart does his homework and goes to bed. He gets a later bedtime on Saturdays. But I'll be back to keep an eye on what you're doing."

"Okay. We'll be here."

"Just try not to interfere with *their* bedtime. Maybe stay right here until the house gets quiet. I'd appreciate it." Chelsea closed the door behind her as she left.

Chapter Ten

As observations went, it was our simplest one in a
while. There was nothing to watch but the one closet.
As requested by Chelsea, we stayed sequestered in our
rooms, quiet and out of sight until the residents had
gone to bed. Over our microphone, I could hear Arden
snoring, while Georgette shifted frequently on her bed,
muttering.

Chelsea walked into our room with one of the
cheap, uncomfortable plastic chairs from her office.

"You can have my chair." I hopped out of the
wingback and went to sit with Stacey on the bed.

Chelsea set aside the plastic chair and took the
more substantial and comfortable wingback. "So this is
it? We just watch the closet?"

"Unless something happens, this is it," I said. "It's
basically a stakeout."

"Okay." Chelsea yawned and stretched. She fell asleep within twenty minutes, head leaned against the edge of the chair, lulled to sleep by the monitor's long, unchanging image of a simple closed door.

"I think she had a rough day," Stacey whispered.

"Rough year, from the sound of it."

"Want a snack?" Stacey unzipped a lunch cooler and offered me a compressed nut and granola bar from Stoneground, her favorite brand for some reason. "Granola?"

"No, thanks."

"Raisins?" She held out a red Sun-Maid box instead.

"Sure."

We snacked, and I drank an iced coffee. I tried to research the Heusinkveld house and family online, but there wasn't much to find, mostly just snapshots by hobbyist photographers interested in old houses with unusual architecture. I couldn't find too much about the town, either. It made me kind of curious to go outside and explore it.

We waited for the entity to arrive, which it finally did around ten-thirty p.m. Even the ghosts kept earlier hours in this house.

"Ellie," Stacey said. her tone told me something was up.

I looked away from my phone—neither of us could really stare at a door nonstop all night, so we took turns —and toward the thermal-camera monitor where she pointed.

The temperature was falling fast inside the closet, a cold spot forming near the back wall. It moved forward, its dark blue shape suggesting a human torso, arm, and maybe part of a neck and head.

"Go for the trap," Stacey whispered, fingers crossed on both hands. "Go for the trap."

The vaguely person-shaped cold spot reached the trap and paused there, as if perusing its contents.

"Get inside, get inside," Stacey whispered, fingers crossed more tightly.

I held my finger on the remote control, ready in case the entity went inside the trap but failed to spring its automatic sensor response.

Despite Stacey's whispered pleas, the cold spot passed on by the trap and moved to the closet door.

On the night vision camera, the door inched open, as if it simply hadn't been closed all the way and had been nudged by a draft or the house settling at night.

"Let's go over there," I said. Stacey nodded. The entity was entering the room of our snoring client and her tossing, turning roommate, and we had to be ready to move in and try to protect them.

We dashed down the hallway, trying to keep our footfalls light so we didn't awaken the residents.

As we approached the closed door to Arden's room, I could hear a woman's voice whispering.

"I see you there," she said. "I see you. Come on out."

With a glance at Stacey, I shrugged, turned the knob gently, and eased open the door.

Arden continued snoring on her simple single bed, her plain brown bedsheet still somehow perfectly made even as she slept under it.

Georgette sat up in bed, looking toward us, smiling. She'd taken a curly red wig from the dresser by her bed and wore it along with her emerald green nightdress.

"Come on," she said.

"Okay." I stepped forward, and then I felt the cold.

She wasn't looking at us, but at the closet door beside us, the same closet where Arden had seen her father's ghost. The closet door opened wider as Stacey and I entered the room, but it blocked our view of whatever was inside the closet.

Georgette could see into the closet from her bed, though, and she was smiling at the cold entity.

A round, dark shape emerged from behind the door, low, clacking over the hardwood floorboards toward Georgette, who suddenly gaped at it.

The black shape bulged forward, followed by a sharp curve of shiny red metal. It was the front tire of a tricycle rolling toward Georgette's bed, pedaled by a boy of four or five with big blue eyes and a long rat tail of sandy hair running down his back. He wore a sleeveless muscle shirt and high-waisted jeans with a bright woven cloth belt.

"Dex!" Georgette sighed. "You finally came to visit. I was getting worried."

"I missed you, Mama," the little boy said, his voice scratchy and distant like an old record. He dismounted the tricycle.

"I missed you, too, honey, but now I have all the time in the world." She embraced him and swept him up onto the bed as if he were light as a cloud. She held him close, sniffing the top of his head fervently, as if desperately searching for a long-lost scent.

"Where were you, Mama?" he asked.

"I told you, honey, I had to work."

"I was scared. You left me alone for so long, I almost forgot what you looked like."

"I didn't mean to. I'm sorry. I'm so…" After all her tossing and turning, Georgette finally lay back in the bed, eyes fluttering closed, breathing shallow.

The child embraced her, grinning.

"It's feeding on her." I flipped on the overhead lights, and Stacey and I charged into the room. "Leave her alone! I cast you out, spirit!" Hey, it's been known to work.

The child's head twisted toward us, unnaturally far and unnaturally fast, going full *Exorcist* with his neck bones creaking and popping. He hissed in fury, baring his teeth.

Then he leaped down onto his tricycle and rode toward the closet.

I blocked his path, pointing my searing white light right at his face, and he shrieked and swerved at the last second. The tricycle grazed my leg, slicing my calf with a sting like sharp, cold metal.

The boy apparition left through the bedroom door instead, out into the hall. As the flash-freezing wore off, I felt warm wetness creep down my leg. My blood. My flesh had been cut by the ghost tricycle, though my jeans were still weirdly intact on top of the wound.

"Let's get it!" I limped after it, furious about my injury.

"Get it how? It ignored the trap." Stacey followed. "Hey, are you hurt?"

"I'll deal with it later." I rounded a corner, following the apparition down the winding hallways of the second floor.

The red tricycle was turning to rust. Little holes opened all over it like pockmarks. It deteriorated quickly, and soon looked as if it had been left out in the rain for years. The child apparition looked back at me with solid black eyes, his face losing its features, becoming skull-like.

His tires thumping over the old floorboards, the dead boy passed through the closed, locked door to Chelsea's office, which connected to the private apartment where Chelsea's son was currently all alone.

"Go get Chelsea," I told Stacey. "I'll try to reach the kid inside."

Stacey nodded and ran away.

I could have dropped to my knees, drawn my lock picks from my belt, and teased open the lock, but when I thought about the eight-year-old in there alone with the apparition of death on wheels, I decided speed was the way to go.

Among the many things Calvin had taught me, drawing on his police experience, was how best to break down a door when no pry bar or battering ram was handy. I raised my foot and stomped my sole into the door just beside the lock. The door rattled but stayed in place.

I stomped again, and again. The door splintered and finally swung open.

On the other side, a child-sized shape shrieked at me, and I flooded it with blinding light.

It was not the same kid I'd been chasing. I recognized Taggart from the picture on Chelsea's desk. He had his mother's black hair and brown eyes.

With a scream, he swung a baseball bat at my flashlight, knocking it out of my hand. It spun away and landed on Chelsea's desk, where it sent a stack of files toppling to the floor. Fortunately, the bat had missed my fingers, or I might have suffered a fractured finger or two.

Taggart drew back his bat for a second blow, and this one was going to hit me somewhere I could feel it.

"Wait!" I shouted.

"What's going on?" Chelsea arrived with Stacey and cast a stunned look from her broken door to her yelling, bat-wielding son.

"She broke in!" Taggart pointed to me. "She's a cat burglar!"

"She's not a cat burglar, Tag. Everything's fine." Chelsea flicked on the office light and looked at the damage. "Why did you break the door?"

I was hesitant to describe what had happened because I didn't want to scare the little kid. "I thought I saw something," I said, hoping Chelsea would get the hint about waiting until later for details.

"And so you destroyed a door? Scared my son? You know this leads right into my apartment?" She glanced at the open door to the living room behind her desk, through which Taggart had entered the office.

"That's why I was so eager to get inside and make sure everything was okay."

"It couldn't wait a few seconds? Do you know how much a replacement door costs?"

"I'm really sorry," I said, feeling at a loss. The apparition had been horrifying, and I'd been scared for the boy's safety, but I didn't want to say any of that aloud while he could hear it.

"Tag, wait here while I deal with this." Chelsea stepped back out of the office and began to shut the broken door.

"Can I watch TV?"

"Keep it muted and read the closed captioning. And

no horror movies!" Chelsea closed the door and shook her head as she walked back through the hall.

"I can explain what happened," I told her in a much lower voice, but Chelsea strode on ahead, hurrying to Arden and Georgette's room.

Arden was awake, lying on her side with hair sticking up, looking baffled and disoriented, as one often does when suddenly awakened from a deep sleep in the middle of the night.

Georgette was still sitting up, sobbing now, her bulky red wig askew to sparse, thin strands of cotton-white hair below.

"Georgette? What's wrong?" Chelsea ran to her side.

Georgette slowly raised an accusing finger at me. "They ran off my son." Her voice was the weakest I'd ever heard it. "I waited and waited for him, and they ran him off."

"I can explain…" I began, but then realized I couldn't, actually. I looked at the picture of the fiftyish man with the balding mullet and purple-ruffled tuxedo. "Isn't your son still alive?"

"Of course," Georgette said. She looked exhausted, like every word she spoke took a huge effort. "He's very busy with his career. He's a magician in Las Vegas."

"But I saw a little boy on a tricycle," I said.

"Sometimes he comes as a little boy," she said. "I *like* when he's a boy. I didn't get enough time with him as a boy. Those little years get by you so fast, and you never get them back, no matter how much you might wish…" Her voice trailed off, her eyes drooping, and she fell silent.

"Are you feeling drained of energy right now?" I asked.

"Uh-huh." She sounded like she was drifting off to sleep in spite of her anger at us.

"What's happening?" Arden sounded bewildered.

"Okay, this was clearly a bad idea," Chelsea said. "We gave it a try, but now I think it's best that you pack up your cameras and go."

"But we did detect an entity here," I said.

"We can show you the thermal recording of the cold spot," Stacey added.

"A cold spot, really?" Chelsea asked.

"And then the door opened by itself—" I began.

"Let me guess," Chelsea said. "You'll need to continue investigating, racking up more charges to add to your bill—"

"It's not about that," I said. "If you'd seen what we saw tonight—"

"But I didn't," Chelsea said. "I saw you kick down my office door, menace my child, and upset my residents."

"If you'd let us explain—"

"It's very late," she said. "You can explain in an email and I'll read it tomorrow."

"I really think it would be best if you let us continue," I said, struggling not to lose my cool. What cool I had, anyway.

"I think it would be best if you bought me a new door," she said. "But right now, it's time to go, or I'm bringing the police into it."

"Okay, we'll go," I said. "Stacey, let's break it down."

"You'd better not be talking about another one of

my doors," Chelsea grumbled.

Stacey and I packed up and hauled out our gear as fast as we could. Georgette slept through all the noise we made. The entity taking the form of her son had drained her like a vampire, taking life energy instead of blood.

"Did you get him?" Arden asked as we made our last trip, rolling the heavy stamper out on a hand truck.

"Sorry," I said. "We didn't. But it may not be your father, anyway. It might be something that changes form. Georgette saw it as the childhood version of her son—"

"I think that's enough," Chelsea said.

"I'm having a conversation here," Arden said. "With my guests."

"Your guests broke down my office door, so if you want to pay for that now, I'll let them stay as long as you like."

"I guess it can wait until tomorrow, if you want to be like that about it," Adren said.

Chelsea kept a close eye on Stacey and me, including riding the elevator down with us and escorting us to the front door. She seemed relieved to finally be throwing us out, probably feeling back in control of her house again.

As we were about to leave, she said, "Wait."

I turned to see what she wanted. She was looking at the dark, wet patch on my pants leg.

"Are you bleeding?" she asked.

"Yes. The entity cut me on its way to your apartment, before it disappeared."

Chelsea sighed. "Come on. Let me patch you up before I kick you out."

"I appreciate it, but we have a first-aid kit in the van."

"I've seen your van, and I have trouble believing it's a hygienic environment. Come on."

I shrugged at Stacey. "I'll be right back."

"I'll roll this on out. It's so nice to have a ramp!" Stacey tilted the hand truck and moved off along the front porch.

Chelsea led me to a bathroom with a shower fitted with a hose and sprayer. She helped me remove my jeans and wash off the wound, then frowned as she inspected the injury.

"What did this, again?" she asked.

"The tricycle."

"The ghost rode a tricycle?"

"It took the form of Georgette's son from when he was a kid."

"Why would it do that?"

"To get close to her," I said. "To feed on her. Drain her energy."

"Does that hurt her?"

"Definitely. It's predatory. I know it's hard to believe all this is real, but it can have a real impact on people's health, especially vulnerable ones."

Chelsea applied a bandage and gauze. "I'll need to think this over. It's hard to see the right path to take."

"I understand. All I can tell you is that this entity is dangerous. I'm not eager to face it, but I suggest that you let us. For the safety of yourself, and your residents, and your son."

"I suppose you'll need to borrow some pants now. You can't put those back on."

"I'll be fine."

"You will not go out in the middle of the night like that. I'll give you my least favorite ones." She left briefly and returned with some orange sweatpants with holes at the knees.

"Thanks." I pulled them on. As she walked me to the front door, I asked, "Should we plan to return tomorrow?"

"Not tomorrow," she said. "I'll get back to you."

"Don't wait too long," I said. "That's my advice."

Then I turned and walked to the van, wondering whether she'd take the advice or not.

Chapter Eleven

We drove home to Savannah, encountering no other midnight drivers until we left the empty country highway for the busier interstate.

"Did we get fired?" Stacey asked me from the passenger seat. She'd offered to drive, on account of my leg, but I still preferred to do it myself.

"Arden didn't fire us, but we can't work the case if we can't access the house."

"Should we get Arden to sneak us into the house like a teenager's boyfriend?"

"I don't know if you're joking—"

"I'm joking."

"—but I'd almost be willing to sneak in there. Did you get a look at that kid?" I asked.

"Which one? The one you scared half to death? Or the Creepy Toddler?"

"Creepy Toddler. It was like his face was peeling off. Maybe his disguise was slipping as he got away from Georgette and gave up on feeding on her. He looked horrifying."

"I saw," Stacey whispered. "So, if he's not really Georgette's kid, who is he? Arden's father? Or is that another disguise he wore?"

"Those would be good questions to look into if we could continue the investigation. I thought I was getting through to Chelsea while she was bandaging me. But then I thought pressuring her too much would backfire."

At the office, we swapped out cars and drove our separate ways.

At home, my cat Bandit actually leaped up on the couch arm to greet me with a quick meow and take some petting.

"Good to see you, too, pal." I looked out the glass balcony door to the drizzling rain outside. I thought about calling Michael, but it was crazily late. He'd returned via Greyhound bus from North Carolina after leaving Melissa and her car at Duke University, but we hadn't seen each other in person since then.

Unable to sleep, I studied online back issues of the *International Journal of Psychical Studies*, reading up on shapeshifting entities. I'd encountered a few, including a parasitic spirit type called an aufhocker, accidentally summoned by a bereaved professor attempting to bring back his dead wife through arcane rituals. The aufhocker could take on many shapes, such as a sad woman, a friendly traveler or animal in need of help, or a horrific shaggy beast.

Another entity we'd encountered was a fearfeeder, a

dangerous one that had damaged my mentor Calvin's spine and left him in a wheelchair for life, starting him on the road to hiring Stacey to help me so he could retire from active investigations. A basic boogeyman, it was a type of entity known by different names around the world, an evil ghost taking the form of its victims' fears in order to prey on their energy. They especially preferred to feed on children, who had so very much energy to steal.

I considered the entity at Sunshine House. Arden certainly seemed afraid of the ghost of her violent father. Was Georgette afraid of her son, though? In the form of a little kid riding a tricycle? She hadn't seemed to be. She'd welcomed the entity with literal open arms, and it had fed on her.

"Not fear," I said aloud, startling my cat. "Maybe it takes the form of someone you love? Or used to love? That sounds closer, doesn't it, Bandit?"

"Mrow?" At the sound of his name, he jumped down from the couch and walked to his dish on the kitchen floor.

"Great insight, thanks," I said, then went to open a cat food can.

The next day, I called Calvin for advice.

"I don't have to tell you that you need to be very careful around this kind of entity." His voice was heavy with the weight of things unsaid. We both knew he was referring to the shapeshifting malevolent ghost that had left him permanently disabled. "They're conscious, they're strong, and they can manipulate your perceptions."

"I remember," I said. "But I'm not sure it feeds on fear."

"It opens up powerful emotions in the victims' minds in order to feed," he said. "It doesn't necessarily have to be fear. Find the pattern in the forms it takes."

"I'm trying. Our other big problem is Chelsea not actually letting us investigate. Visitor hours end at eight, and honestly, most of the residents are in bed by then. Even if we're invited guests, Chelsea will kick us out right when our observation ought to begin."

"Would she let you stay out in the van?"

"At this point, I doubt she'll even let us on the property during daytime hours as Arden's guests. We're lucky Arden is so adamant and persistent, really."

"And you said the other residents were also supportive of the investigation?"

"They're all on Arden's side. That's the only reason Chelsea let us try for one night, but she was looking for a reason to stop it, and we gave her more than one."

"Replace her door," he said. "Out of the company account."

"Are you sure? The company account's not that thick."

"Then the replacement door won't be, either. Think of it as reputation management. Damage control. If it enables you to continue the case, you'll earn it back."

"If you think that's best."

"Harness your support among the residents," he said. "Use the power of their stubbornness to get yourself and your equipment back into that house before the entity drains someone to death. It may have been doing so for years, in fact. Because elderly residents periodically dying in a retirement home is not likely to raise any special alarms."

"That's grim," I said. "But I see what you mean. A

killer ghost could go undetected for a long time in that environment, if it wanted to."

"Well, this case is starting to hit a little too close to home for me. I'll have to go play bridge at the community center so I can feel young again."

"Any plans to come up and visit?"

"I'm not sure, Ellie."

"Good, because I rented out your apartment for some positive cash flow."

"What?"

"To art students."

"Ellie!"

"I'm just kidding, Calvin. Nobody's even answered the rental ad yet. But I did say art students preferred."

After my call with Calvin, I thought over the case, the residents, and the conversations we'd had.

Finally, struck with the early glimmer of an idea, I called Arden.

"Did you still want us to continue the investigation?" I asked her.

"You know I do, but Chelsea's being a roadblock. Seems like she ought to listen to the people who write checks to her every month. Meanwhile, I'm the one who has to live with this awful thing in my room. I'd be better off living at a Howard Johnson."

"I had some thoughts on how we could keep the investigation going, but we'll have to recruit the help of other residents."

"To do what?" she asked, and I told her.

Next, I called Stacey.

"Get ready," I said. "We're going to a tea party at The Sunshine House."

"Huh? They invited us back?"

"Apparently, it was the wildest party they'd had in a while. We really blew the doors off."

Stacey and I showed up at the house in the middle of the afternoon. Chelsea met us with a stony expression at the front door. She examined the new door we held between us, complete with a shiny new key inserted into the lock.

"Fine," she finally said, and she let us inside for the moment.

Chapter Twelve

Chelsea kept an eye on us while we took the damaged old door down to the van and installed the new one. Taggart came to watch, and I apologized profusely for scaring him the night before.

"I wasn't too scared," he said. "I could have knocked you out."

"That's true. You were heavily armed."

"He's one of the best batters on his team," Chelsea told me.

"Like fourth or fifth best," he said cheerfully.

"I believe it," I told him, then grunted as Stacey and I lifted and dropped the new door into place on the hinges. I tested it out by closing Stacey inside the office and turning the key to lock her in there.

"Hey!" Stacey rattled the doorknob.

"It works." I unlocked it and let her out, then

passed the key to Chelsea.

"Thanks," Chelsea said. "Now, my residents have a busy afternoon ahead—"

"Oh, yeah, board game Saturday is a real day at the fair." Arden arrived from the direction of her room. "I want an update on my case. I want to see the video from last night, which I was so rudely denied."

"You didn't ask to watch their video last night," Chelsea said.

"I did, but nobody listened to me, as usual!" Arden snapped, though I had no recollection of that. Arden was possibly just churning up grievances to complain to Chelsea about. "I don't know what I pay for around here. Now, since you ain't dealing with my problem, Chelsea, and these ladies are trying to, I want to visit with them."

"Oh, look, Arden has guests." Spencer emerged from the elevator area, and Chelsea narrowed her eyes, possibly noticing the elevator hadn't made its characteristic bell sound in a while. Spencer had been hiding nearby, awaiting his cue. "I was just on my way to say that Wallace and I accidentally made too many pastries to have with our tea—well, *I* accidentally made too many—and here I was, hoping to collect some guests."

"You were coming up to invite Arden for tea? Just now?" Chelsea asked.

"We must fortify ourselves for the rigors of board game Saturday," Spencer said. "Perhaps you and your guests could join us, Arden?"

"Let's go." Arden turned and started for the elevator.

"Why, we would enjoy some tea also. What a

lovely invitation and complete surprise," Stacey said, overacting a bit.

"Sounds great to me," I said.

Chelsea watched the four of us suspiciously. Spencer and Arden took the elevator, while Stacey and I took the stairs.

Downstairs, Spencer and Wallace shared a long room with a private porch. It was cheerfully decorated and much more sumptuously furnished than the other rooms in the house, as if they'd brought a number of fine items with them, including porcelain vases, a bust or two, and a number of paintings of European cities in ornate frames. Vivaldi played on the stereo.

Tea was served on the porch, where Wallace already waited, his wheelchair placed in a prime spot to watch the neighborhood of birdhouses suspended from the trees on the side lawn.

"Welcome back," Wallace said when Stacey and I emerged onto the porch. The table had four matching chairs and held a platter of tiny raspberry pastries and thimble-sized muffins. "It's so nice to have someone to eat the sweets for us."

"We look forward to it," I said.

Spencer poured mint tea for everyone before taking his seat.

"Well, I'm gonna try one if nobody else goes first." Arden popped one of the triangular raspberry pastries into her mouth. "Nice. I like how the jam squirts in your mouth when you bite down. Good work, Spence."

"Thank you, Arden. Baking is among my current favorite ways to waste time," Spencer said.

"And thanks for helping with all this other nonsense, too, helping us end run around Chelsea,"

Arden added. "I mean it."

"We wouldn't dream of being left out of an exciting scheme," Spencer said.

"It won't be hard to show you how to use the cameras," I told them. "But what about Georgette? Is she mad enough to veto having the gear in her room again?"

"I think she's still in shock," Arden said. "I'm still trying to understand it all, too. You're saying my daddy's ghost isn't haunting me? Because it sure looked and sounded like him. Smelled like him, too."

"We believe this entity changes its appearance for different people."

"Playing mind games," Arden muttered.

"Then what is it, actually?" Wallace asked. "Underneath the disguise?"

"We're not sure yet. It could be an entity consumed by past trauma, like something negative that happened here that left it haunting the place, maybe a murder or other tragic death."

"The Heusinkveld family had no shortage of tragedy," Spencer said.

"The entity might also predate the house," I added. "We need to learn what was here before it, if we can. Does anyone know?"

They looked among each other, but nobody seemed to know.

"The house has been here all my life," Arden said.

"It may have simply been an empty lot," Wallace said. "The courthouse records room would know."

"Ellie *adores* county records," Stacey said. "Especially really old, yellow, hand-written ones that you can barely read anymore."

"I have a fondness for old paperwork myself," Wallace said. "There's always a sense of history even in the most pedestrian of documents, offering a tiny window of insight into the past, into moments of lives that have come and gone."

"You two should definitely hang out, then," Stacey said.

"Let's show them what we recorded in Arden's closet, Stacey," I said, and she played the video on her tablet.

"I see it!" Arden pointed her finger at the blobs of cold. "That looks adult-sized, not like a little kid."

"It didn't take on the form of the little tricycler until it emerged into your room," I said.

On the recording, the door opened when the cold spot reached it. Stacey switched to the night vision video of the door opening.

"Where did it go?" Wallace asked. "I don't see anything."

"The entities don't always get captured on camera, even when people in the room can see them," I said. "Just to be clear, Georgette only has the one son? She didn't have another one who died long ago as a child, or anything?"

"Not that I know of," Spencer said.

"The pictures on her nightstand are both the same person," Arden said. "I know that much."

"She always says her son's coming to visit," Spencer said. "The truth is, he hasn't been here in more than a year. It's rather sad. I think she still mails him money. He's a struggling stage magician, not exactly a growth industry. The days of David Copperfield's big budget network specials are long past."

"I'm not sure what those are," I said.

"Exactly."

Chelsea emerged onto the porch. "Sorry. The door opened when I knocked."

"If that's true, you need to fix it," Arden said. "Along with about fifty other problems around here I could list. Like the water pressure in our shower head. I had a massage head in my last apartment. Should have brought that with me."

"Chelsea, I'm glad you're here," Wallace said, the strong baritone voice coming from his scrawny, shrunken frame like the voice of a larger man. "As executive producer of the upcoming house-wide talent show, I'm happy to present our video production team."

"I thought y'all were private detectives," Chelsea said.

"We moonlight," I said. "Stacey has a film degree from Savannah."

"We were happy to persuade them to donate their services," Wallace said.

"Uh-huh. Is that what's happening here?" Chelsea asked.

"And they're still working my case," Arden said. "Which I'd say is everyone's problem now, not just mine. Show her."

Stacey played the video clips for Chelsea, who looked unsettled but not persuaded. "That's the thing that cut you?" Chelsea asked me.

"It is, and it could harm anyone in the house if it's not stopped," I said.

"Visiting hours end at eight," Chelsea said, after looking at us quietly for a few moments. She clearly didn't trust us yet. "That means all non-residents need to be out of the house."

"Can we be on the driveway?" I asked.

"Off the property. We close the gates at night to keep out unwanted intruders." Chelsea stared at me as she said this.

"Okay," I said.

"You don't need a camera crew, Wallace," Chelsea said. "I can record the talent show on my phone."

"On your phone?" Spencer looked scandalized. "The culmination of a lifetime of craft? Featuring outlaw country princess Georgette Chambers? On your phone?"

"I'm not sure she counts as outlaw country," Arden said. "She's certainly something of a princess, though."

"She had a 45 released by Sun Records," Spencer said. "And the radio stations never play her. What more do you want?"

"Besides, Chelsea, you'll be too busy performing in the show," Wallace said.

"Me?" Chelsea scowled and drew back. "I'm not going to be in the show."

"Yes, you will," Arden said.

"What would I do in a talent show?" Chelsea asked.

"I don't care if you dance around in funny glasses and bunny ears," Arden said. "Spencer wants a third act, and it ain't gonna be me."

"We do need a third act, although I hope for at least five," Spencer said. "The more the merrier. Shall I add you to the list, Chelsea? No audition required! Try getting an offer like that on Broadway."

"I don't think so." Chelsea left, shaking her head.

After tea, Stacey and I set up our gear in Arden's

closet all over again. Georgette drifted into the room and watched.

"Did you get any pictures of my son's visit?" she asked.

We showed her the videos. She frowned at the cold spot in the closet, then at the night vision of the door opening with no visible sign of the entity. "I don't see him."

"No," I said, trying to make my tone as gentle as I could. "Georgette, we don't believe it's really your son visiting you, or Arden's father threatening her. There's something in this house that can look like different people."

Georgette stared at me for a minute, then looked over at the two pictures of her son, the adult man and the tricycle boy who looked identical to the one who had attacked me.

"Well." She sagged down onto the frayed old armchair by her bed. "I suppose I should have known. At first, I thought I was going crazy, or maybe it was a miracle. I wanted it to be real. To have more time with my little boy again. If I could wish for anything in the world, it would be that." Her arms clutched at empty air, as if trying to embrace a child who was no longer on her lap, who hadn't been for decades. "But life would never give me that. I should have known better." She took a tissue from her vanity table and dabbed at her eyes, smearing layers of mascara and eye shadow. "I hope he's happy out there, I really do."

"I'm sure he is," I said. "And I'm sure you were a great mother to him."

She barked a laugh. "Oh, honey, I was not. I was young, you know, and not married. I had the one record, I was touring, I had a hot little career for a while there. Then I got careless and pregnant. I stopped touring for a while, but when he was about two or three, I tried to get it all going again. I left him with relatives, sometimes my mom, sometimes my aunt, sometimes my sister, while I got back to playing little shows, trying to land a second record deal, but… sometimes you miss your chance. Or maybe I went as far as I was ever meant to go. Life's like a big audition, you know, and not everybody's gonna make the cut. I missed his whole childhood chasing my own dead-end dream."

"I am so sorry." Stacey grabbed a tissue for herself.

"Me, too." I felt guilty for how painful the conversation had turned. "I'm sorry we had to tell you this."

Georgette didn't say anything, just looked quietly at the closet from which her son had seemed to visit her, bringing an illusion of the past back to life in exchange for literally sucking the life out of her.

"What is this?" Chelsea stood in the doorway, scowling at the camera. "Don't tell me you're planning to stay again."

"We're letting Arden borrow the equipment," I said. "She'll record anything that happens, and we can review it during normal daytime hours."

"This is quite a plan you've all cooked up." Chelsea glared at me.

"Did you have a different, better plan to offer?" Arden asked Chelsea. "Maybe you want to lay it out for us right now? Because doing nothing is not an option, Chelsea."

Chelsea kept glaring at me, then slowly turned

away. "This is not tenable," she said, then stalked out of the room.

This is not tenable, Arden mouthed mockingly at Chelsea's back.

Stacey gave Arden basic instructions for operating the gear, showing her how to turn it on at night and off in the morning. Everything was plugged into wall outlets, so batteries weren't an issue.

Georgette paid attention, too, and was more than happy for us to test the camera on her, and actually kind of insisted on it. She waved and danced a little, though stiffly and with visible effort. For a moment it was easy to imagine her in her youth, singing and dancing until the early morning hours in the nightclubs of Nashville.

"If it comes back, use these." I gave them each a tactical flashlight. "They create thousands of lumens of white light, like a sunbeam. Keep them by your beds. Turn on your lamps, too. Remind yourself the entity is not who it's pretending to be. And play music, sacred music. Light and sacred music can help drive it away."

"I can put my *Best of Bluegrass Gospel* CD into my stereo!" Georgette said. "It has a remote control."

Afterward, Georgette, Arden, Stacey and I went down to the window-lined sunroom, painted in rich hues of burnt orange and ember red by the setting sun. Coach Joe and Karl were playing checkers. Georgette sat down at the piano, while Arden claimed an overstuffed chair by the magazine rack and picked out a copy of *Time* magazine.

"Well, hello again," Coach Joe said to Stacey and me. "Is there another dinner party already?"

"We were just going to listen to Georgette play a

song, then head home," I said.

"How about a little Jerry Lee Lewis?" Coach Joe asked. "'Great Balls of Fire' is a real hoppin' tune."

"I feel a little more like…" She began to play "I Fall to Pieces" softly with her eyes closed.

Near the end of the song, Karl stood and left the sunroom. When his back was to everyone, he removed his glasses and wiped his eyes.

Taggart arrived, and Georgette immediately stopped playing to welcome the eight-year-old with a hug. "Well, hello, sugar. Are you ready for your lesson?"

The boy nodded, and Georgette began to guide him in playing "Puff the Magic Dragon." He plonked the keys heavily and slowly, and she kept encouraging him and correcting him, gradually extracting the fanciful, melancholy song from the piano's hidden strings.

Chapter Thirteen

Stacey and I left soon after, making it clear to anyone listening that we were heading back home to Savannah and definitely *not* hanging around for the night monitoring the equipment we'd set up in Arden and Georgette's room. Nope, not us.

We drove through the quiet downtown and turned at the railroad tracks. The hilltop house had a commanding view of the town's main street, so we parked well out of sight behind a shuttered warehouse-style building of aged brick. Faded signs indicated that the block-long building had once been the Heusinkveld cannery, economic engine of the town.

"Do you think this is far enough away?" Stacey asked.

"Now that it's dark, we can poke around downtown. We'll just have to avoid the streetlights."

"Doesn't look like there's much to poke. Or many streetlights." She frowned at the dark alley around us.

"Would a meal of authentic local cuisine cheer you up?" I asked.

"Sure, I could go for some farm-fresh fruits and vegetables. Maybe that last produce stand we passed is still open."

"I was thinking Topsy's Diner."

"Oh, the one restaurant in town?"

"The Horse and Bull might serve food." I nodded at the dim bar down the street with a small row of motorcycles out front.

"I'd rather take my chances with Topsy's," Stacey said. "They're not serving to drunk people in the dark. Their standards have to be higher."

We took the back way, keeping out of sight of the house, though hopefully Chelsea wasn't staring out the windows watching for us, anyway.

A couple of dark alleys later, we approached the glass front door of the old diner. The OPEN sign was lit high in one window, though the "N" was flickering like it wasn't too sure whether to stay on or not.

Inside, the diner smelled...diner-y, like years of grease and steam generated by untold thousands of servings of sausage and coffee. The tile floor looked worn to the point of exhaustion, as did the clunking old appliances and chipped plates. An ancient, dusty jukebox squatted in a corner, next to an incongruously new glass-fronted cabinet offering CBD oil and vaping accessories under lights so bright someone could have performed heart surgery by them.

The only customers were a few teens in a back booth. They wore heavily ripped dark clothing and had multiple piercings, including one girl who looked like she'd drawn on her makeup with black marker and dyed her hair a matching inky black.

A tired-looking old man in a smudged apron scraped the grill behind the counter. He sighed as he looked over at us, like he couldn't believe how busy it was getting. Or maybe he'd just had a long day on his feet, frying eggs and potatoes. He seemed to be the only worker.

"Can I help you?" he asked crankily, almost like he expected us to try to sell him scammy magazine subscriptions or questionably sourced essential oils.

"Is it too late to order food?" I asked.

"No soup. I already cleaned out the pot."

"That's fine." I took a booth near the counter rather than by the window so he wouldn't need to walk too far. "What do you recommend? What's popular here?"

"Popular?" He shook his head. "I'd go for the chicken-fried steak, but y'all don't strike me as chicken-fried steak eaters. I could do grilled chicken, BLT, or a salad. Salad's got fresh ingredients, but only three or four of them. I do quality over quantity."

"Grilled chicken and salad sounds great, thanks," I said.

"I feel like I have to defend my honor and try the chicken-fried steak," Stacey said. "With the…" She scanned the side options, written on a wall-mounted chalkboard. "Homemade macaroni. And collards."

"All right, consider me impressed, country girl." He turned toward the grill and got to work.

While his back was turned and his grill hissed with the sound of my chicken, the gang of four teenage kids left their booth, having consumed their four cups of coffee and single order of hash browns. They slunk toward the glowing CBD cabinet, which looked like it had just landed from outer space with all its lights and reflective chrome.

The teens slowed as they moved close to it, and started elbowing and pushing each other, as if daring each other to move on. One pointed at the bright green leaf decal on one side of the cabinet and snickered.

"Hey, interesting CBD oil selection you've got there," I said loudly, hoping to draw the cook's attention before they vandalized something.

The teenagers turned their heads sharply toward me.

"Yeah, it looks really interesting!" Stacey added, after seeing what I was seeing.

"Yeah, folks seem to like it," the cook said, turning to look. "For the longest, time, we had a bookcase of videotapes to rent over there, but that kinda died down after…Hey, get away from there!"

The girl with what looked like black marker make-up was the one who finally broke from her friends and charged ahead, right up to the CBD display. I started to rise from my seat in case the old cook needed help.

"Don't you dare!" The cook ran out from behind the counter clacking a pair of greasy metal tongs at the teenagers.

Smirking, the girl passed by the cabinet and jammed a quarter into the jukebox. This did not pacify the cook at all.

"I mean it!" he shouted, while she punched the worn plastic buttons, selecting a letter and two numbers.

Then she turned and raced for the door, along with

the rest of her pack, howling with laughter.

The cook chased them out, then stood at the door, clacking his tongs in impotent fury, and watching them run across the parking lot and away down the street. Apparently, they'd arrived on foot. They turned down an alley, out of sight, hopefully not on their way to discover our van and vandalize it.

A loud *clunk* sounded from an overhead speaker.

"Achy Breaky Heart" by Billy Ray Cyrus filled the diner.

"I hate those kids." The cook shuffled back to the jukebox and pulled the plug to silence it. "I ought to update the music, but it's not worth it. Maybe should take the jukebox out back and put it out of its misery. Dang thing's still got 'La Vida Loca' on it. Wait'll the kids figure that one out." He shuffled back behind the counter and flipped my chicken.

"So, are you Topsy of Topsy's Diner fame?" Stacey asked, a question that surely would have sounded sarcastic out of my mouth yet seemed perfectly amiable out of hers.

"I'm Vernon. Topsy was my great-grandfather." He nodded at framed black and white pictures on the wall. "He was a dive-bomber. They said he flew all topsy-turvy to avoid the German ground fire, back in World War I."

"And now the diner's named that!" Stacey said. "How neat."

He served us on large, oval plates that looked like they'd seen many years of service, accumulating chips and hairline cracks. I drizzled a packet of ranch dressing over my salad, which was just lettuce, tomatoes, and cucumbers, but as promised, they all looked garden-fresh. "This looks great, thanks."

He nodded. "Are y'all visiting family in town? Or did you take a wrong turn at the exit?"

"We're actually collecting images of old architecture from small towns," I said, thinking of the websites and social-media groups I'd encountered while trying to research the house. "Do you know anything about that mansion on the hill?"

"There's a lot to know," he said. "That house's past reflects the town. The family that built it, the Heusinkvelds, they used to be real big around here."

"How did they become so big?"

He told us what we'd already learned about the cannery. "They used to make pralines. My grandpa would buy 'em for me. That was gone by the time I was a teenager. This diner was still hopping, though. Everybody came here, dawn 'til dusk. It was the place to go after a hometown ball game. Well, here and the Dairy Queen, before that closed. We had my grandma's blueberry pie, but it couldn't compete with those Buster Bars in the summertime."

"The house gives me kind of a spooky feeling," I said. "Did anything tragic ever happen there?"

"All kinds. Some of it self-inflicted. The men had a habit of drinking themselves to death. One of 'em got drunk and fell off a balcony. That's a different way of drinking yourself to death, I suppose."

"So, they basically partied to death," Stacey said. "Kind of like I'm doing with this chicken-fried steak." She put a breaded, gravy-coated slice into her mouth and closed her eyes. "Mmm. Good."

The cook nodded quietly, taking in her approval.

"What else can you tell us about the house?" I

asked.

"It's an old folks' home now."

"Do any of the original family live nearby?"

"The only one who might still be alive is Harold. He was a couple grades behind me in school, but I knew who he was. We all did."

"What kind of kid was he?"

"Quiet. Kept to himself. Didn't play any sports, join any clubs. People thought he was maybe full of himself and believed he was above everyone else. I'm not sure that's right, though."

"What was your impression?"

"He had real bad color, real white, like maybe he was sickly and didn't spend much time out in the sun. Like he had a disease, or something wrong with him. I don't know what. I didn't really know him well."

"Can you think of anybody who might have? Maybe an old school friend of his?"

Vernon shook his head. "I'm not sure he had any friends, to be honest. Seemed kinda sad and lonely, looking back on it, though everybody in school thought he must be happy because he was rich."

After dinner, we stepped out into the dark night. The diner's lights clicked off behind us, and I glanced back to see the proprietor lock the door and turn off the sputtering OPEN sign.

The town's two traffic lights and a couple of streetlights provided some light, as did the beer signs at The Horse and Bull, the only place still open.

"We may as well take the grand walking tour," Stacey said. "See the sights."

"That'll kill fifteen minutes."

"Or we could hang out at The Horse and Bull."

"If that's the other option, then sign me up for the walking tour."

We strolled along the main street, keeping away from the streetlights as well as the bar, and reached the picturesque church, with a brick foundation and a white wooden steeple with a shuttered belfry.

"The graveyard's well-constructed." Stacey nudged the sturdy wall, made of more brick, the steel gate closed. "That's always good, right?"

"Especially if there's something you need to keep inside." I looked among the headstones, many dating back well over a century. The largest grave markers belonged to the Heusinkveld family. The original patriarch and cannery founder Andries had a solid pillar of Georgia marble, as if to represent his place in the community. He lay beside his wife Gerda, who'd died decades earlier than him.

Their sons were buried nearby, Isaak's marker small and modest, the spouse side left blank for all eternity. He'd died as an unmarried young man, it seemed. The other second-generation son, Pieter, had lived many years longer and was buried under a formidable slab of white marble next to his wife Rhea, who'd outlived him until the unfortunate day she'd been pushed down the stairs. Their son Gerrit—the third generation—was buried nearby, next to his own wife Dorothy, whose side of the gravestone was embellished with a couple of stone cherubs.

I scribbled down these names in my notepad, hoping there wouldn't be a quiz later.

"Where's Rhea's other son, Bartel?" Stacey asked. "I don't see him."

"Murdering his mother may have gotten him kicked

out of the family churchyard. He might be buried near the prison, if he died there."

"Makes sense. Hanging out with a family member who murdered you could make for an awkward eternity. But hey, nobody's family is perfect."

After taking our time looking around downtown, we returned to the van.

Headlights off, I drove toward the Heusinkveld house from the side opposite Chelsea's second-floor apartment. This put us out of her room's view and also not far from Arden's room, from which we'd be picking up the audio and camera transmission.

We parked in the darkest spot on the street, away from the scattered streetlights, by an enormous dogwood tree growing on the mansion's grounds. We turned off the van's overhead light so it wouldn't draw attention if we opened a door. Darkness was our friend that night.

In the back of the van, we turned on two screens and a speaker to monitor the gear in Arden's room. We sat on the narrow, uncomfortable drop-down cots built into the van's walls, which were terrible for sleeping but somewhat okay for sitting.

"So, what do you think it'll be tonight?" Stacey asked. "Evil Dad or Creepy Toddler?"

"I'm not sure which is worse," I said.

"Do you think it'll still have the same power over them, now that they know what it really is?"

"I'm not even sure *we* know what it really is."

"But they know it's not their relatives," Stacey said.

"I hope knowing the truth helps them," I said. "And they're ready with basic defenses. If something threatens them, we'll have to get inside to help. I can handle the door lock, but I noticed a burglar alarm system. The main panel for that will probably be in Chelsea's room."

"I bet we could climb up that oak tree over there to that third-story balcony. They might not have wired the windows that high up."

Following her pointing finger, I could sort of see the possible path from limb to limb up to the high balcony, but the idea of climbing such a treacherous course make me feel queasy. I'm not a fan of heights—ghosts can too easily use them to an advantage, pushing someone over an edge while being in no danger of falling themselves. They just float there, untouchable, watching you go down.

"For all we know, the balcony access has been locked or nailed shut," I said. "And the balcony doesn't look like it would pass an OSHA inspection."

"Okay, well, it's an option to consider."

"I disagree." I kept watch on our client's closet, waiting for the hour to grow later, and for the ghost to arrive.

Chapter Fourteen

It was about ten-fifteen when the cold spots appeared once again in Arden and Georgette's walk-in closet.

"It's the same as last night, right?" Stacey whispered. "The same shape, the same pattern of movement..."

My hand crept toward my flashlight as I readied myself to barge inside the house, burglar alarm or no, and protect those women from the evil thing that had taken up residence in their closet. I definitely wasn't climbing up a tree to the top-floor balcony, though. I wasn't completely crazy.

The cold spots vanished. On the other screen, the night vision showed the outside of the closet door, still closed. I tensed, holding my breath as I waited for it to open, to reveal what form the spirit had taken, what mask it wore tonight.

"Here it comes," Stacey whispered.

We stared at the door.

The door did not open.

"Huh?" Stacey looked back at the thermal display inside the closet, but the entity hadn't returned. "He's just gone? Neither here nor there?"

"Maybe he could sense that his victims were prepared for him."

"Yeah, we laid out a good defense. Georgette's stereo speakers are pointed right at the closet door."

We kept watching, but the entity was gone.

"Okay," Stacey said. "I guess it gave up on our tough old gals. That's good, right?"

"But it could move on to other victims." I looked over at the darkened windows of the house, the rooms concealed by thick, heavy drapes. On the covered porch where we'd had tea with Spencer and Wallace, the empty chairs at the table faced each other like a gathering of invisible guests.

A few minutes later, a first-floor light switched on behind closed drapes, but it wasn't in Spencer and Wallace's suite.

"What part of the house is that?" Stacey asked.

"I'm not sure. I'll get a closer look." I opened the van door.

"Ooh, are we going to climb that tree?" Stacey asked, voice brimming with hope.

"Absolutely not." I pulled on my radio headset. "You stay and watch over Arden's room in case the entity doubles back."

I hopped out and softly eased the driver-side door shut.

Then I tiptoed along the fence to get a better view of the lighted window.

As I moved past the dogwood tree, that light went dark. A different light came on somewhere at the back of the house, casting a glow onto the trees in the back yard.

I followed the fence to the street corner. The lights were on inside the spacious western-facing sunroom where the residents gathered for recreation.

Karl hobbled past the room's tall windows, leaning heavily on his cane. Then he hobbled back the other way, pacing. His face was pale, and he trembled.

"It's Karl," I told Stacey over the headset, my voice extra low. "He looks scared. I want to hop the fence and check on him, but I don't think my face suddenly popping up in the window in the middle of the night would have a soothing effect."

"What do we do?"

"Try to find his cell phone number. Karl Moller, this address—"

"Got it."

"You already logged into the data fusion app?"

"Nah, I just used a regular search engine. You know, privacy is not what it used to be." She texted me Karl's number, and I hung up on her and called him.

Inside the sunroom, Karl looked startled. He fished out his phone from the pocket of his checkered bathrobe and squinted at the caller ID, like he couldn't read it without his glasses, but he answered it anyway.

"Hi, Karl," I said, keeping my tone gentle since it looked like he was having a rough time of it. "This is Ellie Jordan, the investigator Arden hired about the strange events in her room."

"It is?" He rubbed the temple on the non-burned side of his face, his startled look giving way to confusion. "How'd you get this number?"

"The internet. I'm sure it's weird to have me call like this, but we're actually staking out the house for Arden tonight. We didn't mention it to many people—"

"Because you don't want Chelsea to know," Karl said, nodding. "Makes sense."

"We noticed you were up and wanted to make sure everything was okay."

"I wouldn't say that. Not at all." He sat down heavily, as though he'd lost all his strength. "I saw someone tonight. Someone who couldn't have been there."

"Did you recognize the person?"

"Not at first. At first it was just a solid black cloud just inside the bathroom door. Normally, I can see the reflection of the moonlight in the bathroom mirror, but tonight there was something dark in there, filling up the room."

"Then what happened?" I asked.

"It moved closer, and I realized it was Wendy. Just like I remember her, not a scratch on her, like the accident never happened."

"The accident?"

"The one that ended my life almost fifty years ago."

"I'm sorry?" I said, feeling stupid. If Karl was a ghost, yet he could take calls from the living, he must have had amazing cell service.

"I was a pilot. Did you know that?"

"I didn't, no."

"Real hotshot, too, or I thought I was. Legend in my own mind. After Vietnam, I got a job with Pan Am.

Let me tell you, if you want to have a great, wild, crazy life, you can't go much better than being an airline pilot in the 70s. Whew. Wendy was an air hostess, and I'll tell you, I could barely keep my mind on the job when she was onboard. We got married in '72. In '75, we went out on one of those wild nights, saw the Stones play the Cotton Bowl, along with my brother and his girlfriend. Then we hit one or two clubs in downtown Dallas.

"In those days, I liked to drive like I was flying. I had a Stingray, and my brother had a GTX. You could say we were a might bit competitive. We got to racing, and I don't remember much, but they say I missed a hairpin curve, flipped the car. Ruptured the gas tank, that's how I got all my unique good looks." He gestured at the burned side of his face and his patched eye. "Wendy lingered for a while, but never recovered. I never really did, either. Never remarried, despite all the ladies lining up to kiss this mug. Quit flying, went into ground maintenance, then sort of fell into janitorial… Where are you, exactly?"

"Down at the street corner. To your right."

He hobbled toward the wall of windows, leaned his face to the glass, and cupped a hand around his good eye. I moved to the brightest patch of moonlight I could find and waved at him.

"I can't see you," he said.

I pointed my flashlight at the sky and clicked it on like a beacon.

"There you are," he said. "I suppose it's nice to know you're out there, since you seem to know what you're doing. I won't be going back to my room anytime soon."

"I'm so sorry to hear about your wife. What happened when you saw the apparition of her tonight?"

"Like I said, she was fine at first, just like I remember her back in the good times. Then she started to change. To burn up. To become…the way they found her, I guess. And I told her I was sorry. Begged her to forgive me, while she stood there, staring, her hatred burning me like an overheated engine. I thought I might die, too. But I didn't. And when I couldn't apologize anymore, when I felt all empty inside, she left. She left me to think about what I did to her."

"What you saw was not really your wife," I said. "It's an entity that changes form. It can take on the appearance of someone who was important to you."

"Why would it do that?"

"To feed on you. We explained this to Arden and Georgette earlier."

"It sounds like you should have explained it to all of us," Karl said. "What can we do about this thing?"

"We're working on a solution," I said. "Until then, I could come inside and have a look at your room for you."

"Aw, I wouldn't feel right having you do that."

"It's my job," I said. "And you'd be doing me a favor, because I'd really like to take some readings after what you saw. The main problem is the burglar alarm."

"I can get you past that," he said. "I saw her punch in the code."

"Perfect. Should I meet you at the front door?"

"Back door's better. By the sunroom."

"Okay. I'll see you there." I hurried to the van and grabbed a backpack.

"Should I come with you?" Stacey asked.

"Nope. Keep watch over the monitors," I said. "Let me know if anything happens in there."

"You do the same," she said as I closed the door again.

I climbed carefully over the wrought-iron fence and landed in the soft soil of the lawn. Not much grass grew in the shade of the towering old trees. The lawn was mostly clover with patches of bare dirt.

The back door was recessed under a small roof, and I had to climb half a dozen worn brick steps to reach it. Karl opened it when I arrived. We crossed through the sunroom and down a hallway to Karl and Joe's room.

"I already woke up Joe when I turned on the lamp, so don't worry about tiptoeing around him," Karl said as he opened the door and led me inside.

The room shared by Karl and Coach Joe had a very different look than Spencer and Wallace's. The furniture was plain and worn, including a futon on Karl's side of the room. The two sides were easily distinguished. Coach Joe's side was hung with pennants, trophies, and framed faded team pictures, while Karl's was sparser, decorated with a couple of model biplanes.

"Oh, ho!" Coach Joe sat up in bed. "Karl, if you're going to have lady friends in the room, you're supposed to hang a necktie on the door. That's the gentlemanly thing to do."

"That's a real knee-slapper, Joe." Karl frowned, shaking his head. "I just brought Arden's detective in to have a look at what I saw."

"You never told me what you saw," Joe said, frowning at the bathroom door.

"Something strange. I don't know." Karl shrugged,

apparently unwilling to open up to Joe about his wife like he had to me.

"This won't take long." I brought out my EMF meter and stepped into their shared bathroom, which wasn't exactly loaded with decorative soaps or potpourri. Worn gray towels hung over a pair of towel racks. Toenail clippers sat beside a toothbrush at the sink.

"What are you looking for, specifically?" Karl asked.

"Any strange electrical activity, though it's hard to determine that without a baseline reading. It also checks the temperature to help me measure cold spots, but I'm not finding any of those so far." I brought out my voice recorder. "I'm just going to ask a few questions for any entities that might be present. Even if we don't hear anything, we might record something we don't notice until we review the audio."

"Let me guess," Coach Joe said. In the mirror, I saw him sitting on the edge of his bed, watching me. He raised his hands and wiggled his fingers. "They like to say 'boo!'"

"I'm not sure I've ever recorded one saying that, though you'd think at least one might have done it as a joke. I'll start now. If y'all could keep quiet and help me listen, that would be great."

"Keep quiet, she says." Coach Joe chuckled. "You remind me of my first wife. She couldn't stand for anybody else to be the center of attention."

Karl eased down into a faded green La-Z-Boy recliner. He nodded at me to begin.

I turned out the overhead light and started recording.

"Is anyone here?" I asked. "Anyone with a message for the living?" I paused. "I can help if you need it. I'm here to listen."

"Shoot, are you trying to get rid of the thing or be its mommy?" Joe grumbled.

"Quiet," Karl told him.

I closed the door, partly to help me ignore them, partly to plunge the room into complete darkness. The bathroom window was heavily draped like most of the windows in the house, blotting out any natural light.

"Hello? Is anyone here?" I asked again, as if trying to strike up a conversation via Ouija board. "Please speak up. I want to hear from you."

I waited. The bathroom felt colder than the bedroom had been, but no voice answered me as I stood alone in the dark.

A hand touched my arm.

I gasped and jerked back, crashing into the door. Then I covered my mouth with one hand to shut myself up and drew my flashlight with the other.

The shape in front of me looked like a short, petite woman in a paisley mini dress. She was slashed and mangled, and the stench of hot metal and burning gasoline wafted from her. Her burn injuries reminded me of Karl's, only much more severe. She wept, her tears sizzling to steam along on her burning cheeks, and looked so sad and helpless I almost wanted to reach out and help her.

Then I reminded myself of what she was, or at least what she wasn't.

"You're not Wendy," I said. "I already told him. You may as well take off your mask and show your true face."

She recoiled from my light, baring her teeth in hatred like a vampire being offered a garlic pizza. I blamed this predatory entity for making me think of vampires so often lately.

"You okay in there?" Karl asked, rattling the door, probably in response to my crashing against it.

"Don't ask her if she fell in," Coach Joe said. "It's not polite."

The apparition grew less distinct, collapsing into a faceless dark cloud. It retreated toward the narrow door to the linen closet and disappeared. I flung that door open but found only folded towels quietly waiting to be used.

The bathroom door opened, bringing in all the light from the bedroom, and I turned off my flashlight.

"I saw it." I turned to face Karl, but it wasn't Karl standing there, or even Coach Joe.

It was Chelsea, her short black hair rumpled, wearing a housecoat and slippers, and the fury in her eyes was so intense they seemed to glow.

"What are you doing in my house?" She pushed the words out through curled lips and bared teeth.

"Um," I replied, feeling not so quick on my feet at that moment.

"Give me a reason why I shouldn't call the police." Chelsea waved her phone at me like a weapon.

"Ellie, what's happening in there?" Stacey asked over my headset.

"Not now," I whispered.

"Why not?" Chelsea asked, moving her finger close to her phone.

"Sorry, I was talking to…" I touched my headset and cleared my throat. "The important thing here is that the entity isn't restricted to Arden and Georgette's room. Karl encountered it tonight—"

"And y'all drove all the way here from Savannah just now? In the middle of the night? That's what I'm supposed to believe?"

"As it turned out, we never actually went back to Savannah—"

"Is that how it turned out? And now you're lurking around in residents' bathrooms?"

"Karl saw the entity in here."

"Really?" Chelsea whipped around on Karl so fast he leaned back in his recliner like he was accelerating for takeoff. "Is that right, Karl?"

"Yeah, I saw it. It's coming for all of us, Chelsea." Karl folded his hands in his laps, fingers twitching nervously. "It can get inside your head and play tricks on you."

"I'm starting to believe someone around here is good at that, yes." Chelsea stared at me, not too subtly at all.

"Aw, don't call the police," Coach Joe said. "These two ladies and Arden's ghost stories are the most interesting thing we've got going around here lately."

"If you're bored, sign up for the talent show," Chelsea told him without moving her eyes off me. "Spencer's looking for a third act."

"Nobody's roping me into that mess." Coach Joe waved his hands across each other and shook his head as if canceling a play from the sideline.

"I assume your little blonde friend is here, too?" Chelsea asked me. "On the other end of that headset? In that ugly van?"

"Pretty much," I said. "Look, I apologize for all

this, but Arden and Georgette were still very concerned, so we decided to stay nearby in case problems happened."

"I will talk this over with our residents in the morning," Chelsea said. "For now, you need to go. I would have you remove the cameras out of Arden's room, too, but I don't want to interrupt their sleep."

"Aw, don't make 'em go—" Joe began.

"I will or the police will," Chelsea said. "That's it."

"No need for that," I said. "I'll leave."

"Good," Chelsea said. "Try leaving town this time. The interstate is that way." She pointed toward one of the bedroom's curtained windows.

"Thanks for the tip," I said, and I headed for the front door.

Chapter Fifteen

"I don't think we'll be welcomed back anytime soon," I told Stacey as I climbed into the van and put down my backpack.

"What about our gear?"

"Hopefully Arden will run it in our absence." I started up the van. "Time to go home."

"Like, actually go home, or 'go home' but really stick around?"

"Actually go home."

"Then we're done? Off the case? Handed our walking papers? Given the boot?"

"I'll check with Arden in the morning," I said. "But our odds don't look great."

I drove toward the interstate, which was more or less in the direction Chelsea had pointed when ordering me out of her house.

At home, I spent some quality time with my cat. He wasn't interested until I pretended to read a paperback novel. Lured by this irresistible trap, he walked over and sat on the pages, close enough for me to pet. He started purring after a minute. He wasn't usually quick to purr. He was more like a rickety engine that took a few false tries before it finally sputtered to life.

After clamping my blackout curtains together so no drop of the sunrise would reach me, I went to sleep. Strange, eyeless figures chased me through the dark rooms of my dreams. Typical night for me.

Arden called at six in the morning, my ringing phone shattering my unpleasant slumber.

"Is everything okay?" I asked, yawning and trying to rouse myself. "Is there an emergency?"

"No, I just thought I'd call you after breakfast to catch up on things," Arden said.

"Okay. Good." I stood and stretched. "What's happening? Is Chelsea pulling the plug?" I winced at the term after I heard myself say it.

"She's in a fury, but she can't call *all* of us crazy. The only crazy thing I did was move into this place. Old house, understaffed, and poor quality control on the tomatoes." Arden sniffed.

"I was going to talk to you about the staff. I'd really like to speak with any of them who've quit. Chelsea mentioned nighttime workers named Emmanuel and Veronica who left abruptly."

"I'll see what I can do."

"Thanks. Just call back and let us know—"

"Georgette!" Arden shouted, her voice blaring into my ear over the speaker. "Georgette, who can get us in touch with Emmanuel or Veronica?" Georgette murmured something, and Arden said, "I'll call you back."

"Thank you."

After the phone call, I intended to go right back to sleep for a couple of hours, but I felt restless as I lay there in bed.

I finally grabbed my laptop and looked up Harold Heusinkveld, the former owner of the old house. His uncommon Dutch surname was a big help. The data fusion service showed me he'd rented an apartment in Tallahassee, Florida, a couple hundred miles southwest of his hometown. His cell phone number still had a 912 area code for southern Georgia instead of 850 for northern Florida. I'd wait until a bit later to call him, in case he wasn't an early bird like Arden.

I made coffee and called Stacey instead.

"Seriously?" Stacey said when she answered. "It's so early. And a Monday."

"Don't be a Garfield. We're heading to Reidsville, home of the Tattnall County Library and the local newspaper of record, *The Tattnall Journal Sentinel.*"

"They should have called it *The Tattnall Tattler,*" Stacey said. "They totally missed the boat on that one."

"Hopefully, the paper spent a lot of time tattling on the Heusinkveld family down in Burdener's Hill, because we need to learn all about them."

"I guess I'll put on my library shoes," Stacey said. "It's rainy, too. What a day for a drive."

I pulled aside my window curtain and looked out. A thin gruel of rain drizzled from the dim gray morning sky above, not exactly inviting. "It does look bleak. Not ideal road-trip conditions."

"I'll make an upbeat playlist for the car."

"Not too upbeat, though."

"I'll keep it mellow. Maybe some Creedence."

We decided to take my semi-ancient black Camaro since it was faster and lighter than the van full of equipment. The Camaro had been my dad's and was sort of my last tangible connection to him. Being inside made me feel almost like I was surrounded by his memory, by whatever residual spirit he'd left behind. I could remember him standing in the driveway with the hood up, his checkered sleeves rolled back while he tinkered with the engine. He'd been in construction, a guy who worked with tools and was good with his hands. He'd been a lot like Michael in that way, I supposed, but decided not to think too deeply about that. I had work to do, no time for self-analysis.

I drove through the rainy streets of Savannah to pick up Stacey at her apartment. She wore a green weatherproof hoodie that was much more streamlined and stylish than the black raincoat I'd brought.

Reidsville, the county seat, was farther away from Savannah than Burdener's Hill. I drove as fast as I could without becoming an obvious revenue target for the local police.

The library was a small red brick fortress of a building fronted with a covered portico featuring narrow cutout archways. I almost expected archers to pop up inside and shoot arrows as we approached.

That didn't happen, though, and while the library's exterior might have led us to expect beefy medieval warriors feasting next to roaring fireplaces, it was just a normal little modern library on the inside, with bookshelves and computers under fluorescent lights.

Our first task was to look through the local

newspaper archives and put together a family tree and timeline for the Heusinkveld family, noting any strange deaths or hints of other unusual occurrences.

Much of what we found concurred with what Wallace and the other Sunshine House residents had told us. Andries Heusinkveld, founder of the cannery, was shown in a picture from 1900, along with a smiling blonde wife, Gerda, and two small children, a toddler called Isaak and an infant called Pieter. The article was basically a puff piece about the family following an expansion of the cannery.

"He doesn't look friendly," Stacey said. In the picture, Andries had small, dark eyes and large sideburns extending almost to his chin, which combined with unkempt dark hair to give him a feral-animal look, like he might bite you if you got too close and leave you with a bad case of rabies. His dark suit, stiff-collared shirt, and necktie barely lent him a veneer of civilization.

A society page photo from 1910 showed the same family, the infant Pieter grown to upper elementary age, the older boy Isaak grown to his early teens. They stood on the front steps of the mansion that would become The Sunshine House, but the house was brand new, with potted plants and baskets of flowers on every windowsill and balcony. The article spoke of a lavish "Harvest Party" at the house, which all the local fancy-pants types had attended, including the banker and the mayor.

"Aw, look at this," Stacey said a little later, showing me an obituary. "Poor Gerda died soon after they moved into the house. She barely got a chance to enjoy it. Her boys were still pretty young, too."

A 1920 wedding announcement featured a formal photograph of the younger boy, Pieter, by then a youthful veteran of the First World War, standing beside a striking, cheerful-looking young woman with big, catlike eyes, cutely bobbed hair, and a beaming smile she could barely contain. Pieter Heusinkveld would be marrying Rhea Loundes, daughter of Buck Loundes. Pieter had developed some of his father's rough, wild look, and his eyes stared off into the distance as if shell-shocked, which I supposed was a real possibility.

We later found birth announcements for Pieter and Rhea's sons, the family's third generation, Gerrit and Bartel. The younger one, Bartel, would eventually go to prison for murdering Rhea.

In between these events, there had been tragedy. Pieter's older brother Isaak died in an accident falling from a third-floor balcony.

"Probably the same balcony you wanted us to climb up to," I told Stacey.

"I still think we could pull it off," she said.

Tragedy struck the family again in 1936, when founding patriarch Andries died of an unspecified illness at age seventy-one. Three years later, Pieter died of a liver ailment. In all his pictures, he'd looked thin and haunted, as though he'd never really recovered from whatever horrors he'd seen in the trenches of wartime Europe.

Happier news arrived with his son Gerrit's wedding announcement to Dorothy "Dottie" Meadows in the late 1950s, followed several years later by the birth of their son Harold.

Then Gerrit died in 1967, of liver failure in his

early forties just like his father Pieter, leaving Dottie and five-year-old Harold to live with Harold's grandmother Rhea and uncle Bartel.

"Wow, this family cannot catch a break," Stacey said.

"It only gets worse." I pointed to an article on my own microfilm projector about Bartel's conviction for his mother's murder about a year later, after rolling her down the attic stairs in her wheelchair. "Imagine the effect on Dottie. Her husband dies, her brother-in-law murders her mother-in-law, she's left alone with the kid."

"And that poor kid!" Stacey shuddered. "His whole family wiped out by a wave of death and murder. And to keep living in that house afterward! I mean, it's a nice house, but yeesh, that's a lot of death. It's like having the Grim Reaper for a roommate. And you just know he leaves those black robes hanging all over the bathroom, too. Probably drinks your OJ right out of the carton. I've had some bad roommates."

I kept reading. Dottie had operated the Heusinkveld house as a group home for senior citizens until her death seventeen years later. Harold had earned a degree from Georgia Southern, close enough for him to live at home during college, and kept the place going until he'd finally sold it to Chelsea and retired.

"It sounds like Harold basically lived here his whole life, from childhood onward, taking care of patients," Stacey said. "I wonder what that was like."

"I haven't found any wedding or birth announcements associated with Harold. Looks like he's the end of the Heusinkveld line. We need to get in touch with him. Now it's lunchtime, which is a good time to try to cold-call someone."

"And also a great time to get lunch!" Stacey eased her phone out of her pocket. "Shall I search up colorful local places?"

"I'd rather you look for Bartel Heusinkveld's obituary," I said, and she sighed as I headed for the door.

Outside, I stood in the library's dark covered portico, grateful for its shelter as the rain gushed down just beyond the narrow archways.

Unfortunately, but not surprisingly, Harold didn't answer a voice call from an unknown person. I tried to throw all the charm I could into my voicemail, though charm isn't especially my strong suit. "Hi, Mr. Heusinkveld! My name's Ellie Jordan, and I'm doing historical research around Burdener's Hill. I'm hoping to ask you one or two questions about the town's past. I would love it if you could give me a quick call back as soon as you can…"

As I turned to start back toward the library doors, I found myself face to face with a rough-looking man with shaggy hair and small, dark eyes. For a moment I thought it was Andries Heusinkveld, based on his old pictures, but it was a black and white arrest photo from 1968.

"Bartel Heusinkveld," Stacey said. "Convicted of murder in 1969, died in Georgia State Prison in 1999."

"That's not far from here," I said. "Home of the state electric chair."

"It's kinda disturbing you know that right off the top of your head, Ellie."

"Did Bartel get the chair?"

"Says he died of heart failure." She showed me

another page, which was a print-out of local obituaries from 1999. "His obituary is more of a short death notice. It doesn't say much."

"He's buried at the prison cemetery," I said, looking it over. "We should visit his grave while we're close by."

"Sure, a prison cemetery on a gloomy day, that could be fun," Stacey said. "Maybe after lunch—"

"I'm really not that hungry. Let's go to the grave first."

"You're killing me, Ellie. I haven't had anything today except strawberries, raisin toast, and a few eggs with cheese."

"I've only had coffee."

"That's super unhealthy. You need a balanced diet with a complete set of nutrients."

"Maybe after we check the land records at the courthouse."

"Ugh."

After the library, we studied the courthouse records of land ownership, looking at both the Heusinkveld house and business properties.

Our biggest discovery was that the previous owner of Heusinkveld's grocery, Edgar Morgan, had no heirs and left the shop and his own small house to his young employee Andries upon his demise. Andries had expanded the grocery business and added the more profitable cannery, and eventually demolished Morgan's little house to build the mansion.

The cannery closed in 1965, unable to keep up with national competition, and the building now belonged to a national banking chain that had absorbed the town's local bank and later closed it. The family grocery store lasted a little longer, closing down in 1967.

"We could pretty much walk to Tacos La Chona." Stacey gazed at her phone, licking her lips.

"In this weather?"

"Maybe not in this weather, but we could drive there in an eyeblink. Look at these pictures. I could go for a barbacoa burrito right now."

"You can sell me on it while we visit the cemetery," I said.

"Seriously? You are killing me, Ellie."

"Think of the barbacoa burrito as your reward for going somewhere awful."

She nodded. "I get it. It'll take the full cheeriness of a Mexican restaurant to wipe away the bleakness of a prison boneyard."

We drove south out of the little town, into farmland. The road was similar to our drive to Arden's old farmhouse, a black ribbon of asphalt with occasional dirt roads branching off to one side or the other. We passed overgrown houses, barns, and a warehouse building that may have been some kind of machine shop but didn't have a sign to explain itself.

The state prison soon loomed by the road, its towers and walls surrounded by chain-link and razor wire. The prison had closed in 2022 after decades of holding death-row inmates and other violent criminals.

"People were wrongfully executed there, too," Stacey said, reading aloud from her phone. "Like Lena Baker, a black woman sent to the electric chair for killing a white man in self-defense. She was pardoned sixty years after her death."

Reflecting on the prison's grim past, we turned down a country lane through more farmland and stands of tall pine trees.

After a minute, down an isolated stretch of road, the cemetery appeared on our left, with rows of identical white crosses marked with numbers instead of names. I pulled off and parked on the short stub of gravel road leading to the small, perfunctory concrete sign identifying the prison cemetery.

The desolate cemetery was bounded by fenced pastures on both sides, as well as across the road, as if nobody wanted to build a house or even a barn in sight of it. The wire fences and metal gates in every direction echoed the atmosphere of a prison.

"This is eerie," Stacey said.

"There's no fence around the cemetery itself," I said. "And it's right by the road. They're basically inviting all these spirits to leave their graves and go traveling."

"And Bartel Heusinkveld wouldn't have too far to go if he wanted to visit home," Stacey said.

"A murderer who spent thirty years in a prison full of violent criminals could become a very twisted soul," I said.

"Just imagine all the evil vibes he might have soaked up." Stacey shivered. "Have I mentioned how much the numbers instead of names on these headstones is weirding me out? I guess we'll have to leave since there's no way of finding Bartel's grave."

"The internet might help us." I searched with my phone. "FindAGrave has a long list of the graves here, giving names to the numbers. Thank goodness for cemetery enthusiasts." I opened the driver-side door onto the dark, drizzling afternoon outside.

"Uh, yeah. Thank goodness for those folks." Stacey

reluctantly pulled up her green hood and stepped out of the car. "It got cold out here."

We walked between the rows of graves. The pattering of rain and the persistent wind were like wordless voices around us.

Grass and weeds didn't seem to grow well in the cemetery. Bare patches of red Georgia clay had been turned to mud by the rain, forming red puddles and streams among the rows of numbered white crosses.

We eventually found Bartel's toward the back in the shadows of pine trees.

I knelt in front of it.

"Bartel Heusinkveld," I said, doing my best to pronounce the last name correctly. "If you're causing trouble at your old house, you need to move on. Your family has left, and you do not belong there anymore."

The cross sat indifferently in front of me. I didn't hear or see any response, other than the wind picking up and blowing the rain sideways, flicking it into my face.

I removed a glass jar from my raincoat pocket and unscrewed the lid. I scooped up red mud from the base of the cross, a sample of the earth in which he'd been buried, sometimes useful for attracting a ghost's attention into a trap.

"If you don't want to move on, I'll be happy to trap you and bury you—" I looked up and drew a sharp breath.

Only inches away, staring at me over the arm of the cross, was the same rough-looking face with small, glaring eyes that Stacey had showed me earlier, in his arrest photo from the old newspaper. His face was more wrinkled, his dark hair veined with gray and white. He wore the blue-edged white jumpsuit of a state prisoner, and he squatted so his pale blue eyes were even with mine.

I gasped and pulled back, dropping the jar and drawing the flashlight from my belt, though I wondered whether it would be any use against an entity that didn't mind coming out during the daytime. It was cloudy and dark, so maybe a little more light would help me out.

"What happened?" Stacey turned toward me. "I looked away for one second…or okay, maybe five or ten…"

The beam of my light shone on the cross. The apparition had vanished.

"Bartel," I said. "He was right there."

"He still is." She glanced at the wet red earth in front of the cross where I'd been kneeling, right on top of where he'd been buried. "Just, you know, a little bit less of him each year, I'm sure."

"I mean his ghost. He was all in my face, looking at me."

"Yikes." Stacey looked around at the cold, isolated cemetery. "Should we get out of here?"

"No, we should try for more contact."

"Oh, with the murderer's ghost, of course. Silly me, suggesting we leave." Stacey shook her head and followed me as I returned to the car, put away my sample jar, then returned to the grave with a microphone.

"Bartel Heusinkveld," I said. "I saw you already. Can you show yourself again?" I paused a minute, then said, "Do you have a message for me? Or for anyone? Is there any way I can help you move on? Some reason you're stuck here?" After a while, I added, "You need to stop bothering the living. Or we'll make sure you do."

The wind lashed harder, and the rain picked up.

"Can we, uh, skedaddle yet, Ellie?" Stacey asked.

I looked at the place where Bartel had momentarily appeared, but nothing was there except empty space and increasingly heavy rain.

"Okay." I nodded slowly, reluctant to back away from a chance to learn more, but the weather was taking that choice out of my hands. "I meant what I said, Bartel. Go, and don't come back."

After issuing my threat—a fairly empty one at this point—I turned back toward the car. We walked across the thickening, darkening streams of red that covered the earth as a storm swelled in the sky.

Chapter Sixteen

"This is what I needed," Stacey said, biting into a tortilla chip heaped with salsa. Tacos La Chona occupied a compact brick hut in downtown Reidsville, between a neighborhood of well-kept little houses and an empty industrial strip where there had once been an auto parts store and a mechanic shop. A block away stood the windblown hull of a two-story abandoned building whose remnant of a sign identified it as the Dixie Motel.

The Mexican restaurant was cheery enough, though, and offered a shelter full of hot snacks, a respite from the rain outside. I sipped my agua fresca, luxuriating in the refreshing, sugary lime taste.

We barely had time to process our eerie experience at the cemetery before the spicy, alluring tacos arrived, an assortment with grilled chicken, barbecued meat, and birria that smelled like stewed beef and chili peppers. They were folded in soft taco shells along with guacamole, cilantro, and jalapenos.

Stacey's eyes lit up. "I knew this would be good," she whispered reverently.

I started to reach for the nearest taco, my mouth suddenly watering, and then my phone rang.

Scowling, I changed course and drew out my phone instead, hoping for a spam-or-scam call I could confidently blow off in order to focus on the precious tacos. Stacey was already biting into one, and my stomach growled jealously.

"It's Arden," I said.

"Oh, good!" Stacey said after swallowing her juicy bite of green vegetables and spicy meat.

"Not really, because now I have to take it." I stood and headed for the door. "You'd better save me some tacos."

Stacey gave little indication of hearing me as she took another bite, let out an "mmmm" sound, and closed her eyes.

Outside, I stood against the outer wall of the restaurant under the slightly protruding roof while the rain fell in front of me.

"Sorry to call so late," Arden said, because it was almost seven in the evening. "Just wanted to let you know I got Veronica's phone number for you."

"Thanks—"

"She used to be on the night staff but quit. Now there's nobody reliable. Just Chelsea to come when you buzz for help, and she moves slow at night. I ought to get a discount."

"If you could just give me the number—"

"Now Veronica, on the other hand, she would always listen to you and straighten things out like they needed to be. She never acted tired or copped an attitude like Chelsea. Always pleasant."

"I'm glad to hear—"

"Chelsea's interviewing some new people, but I doubt they'll be as good as Veronica was."

"If you could just—"

"Chelsea's still sore about you, if you were wondering. Got a chip on her shoulder as big as Mount Rushmore about the whole thing. I don't know when she'll allow you back."

"I'm not sure about the best approach with her. But we did look into the history of the house, and there does seem to be a pattern of tragedy—"

"Shoot, everybody in town knows that. Just proves you can have all the money in the world and still be miserable."

"We also encountered an apparition of Bartel Heusinkveld while visiting his grave by the prison," I said. "So he's still hanging around."

"That's all we need," Arden said. "A dang murderer's ghost. If the house is haunted, and it's not Daddy's ghost following me here, I think Chelsea ought to be liable for paying y'all instead of me. I probably ought to get a discount from Chelsea, too, since nobody mentioned any shape-changing murder ghosts to me before I moved in. That wasn't on the amenities list. The so-called 'movie theater' is a joke, too."

"I hope Chelsea will come around," I said, keeping it agreeable but vague. I was worried about whether we'd ultimately get paid for this case, but there was no way I'd let a dangerous entity like this one continue to prey on innocent victims just because of a money issue. I'd deal with the entity for free if I had to, but I certainly wasn't going to say that out loud. "We'll continue working your case to the extent we can. Which brings me to that contact information for Veronica—"

"Veronica, yeah. I've got her phone number here for you if you want it."

"That would be great." I jotted it on my trusty pocket notepad as Arden read it aloud. "Thanks. I hope she'll talk to me."

"You tell her it's for me, and she'll do it," Arden said.

"Good to know."

After the call, I returned inside to find Stacey had demolished the tacos. She leaned back in the restaurant booth like an overstuffed dad on Thanksgiving.

"Hey!" I sat down across from her. "What did I say?"

"Relax, I ordered more for you. I couldn't eat another bit." Stacey rubbed her stomach. "You should take some to Michael."

"I wasn't planning to go over there tonight."

"So surprise him with tacos. Who wouldn't like that?"

"They'll be cold by the time I get there."

"Not if you drive fast enough. Especially if we get yours to go. Then you can wait and eat with him."

"That's not happening," I said, my stomach growling as the server brought another round of tacos just for me. I ordered some more for Michael and then, finally, bit into some of the soft, warm taco goodness I'd been denied earlier, full of spicy chicken and crunchy vegetables.

Two were enough to pacify the angry dragon in my stomach. I could have eaten more, but that might have put me into a state of jalapeno-scented drowsiness like Stacey, and I had to drive.

The rain slacked off a little as we drove back to Savannah but clearly had plans to keep falling all night.

I left Stacey at her place and continued on to Michael's apartment building, where the rain lashed against the high turret windows and ran along the labyrinth of rooftops and gutters, cascading in waterfalls in front of the cave-like recessed balconies. A couple of lights were on in Michael's apartment.

In the downstairs hall, I pressed the button for apartment C.

"Hello?" Michael sounded suspicious, like he thought I might be some species of door-to-door scam artist.

"Hey, it's me, spontaneously dropping by."

"Oh, okay, nice," he said, not quite gushing. The door buzzed. "Come on up."

I climbed the flights of dark hardwood stairs to his open apartment door. He leaned against the frame, dressed in some long cotton boxers and nothing else, the muscles of his chest and arm backlit by the low light inside the apartment. He watched me ascend toward him, but with a sort of distant look in his eyes.

"You feeling okay?" I finally reached the small landing at his door.

"Yeah, just distracted. What's this?" He pointed at the temptingly grease-stained white paper bag in my hand.

"Tacos. They're still warm. Ish."

"You know I love warm-ish tacos." He took the bag in one hand and wrapped the other arm around me, pulling me close and kissing me.

"This is how you answer the door?" I ran my fingers over the bare muscles of his back. Looking past him, I saw a pair of jeans and a t-shirt flung casually onto the couch. A pair of dirty socks were just hanging out on the floor, near the closed door to his bedroom.

"The whole apartment is basically my room now," he said.

"I see that." I stepped inside, and he closed the door behind him. "So, it took how many days of living alone for you to regress into a caveman? Two? Three?"

"I was going to roast some mammoth steaks in the fireplace, but now I'll eat these semi-warm tacos instead."

"That's all you'll need, I promise."

He sat down at the kitchen table and took one out. "Mmm. Little soggy, but I like the barbecue."

"I figured you would." My gaze drifted back to the closed bedroom door. Why close it if he was the only person here? "What were you doing when I got here? Reading that Leonardo da Vinci book?" I'd bought it for him as a gift, figuring he would like all the mechanical drawings.

"I haven't been reading much lately," he said. "But I will soon, now that it's so quiet. I never really noticed how much constant banging and thumping there used to be with Melissa running around. But I notice the silence now."

"Have you talked to her?"

"Yeah, texted. She's doing fine. Sounds happy."

"Great. So…does this casual underwear dress code

only apply to you, or is it open to guests?" I began unbuttoning my shirt.

"Most guests, no." He looked at me with his taco forgotten somewhere near his mouth, dripping sauce onto his table.

"What were you really doing, though?"

He sighed. "Like I said, it's quiet. So I got sucked into a project."

"Which one?" I started toward his door. "Can I see? Is it another cuckoo clock?"

"No, it's not…" He put down his taco and stood. "Just let me clear it up first."

I opened the bedroom door and looked inside. "Oh."

"Yeah," he said.

In his room, a grandfather clock made of dark, heavy walnut stood in the corner near his worktable. It had been there for months, draped in an old, paint-stained drop cloth to signify that he'd put it aside in frustration, and also to signify how much I didn't like looking at it. The clock featured little medieval-keep style doors, wooden with metal brackets, opening onto little pathways that curved behind castle-like crenelated walls. The pathways were built in tiers under the clock face, where the unmoving hands pointed to high noon, or maybe low midnight, if that's a thing.

The clock's doors and panels were all open, and many of its guts were on the table—gears, cogs, and carved figurines modeled on chess pieces, meant to emerge from the clock's doors at different hours.

"I thought you were getting rid of that," I said.

"It sells for a lot more if it works. Right now, I'd be lucky to break even."

"Didn't you say it was a lost cause?"

"There's not much chance I'll find all the original parts I need." He looked over the array of clockwork and small tools on the table. Among the carved figures, a robed black bishop seemed to glare at a tall white queen, her crown bristling with little spikes like icicles, her face chillingly blank. A couple of pawns in peasant clothing wore matching looks of fear, like they knew they were destined to be sacrificed. "I'm looking at renting this maker space where I might be able to machine what I need, maybe even 3D print it, though collectors would ding it for authenticity."

"As long as the figures perform their weird little hourly square dance or whatever, that should be impressive enough, right?"

"Some buyers are sticklers. There's a lot to be done on the exterior, too."

"And you were hoping to spend the rest of your evening focused on that?"

"I'm not sure 'hoping' is the right word." He picked up the big drop cloth and draped it over the grandfather clock. "Is that better?"

"Got another one?" I asked, looking at the faceless white queen. Her white knight, a horse that looked like it had been sculpted out of frost, snarled in front of her, as if guarding her.

"What, you don't like the little village people?"

"Calling them that doesn't make them cuter."

He rummaged in his closet and came back with a beach towel featuring giant goldfish wearing headphones, which he tossed over the worktable like a blanket. "Better?"

"Much better. Your dinner's getting cold. Aren't you

hungry?"

He drew me close. "I am."

Then he kissed me, and I was glad we had the place to ourselves.

Later, he slept, and I lay awake listening to the slow rain on the apartment's roof. It was a converted attic, so the sound was fairly close.

The quietness of the apartment was noticeable, like he'd said. The quietness of solitude, of absence. Life seemed increasingly full of absences as it went on, noticeably silent places where people had once been. I thought of my parents, how we'd fought on the night they'd died, leaving us on bad terms at the end. Calvin, my mentor and technically my boss, moved on to join family in Florida. There were no parents in my life anymore, real or surrogate. I was alone with the rest of my life, left to figure it out without any further guidance.

I had uneasy dreams of my parents, and of so many ghosts I'd encountered, memories taken out of place and strewn everywhere, out of any sequence or logical order, like the innards of the grandfather clock spread across the table.

Chapter Seventeen

In the morning, I went to the office and tried to focus on work again.

Veronica, the former Sunshine House employee, didn't answer her phone, but I left her a voicemail explaining that I was looking into problems on behalf of the residents.

After that, I spent time on some pesky paranormal paperwork—unpaid client tabs, utility bills for the office, typing up notes about the current case so I could eventually turn them over to the client at the end of the job, assuming someone did in fact pay us for the work.

Stacey showed up, and we repaired a trap damaged in our last case. Then I paced around a little bit, trying to figure out how best to continue the investigation while being barred from the premises. Stacey reviewed the video and audio footage we'd collected so far, and eventually I joined her on that, taking some of the hours of data for myself.

The phone rang around eleven. Veronica sounded suspicious, and spoke with a heavy Latin American accent, though I wasn't sophisticated enough to identify which country she might have been from.

"Thanks so much for calling back," I said.

"I only worked there a few months," she said quickly. "I don't know much about it."

"I understand, but we have several residents who say they see strange things at night. We were wondering whether you had seen anything strange."

"What kind of 'strange'?" Veronica asked. "Like Chelsea's kitten apron? The kittens' eyes are too big. Like bugs."

"No, but I'm not kitten around about these problems." I cleared my throat. "The residents are complaining of strange, shadowy figures in the house at night. And encountering people from their past, almost like ghosts."

She took a breath. "It is a place of sadness. And… how do you say…bad memories."

"What kind of memories?"

"It makes me think of the past. My past, my home and *familia*. And I don't know why. It doesn't look like anywhere at home."

"Can you tell us what part of the past?"

She was silent so long I thought she might have hung up. Then she said, "Maritza. *Mi hermana*…my sister. I was saving money to bring her from El Salvador. She was a bright student in math. She was accepted to university here. But Maritza was at the market buying fruit, there was a gunfight, and a bullet found her by mistake. She died right away."

"I'm so sorry."

"Maybe if I had sent more money, sent it faster..." Veronica sighed. "I think of her all the time. But in that house, I saw her. Just looking at me. The first time, I was happy. Scared, but happy. Then I saw how she hates me because I did not save her. One day, I could not go back. I quit. I started another job now."

"That's great," I said. "I mean, the new job part. The rest sounds terrible, obviously. I'm sorry."

We wrapped it up soon after, and I thanked her for her help.

"So?" Stacey asked, lifting a headphone away from her ear. Two of the monitors at her workstation showed images of Arden's closet. The third showed video she'd taken of my attempted EVP session at Bartel's grave. "Anything new?"

"Mostly just confirmation. Veronica said her deceased sister haunted her there and left her feeling drained."

"No wonder she quit abruptly," Stacey said. "Probably a smart move with Bartel around. Do you want to hear his sweet little message from the cemetery?"

"We actually recorded something?"

"Listen carefully..." Stacey unplugged her headphones and turned up a speaker.

On the recording, a voice responded to my questions. It was deep and distorted like it was groaning from somewhere below the earth, a voice from a lower, darker world.

"I don't understand it," I said.

"I had to clean it up a lot, and even speed it up,

because it turns out it was really dragging out long and slow. Like it's moving on a different timescale than us."

"Okay. And then you ended up with…?"

"This."

She played it again, the voice still deep and unnerving but at least much faster. Two words came through clearly and sent frosty little spiders crawling down my spine. *"Kill her."*

"Oh," I said, pulling back from the speaker. "Yikes. I mean, nice work there, Stacey."

"Kill her…Kill her…Kill her…"

"You don't have to keep replaying it."

"Gotcha, sorry." Stacey paused the audio. "Who do you think he's wanting to kill? Or is he giving instructions, like telling *us* to kill someone for him? Because I am not doing that."

"It's definitely troubling." I thought of the women in danger at the house—Arden, Georgette, and even Chelsea, who'd decided it was easier to blame Stacey and me for all the problems than to admit they were real. I thought of Rhea, pushed down the attic stairs to her death.

We kept going through the relatively scarce amount of footage and recordings we'd gathered, but there wasn't much left to discover. We'd reached the end of that road until we got more access to the house, or at least received the recordings Arden was hopefully still making.

Much later, around midnight, lying alone in the dark in my bed, I heard the dead man's voice again, another sign that this line of work was slowly driving me crazy. Maybe not even all that slowly. *"Kill her."*

I shuddered, and the phone rang immediately after.

My phone company readily identified it as The Sunshine House.

"Hello?" I answered, assuming it would be Arden.

"I didn't expect you to answer this late," a woman said. Not Arden. "I meant to leave a voice mail."

"Chelsea?" I asked, hearing the surprise in my own voice.

"Yes. Sorry. Should I call back in the morning?"

"No, it's fine. What's happening?"

"I just…can you explain again what this thing is? What you're saying is in my house?"

"Couldn't be happier to do that." I sat up and rubbed my eyes while I gathered thoughts from my drowsy brain. "As far as we can tell, it takes the form of someone from your memories, and it does this to drain your energy."

"So, whatever we see isn't actually real, right? It's not really that person at all?"

"Right. Did you see something, Chelsea?"

She was silent for a long moment, then said, "You can come back if you want. I think we may need your help."

"Okay," I said. "We could come back tomorrow if you want."

"That would be great. Thank you. And…sorry for how I've acted." She sounded drained, and beaten, like whatever she'd experienced had taken it all out of her.

"It's fine," I said. After she hung up, I texted Stacey the update. Something awful must have happened to Chelsea, bad enough to reverse her stance on paranormal investigation. While I was glad to be able to dive back into the case, I worried for everyone living in that house with that entity.

I wondered how long it had haunted the place, draining residents and perhaps shortening their lives. Local elderly retirees had been staying there for decades while the place was run by Dottie Heusinkveld and her still-living son Harold, from whom Chelsea had purchased it. Harold hadn't yet returned my call. I could only hope that he would.

I lay awake for some time, thinking of the dark hallways of the house, the many rooms and closets we would need to watch, and all the people we needed to protect.

Chapter Eighteen

Pablo answered the door the next day, smiling and shaking his head as he let us in. He looked younger than me, and more energetic, and like he spent more time at the gym. I wondered how he felt working with the elderly all day.

"First she tells me not to let you in the door, then today she says to welcome you and give you a hand." Pablo shrugged. "What do you need? I have five minutes before my next round of medicine reminders."

"I'm sure you have a lot to do," I said. "If you'd just let Chelsea know we're here—"

"She knows. I'll show you up to her office." He turned, and we followed.

"How long have you been working here?" I asked.

"Since last year. Maybe ten months."

"What do you think of the old house?"

"It's very nice." He took us up the winding front stairs to the second floor.

"Do you know why we're here?"

"I've heard."

"So, what do you think?"

He shrugged. "Whatever makes them happy."

"Have you ever encountered anything unusual here?" I asked.

"Coach Joe always wants to argue that American football is 'real' football. All the time."

"That's not what I mean."

"You're asking if I ever saw a ghost?" He paused at the top of the stairs before continuing to the upstairs hall.

"I am."

"No. Nothing like that. I see why people could feel scared by this old house, but nothing has bothered me." He lowered his voice. "Except for Arden. She's always complaining about something. She always doesn't like the food, or the choices on television, or how I fold her towels."

"But you've never seen anything unusual?" I asked. "Like someone who shouldn't be here? Maybe someone from your past?"

"No, nothing like that." He shook his head.

"Do you ever work the night shift?"

"Sometimes."

We walked down the hall toward the office. *The Sound of Music* played on a distant television somewhere behind us, probably over in Georgette and Arden's room.

Chelsea's office door was open. She sat at her desk among the stacks of paperwork, rubbing her temples.

She stood when we arrived.

"Thanks, Pablo," she said. "You can resume your regularly scheduled programming."

Pablo nodded and gave us another smile as he left, most of it directed toward Stacey. Her eyes flicked over him after he passed.

"Thanks for coming back. I know I wasn't exactly cooperative before." Chelsea turned and opened the door at the back of her office, revealing the living room beyond. She'd tidied up since our last glimpse of it— the dirty sneakers and baseball glove were gone, and the *National Geographic for Kids* magazines were stacked neatly on the end table. A television was mounted over the fireplace. A microwave, coffee pot, and mini-fridge were jammed into one corner.

"It's understandable," I said, following her down a narrow blind hallway that had three doors crammed in along one side. It looked like the hall and three rooms had been carved from one or two much larger original rooms. I'd seen that before, when grand old mansions had evolved into more crowded hotels, apartments, or boarding houses over the years.

The first bedroom was clearly the boy's, a narrow space cluttered with baseball paraphernalia. Behind the second door was a tiny bathroom with barely any room for the sink and tub inside it.

The third door led to a larger bedroom, which was somehow gloomy even with the heavy drapes pulled aside from the windows and the glass door to a second-floor balcony. An antique full-length mirror and matching dresser stood against one wall; I wondered if they were original to the house. An armchair sat between a small fireplace and an overflowing bookshelf. The queen-sized bed looked simple and modern, in contrast to the rest of the furniture, a no-nonsense thin steel frame with a basic flimsy engineered-wood headboard colored to look like mahogany.

Chelsea closed the door behind us, as if to make sure nobody overheard us, though her son was still away at school.

"I'm sorry I called so late last night," she said.

"It's totally fine. I'm a night owl. What happened?"

"I'm ready for you to resume your investigation. And I'd like you to, well, monitor this room, as well."

I nodded and approached the folding doors to the wide closet. "Did you see an apparition?"

"Not there." Chelsea cleared her throat, then slowly raised her hand and pointed at the armchair by the bookshelf. "He was there."

"What did it look like?"

"My…" Her voice caught in her throat, and Stacey touched her shoulder, comforting her. Chelsea looked surprised at the gesture but didn't pull away. "My father. He died only four months after we moved here, you know. And at first, I could have sworn I could still feel him around somehow, like I'd turn a corner and he'd be there, maybe reading the latest Jon Meacham book, ready to give his opinion about it to anyone who'd listen. He was a high school history teacher. Before he went downhill, he would take Taggart to museums and historic sites. But eventually there were days he didn't recognize me or Tag at all, and acted like we were strangers. I still haven't leased out his old room. Not that there's a waiting list or anything. Even the ladies' floor is mostly empty since Louise died."

"Can you tell me more about what you saw last night, specifically?" I asked, trying to gently nudge her back on topic.

"He was sitting in that chair all withered up, worse than he'd ever really looked in life, like he was made of dried tree roots. That's the best I can describe it. His eyes were almost blind with cataracts, even though they were actually caught early and lasered off. My sense was he'd been suffering the whole time since he died. That death hadn't freed him at all, and he was more lost and alone than ever."

"I'm so sorry." Stacey wrapped an arm around Chelsea, who stiffened up a little but then hugged her back.

"He wouldn't speak to me." Chelsea closed her eyes. "Just stared past me like I wasn't there. I pleaded to him. I knelt there and I cried, telling him how sorry I was. I basically lost my mind. And he never responded. He just faded away, until I was just staring at the fabric of the chair." She pulled back from Stacey and wiped her eyes. "I'm sorry."

"Oh, come on, don't be sorry," Stacey said.

Chelsea drew herself up and looked at me. "From what you're telling me, that wasn't actually him at all, was it?"

"I don't believe so," I said. "It's almost certainly this other entity, the one that uses your memories against you, bleeding out your energy. Did you feel drained afterward?"

"Of course," she whispered. "Drained and hopeless." She swallowed. "What I need is for you to assure me that it wasn't real. That this...thing in the house, this monster, was just getting into my head."

"That's exactly right."

"So, go ahead," she said. "Bring in your cameras. Put them here, and anywhere you want, except Wallace and Spencer's room. They support the investigation but prefer their privacy."

"Has your son reported any unusual activity?" I asked. "Anything scaring him in his room?"

"Not so far. And I don't want to upset him with any of this."

"Then we'll skip putting gear in there. In fact, Stacey can conceal the equipment in your room so he won't notice it."

"Oh, totally," Stacey said. "I'll use our most compact stuff."

"We're also eager to speak with Harold Heusinkveld, but he hasn't returned my call," I said. "Do you think you could encourage him to talk to us?"

"I'm not even sure how to get in touch with him. Maybe I have his cell number somewhere—"

"I can give you his current phone number."

"Okay. We barely met, you know."

"We'll need to dig out whatever he can tell us about the house. He knows it better than anyone else who's still alive."

"Yeah, it seems like he'd notice a nasty ghost or two during all those years of living here," Stacey said.

"But it didn't scare him into leaving," I said. "He stayed here most of his life."

"Then maybe it's not so dangerous?" Chelsea asked. "If he could live here that long?"

"It'll be interesting to hear what he has to say, if he agrees to say anything at all."

We got to work, setting up in Chelsea's room first,

concealing the gear like we'd promised. After that, we
checked on the gear in Arden's room, which gave us a
chance to catch up with her.

"How have you been?" I asked while Stacey looked
over the cameras.

"My eggs were runny this morning and my hip
hurts," Arden said. "And Kyle got voted off *Bachelor
Island* last night, so I don't know if I'll even bother
watching next week."

"Any troubles of the kind you called us about?"

"You mean dead people in my room? I thought I
saw something the other night, but I used that flashlight
you gave me, and it went away."

"Good. We'll be around if you need us."

We set up our nerve center again in the empty
bedroom where someone named Louise had once lived,
not far from the door to the attic. I tried the attic door,
curious to look up there, but it was locked.

Downstairs, Karl and Coach Joe welcomed us back
to their room. We placed camera tripods at the
bathroom door where Karl had seen the apparition of
his wife.

"My goodness, this is going to be strange," Joe
said. "No privacy. But I guess it's just like a locker
room."

"You've still got privacy," I said. "We're mainly
interested in watching later at night when you're asleep.
You can close the bathroom door when needed."

"And you should," Stacey added.

"Have either of you encountered anything unusual
while we were away?" I asked.

Karl shook his head.

"I saw a couple of hummingbirds fighting at the

feeder," Coach Joe offered. "You think they're innocent, but they're violent little boogers when nobody's watching."

We managed to finish setting up before Tag arrived home from school. The eight-year-old went to the western sunroom for another piano lesson with Georgette. Spencer sat in an antique armchair, nodding along closely as if measuring the boy's progress on the keys. Wallace was parked beside him in his wheelchair, reading the *Wall Street Journal*.

When Spencer saw Stacey and me, he waved us over, his expression urgent. I wondered if he'd seen something troubling in his room since we'd last talked.

"What do you think?" Spencer whispered to us.

"About what?" I asked.

He gestured toward the piano. "Could Tag be our third act for the talent show?" He looked to Stacey for confirmation. "He's new to the performing arts, but he's learning quickly."

"Uh, sure," Stacey said. "If he wants to."

"Fantastic. We'll broach the idea softly." Spencer spoke with all the seriousness of a movie producer trying to close a major deal. "I think he may go for it."

"I know y'all aren't running your jawbones during our piano lesson," Georgette said. "Because that sort of thing would be mighty rude, and y'all ain't rude, are you?"

"Uh, no, ma'am," Spencer said. "I apologize. We were discussing talent show business."

"The talent show?" Georgette turned on the piano bench to face us. "Is that today? I haven't prepared." She adjusted one of the red ribbons in her platinum bouffant wig. She wore full make-up, a sparkling ruby-red dress, and bracelets and necklaces loaded with costume jewels. "Do I look ready for the camera?"

"We actually weren't planning to record you today," Stacey said, and Georgette looked disappointed.

"Though I guess we could do a behind-the-scenes documentary about the talent show," I said, and Georgette brightened. "Maybe put a few cameras around the house."

"Clever idea," Wallace commented, not looking up from his paper.

"We haven't yet finalized the date for the talent show, sadly," Spencer said. "How can we, when we still need a third act?"

"Well, maybe Tag would like to be in the show." Georgette gave the kid a playful bump with her elbow. "Wouldn't that be fun?"

"Me?" Tag looked stunned by the idea, his innocent brown eyes wide. "But I'm not good enough yet."

"Sure you are!" Georgette said. "It's a just little ol' talent show for a few folks here. You know they'll enjoy anything. Shoot, Wallace still watches *Love Boat* reruns."

"For the guest stars," Wallace said. "*Murder, She Wrote* is another good program for guest stars. You never know who might pop up. It's like sitting in a Beverly Hills cafe circa 1985."

"Can I do the dragon song?" Tag asked.

"Of course," Georgette replied, "but we'll have to practice some more."

"I can make my hat into a dragon head." He pulled off his baseball cap. "I'll cut the teeth out of construction paper. My teacher Ms. Spinach showed us how."

"Ms. *Spinoza*," Chelsea corrected. "She doesn't like being called Ms. Spinach. She was very clear about that in the parent conference. Come on, you'll be late for fall ball practice."

"I thought I was carpooling with Keating." Tag replaced his baseball cap and stood up from the bench.

"Keating has a cold, so I'm driving you, and we're late. Are you wearing baseball shoes inside the house?"

"You told me to get ready for practice!"

"We don't wear those inside! Take them off and carry them to the car!" Chelsea looked beyond flustered. "Everyone, Pablo agreed to take charge of dinner tonight, so he'll be cooking instead of me—"

"Thank goodness," Arden mumbled. I hadn't even seen her enter the room from the other hallway. She sat down on a sofa and drew out her phone.

"—and we are interviewing potential new staff next week, so this crunch time for help will be over soon, I promise."

Spencer and Wallace shared a doubtful look, and Wallace shook his head. Karl sighed.

"Well, don't let the boy be late for practice," Coach Joe said. "That's disrespectful to his coach and teammates."

"Right. Come on, Tag."

"Remember what I told you about pitching," Coach Joe told the boy. "And about focus."

Tag nodded quietly and looked away, as if he sensed that too much of a response might invite a new coachly lecture. "Yep," he said.

Chelsea ushered him out the door.

Georgette frowned, seeming unhappy at the loss of her little pal, and closed the piano.

Chapter Nineteen

With the house short-staffed and Chelsea unexpectedly away, Stacey and I decided to help Pablo serve the residents their early-bird dinner of rice, peas, and Salisbury steak. We sat with them at dinner, drinking herbal tea but not eating, since neither Stacey nor I was really in a Salisbury-steak mood. I wanted to get more information out of the residents while Tag was away and before they all went to bed.

"We know Arden just moved here, but who has lived here longest?" I asked.

"Georgette," Wallace said.

"Yes, what?" Georgette, who hadn't been listening, looked over.

"Haven't you lived here the longest?" Wallace asked her.

"Oh, no. Louise was here before me."

"But she's no longer here," Wallace said. "She passed away."

"Oh, yes." Georgette looked around them, blinking. "*Have* I been here the longest?"

"You were sure here when I moved in," Coach Joe said. "I've been watching you sing since day one."

"You and Louise were here before me," Karl said to Georgette. "I used to be at Rustic Pines, but they closed after the health inspection. Wallace and Spencer, and then Joe, moved in after me."

"Lord knows why Wallace moved here," Arden said. "The McMurtry house was bigger and grander than this one. The nicest house in town."

"Well, thank you for saying so," Wallace said.

"Why you thanking me? You didn't build it. Men hired by your grandpa did. Bet he was skimpy with their wages, too."

"That would be my great-great-'grandpa' who built it. Or had it built, as you pointed out. And yes, my only role was to inherit it. However, as you mentioned, Arden, my family's house was both larger and older than this one. A hundred and fifty years of accumulated leaks, sags, rust, cracks, and decay gave the old family place an endless appetite for maintenance and restoration. The house threatened to consume all I'd earned, and more, and for what? For what posterity was I struggling to maintain it? I sold it and instead took a comfortable home here, overlooking the charming little town of my youth."

"And your adulthood," Spencer added, in a slightly needling tone.

"Yes, sadly. I once dreamed of a wider life, seeing the world, perhaps set up practice in a major city, but one family obligation led to another. And for what? Where is that family now, whom I served so diligently? They are buried in the graveyard down the street, and what have I to show for my years of service?"

"The finest suite at Heusinkveld House," Spencer said with a smile.

"Where the staffing is inadequate at best," Wallace said.

"Chelsea's working on it," Karl said, sounding a little defensive. "She's overwhelmed right now."

"I wish we'd been overwhelmed with better local options," Wallace said. "Ironically, my father hated this house. He called it decadent, even European, which was a venomous insult from him."

"Well, it does sorta look like something out of *The Addams Family*," Georgette said.

"I think it's pretty," Arden said.

"Oh, don't misunderstand, I personally admire the lavish architectural style," Wallace said. "I always have. It's amusing to think of my parents seeing me living here at last, having sold off the old family place, the end of the McMurtry line. Wouldn't they be apoplectic?" He chuckled, and Spencer shook his head with a thin smile.

"Now that we have some idea of what's been happening in this house," I said, "I'd like to get an idea of how long this entity has been here. Looking back, can anyone identify possible previous encounters? Times when some powerful memory from your past seemed more real than the present moment?"

"That sounds like every day to me," Spencer said, which got him a few laughs.

"Georgette, how long have you been having those

visits from your son?" I asked.

She frowned, looking hurt. "I can't say for sure. They weren't bad at first. I thought they were just dreams, I guess. Or my mind going, but going in a nice way, at least. But then I started remembering all the things I'd done wrong by him when he was a child, when I had my chance to be there for him, I wasn't. I'd tell him I was sorry. I'd cry. It would never be enough."

"It sounds like the entity uses guilt and regret to drain the living," I said. "It takes on the form of someone from your past. It might prefer to take on the form of dead people, possibly to confuse and frighten, or maybe because once someone is dead, you can't really reconcile with them. Any unresolved regrets just go on, they just stay there like a weight…" I realized I was starting to think about my parents, and maybe talk about them, and stopped myself. "Anyway, I'm not sure how the entity can keep this up now that you all know it isn't who it pretends to be. Knowledge should help defend you, if you encounter it. Remind yourself it's just holding up a mirror to something inside your mind."

The table was silent for a minute.

"Well, as the city boy said at the swimming hole, that's too deep for me," Coach Joe said. "Are we still having peach cobbler for dessert?"

It turned out they were indeed having peach cobbler with sugar-free, low-fat vanilla ice cream. I'm not sure it still counts as ice cream at that point, but anyway, Stacey and I again helped with clearing and serving dishes in exchange for small squares of the sweet, rubbery dessert.

Chelsea returned home, somewhat shocked to see

dinner cleared and Stacey and me cleaning up the kitchen while Pablo handled after-dinner medications for those who needed them.

"Do y'all do windows, too?" Chelsea beamed at the sight of Stacey wiping off the kitchen faucet. "Maybe we should hire paranormal investigators more often."

"It seemed like you needed the help," Stacey said.

"It makes my night easier." Chelsea gave Stacey a hug, I guessed because they'd previously established a hugging sort of relationship. She looked embarrassed and pulled back. "Thanks."

"You bet," I said. "Chelsea, we need to look in the attic, but it's locked."

"It's always locked for safety reasons," Chelsea said. "The staircase is too steep for code. Servants' stairs, someone called them."

"Can we borrow the key?" I asked. "We promise to wait until a late hour to check it out, when everyone's asleep. And we'll definitely lock up afterward."

"Okay, but make *sure* you relock it. It can't be left accessible."

"I promise."

"The key's in my office. Come on, I'll grab it for you."

Upstairs, Chelsea opened a desk drawer. She frowned, pawing through some change and small office supplies like Post-Its and paper clips. She closed that drawer and rummaged through a couple of others.

"I don't know where I put it," she finally said. "I'm sorry, but I don't even know the last time I went into the attic. Can I let you know when I find it? I have to run and check on Tag, and then I have evening procedures. Life's going to be so much easier when we re-staff."

"Of course. Let us know if we can lend a hand with anything."

Later, Stacey and I sat on a screened balcony outside our borrowed room, watching the birds arrive at the birdhouses for evening snacks. A hummingbird floated at a feeder, slurping away the sweet water inside, perhaps ready for a fight if another of its kind dared to show up for a drink.

We ate some snacks of our own. I'd brought cherry tomatoes, baby carrots, and broccoli, with blue cheese dressing for dipping. I was glad to have that instead of Salisbury steak or braving Topsy's Diner again. I wouldn't have minded more Tacos La Chona, but that was all the way across the county.

Stacey had a banana, yogurt, and a can of mixed nuts. She munched contentedly while the sun went down.

Eventually, the house fell quiet as the residents went to bed. We watched thermal and night vision views of all the problem spots where apparitions had been seen so far.

Around nine-thirty, Chelsea's light went dark and the camera's night vision took over, showing the empty chair and some of the nearby fireplace.

"Looks like she's not getting back to me about that attic key." I thumped the slim leather pack of lock picks on my belt. "We'll have to do it the hard way."

"Can't it wait until tomorrow?" Stacey asked.

"I personally think it's important to investigate the old murder scene, on the off chance it happens to be relevant to the house being haunted," I said. "I know it sounds like a long shot."

"Okay, be more salty, Ellie. You bring the lock

picks and I'll bring the cameras, and we'll have a whole attic-investigation party."

The hour grew later and the house grew quieter, though never completely silent. There was the occasional creak or groan of the house settling. A loose windowpane rattled somewhere when the wind picked up outside.

It was past eleven when we finally made our move, walking softly and carrying big camera tripods. I knelt at the attic door and popped the lock while Stacey watched to make sure nobody was coming. Ideally, we'd go in and out without anyone knowing we'd done it.

The door opened onto a steep, dusty set of sagging wooden stairs that were indeed dangerously steep. In lieu of a handrail, a length of old rope drooped through eyelets in the wall along one side.

"Wow, that's so hazardous," Stacey whispered. "The lady in the wheelchair didn't have a chance after she got pushed down those. Nobody would."

We climbed up cautiously. The staircase was more like a ladder, or maybe a set of shelves, than a normal set of stairs, and it was hard to keep our balance. I used a camera tripod like a walking staff, as if we were hiking up a mountainside.

At the top of the stairs was a haphazard pile of cardboard boxes that looked fairly recent; an Amazon logo on one was a clue. They held some paperwork and assorted items, like golf shoes and Hawaiian shirts, that I guessed might have been the property of Chelsea's errant husband.

Past that was an accumulation of furniture and older attic clutter. Shutters on the windows kept the attic permanently dark aside from a hanging light fixture. I found the switch on the wall, but only one of the fixture's bulbs sputtered to life. The roof above sloped low toward the back, the beams and trusses visible. Everything was thick with dust and cobwebs.

Deeper in the attic, a queen-sized bed was pushed against one wall between a cobwebbed wardrobe and an end table cluttered with dusty pillboxes and medicine bottles. A wheelchair made of thick, dark wood sat by the bed.

"That wheelchair's a beast compared to Wallace's modern one," Stacey whispered. "Imagine a sick old lady trying to power that thing."

"I'm sure they had better chair options by the 1960s. It's like they deliberately turned this room into a prison cell." I tiptoed across the room, mindful of people sleeping below, and nudged open the bathroom door. Its Pepto-pink tiles and fixtures indicated it might have been built in the middle of the twentieth century.

"Most of this actually looks kinda new." Stacey reached for the shower curtain, and I tensed as she pulled it aside, but no horrible apparition awaited us on the other side. "Well, not really *new*, but barely used."

"That's true. They renovated the attic into a suite for Rhea, but she must not have lived up here very long before she died."

"And nobody's used it since?"

"Rhea's daughter-in-law, Dottie, must have left it like this and chosen to stay in the apartment where Chelsea is now."

"And her grandson, too? All these years?" Stacey followed me back to the bedroom area. "I guess that makes sense, though, since the grandma was murdered

here. I still can't believe the family stayed in the house
at all."

"Maybe they had nowhere else to go."

"It had to be weird for that kid, Harold. His father
got sick and died, his uncle killed his grandma, and
then he kept growing up here in the aftermath of all that
death, with just his mom. And he even stayed after she
died." Stacey shook her head.

"Despite all the tragedy, it might have been hard for
him to move on from here, the place where all his
family had lived," I said. "But he finally has, now. Sold
the place and moved to Florida, the natural habitat of
the retired."

"Well, good for him! He probably needed a
change."

"I wish he'd return my phone calls, though."

"I'm assuming we want to watch the murder stairs,
right?" Stacey pointed a night vision camera at the
lethally steep staircase.

"Definitely, but also some wide-angle views of the
room, since privacy's not an issue up here. We want to
watch this whole bed and bathroom area, and all the
way to the closet."

"Bed, bath, and beyond. Got it." She set up another
camera.

I slid aside the pair of doors to the deep walk-in
closet, wide enough to rotate a wheelchair in the space
between the racks of clothing.

"Whoa, this is a thrifter's dream," Stacey said,
taking in Rhea's collection of dresses from the Roaring
Twenties, full of chiffon, velvet, and taffeta.

"Let's put a camera in here," I said.

"I'd like to put an offer on some of the clothing,

too, but I guess that'll have to wait." Stacey pulled a small camera from her backpack and placed it on a high shelf to give us the fullest view of the room.

After setting up, we crept back down the steep stairs and eased the door shut. I again knelt at the door, working by flashlight to lock it with my picks. I was a little clumsy with the procedure, since I spent a lot more time opening locks than closing them.

Back at our little nerve center in the recently departed Louise's room, we turned out the overhead light and settled in to watch and listen, going dark and silent to encourage the ghost to come out, in whatever form it decided to take tonight.

Chapter Twenty

The house resumed its quiet atmosphere for a long while. Quiet, but never silent. The residents coughed, sneezed, and shuffled, mostly unseen, out of sight of our cameras pointed at the dark nooks and doorways of their bedrooms. Faucets turned and water dripped. A high wind creaked the hilltop house's timbers like we were aboard an old wooden sailing ship, crossing an ocean by night.

It was close to three when Stacey heard the noise in the attic.

"Ellie, listen!" Stacey seized control of my laptop and switched my headphones to the attic audio.

A rattling sound echoed up there. I looked at the attic camera feeds, but the night vision showed nothing amiss. Empty bed, empty wheelchair, nothing moving.

It sounded again, and we finally did see movement

on the thermal video at the stairs. Someone alive, represented by warm hues of red and orange, was opening the door, the hinges creaking with age. I thought it might be Chelsea at first, but then he spoke.

"Hello?" he whispered. Taggart. His glowing form climbed the treacherously steep stairs into the cooler space of the attic.

On another monitor, he emerged at the top of the stairs, using a plastic glowing *Star Wars* light saber as a flashlight, creating a bright glare in the night vision feed. "Hello? Are you there?" he whispered again, glancing around the attic. After a moment, he added, "Sorry. I know you hate bright lights." He turned off the light saber.

"I'm sure I locked that door," I said. "I double-checked."

"Maybe we solved the mystery of the missing key," Stacey said. "But why's he up there? Who's he talking to? Should we get him out of there?"

"If it starts to look dangerous for him. We might scare him if we follow him up there right now." I was torn, but felt like we needed to see what happened.

"But this can't be good, right?" Stacey asked. "Innocent kid, dark attic, invisible friend, three in the morning—"

"We should definitely be listening carefully."

Stacey took the hint and made a zipping motion over lips, locking them and throwing away the key for good measure.

"—just couldn't sleep. I'm worried about Mom." The eight-year-old boy sat cross-legged on the floor. He looked toward the wheelchair and bed. "Yes, please!" he said after a minute. "Can you tell the one about the wolf who dusts his fur with flour to fool the lambs?" He smiled.

He fell silent for a while, gradually drooping forward to rest his elbows on his knees, his chin in his hands. He seemed to be listening attentively to someone, but his eyelids kept closing.

"No," he finally said, raising his head. "I'm still awake." Another pause. "But I don't want to go to bed."

The wheelchair turned slightly toward him, just an inch or two. It was a small but significant movement, a clear sign that a conscious, active entity was present in the empty chair, chilling to observe.

"Should we go now?" Stacey whispered, removing her headphones and edging toward the door, looking to me like an impatient racer waiting for the starting gun.

"But I don't want to!" Taggart rose to his feet. "I want to hear the rest of the story—huh? Who's coming?"

The heavy wheelchair rushed toward the boy like someone had given it a hard, forceful shove. He cried out and scrambled aside to avoid getting hit.

I pulled off my headphones and ran for the door.

"Finally!" Stacey said, taking off at top speed.

The attic door, just around the corner from our borrowed room, stood wide open, the key still in the lock.

From the darkness above came a high-pitched wail, like a woman or child in severe pain. I reached for my flashlight, barely keeping ahead of Stacey.

As I stepped through the attic door, the crashing sound drew close.

Something rushed down the steep attic stairs and flew out at me, much larger than any barn owl. It was a woman in a yellowed, frayed lace nightgown. Long, stringy gray hair blew back from where her face should have been. She had no face at all, though, just a skull with bare teeth and empty eye sockets.

She occupied the heavy antique wheelchair that had been upstairs, the one that had suddenly rolled toward Tag. Apparently, it had continued past him and gone crashing down the stairs, just in time to meet me.

The wheelchair-bound entity slammed into me and knocked me back against the wall, pinning me to the floor. The corpse-like woman fell from the chair and landed on top of me. Her awful face filled my vision, and her skeletal hands scrabbled over my leather jacket. The smell of decay rolled out from her.

"Ellie!" Stacey grunted as she lifted the toppled wheelchair away from me. The skeletal apparition vanished like an interrupted nightmare, but its face still filled my mind, my memory of it fresh, raw, and horrifying.

"The kid..." I said, with what air I could manage to breathe through my recently slammed lungs. I pointed toward the attic stairs.

Stacey nodded and ran, setting her flashlight to flood mode before clambering up the deadly stairway.

"Taggart!" Stacey and her light ascended out of sight. "Hey, where are you, buddy?"

Footsteps ran toward me from elsewhere on the second floor. The overhead light in the hall turned on. Chelsea stood over me in kitten-print cotton pajamas, looking scared.

"What happened?" she asked.

"I'm still piecing that together." I let her help me up, wincing at a bruised area on my side where the solid wooden arm of the wheelchair had jabbed me in the ribs and knocked the air out of me. I staggered through the door to the stairs. "Stacey?"

"He's fine." Stacey appeared at the top, gripping Tag's arm like she was afraid he would stumble and fall down the stairs. The boy looked weakened, his face bone-white. I knew just how he felt, especially after my up-close encounter with the lady in the wheelchair.

"Tag? What are you doing in the attic?" Chelsea stepped onto the bottom stair. "I told you it's off-limits! It's not safe for anyone."

"What happened to Mrs. Hoosie?"

"Who is Mrs. Hoosie?"

"The lady who lives in the attic."

"Nobody lives in the attic, Tag."

"The bad man pushed her down the stairs. Is she hurt?"

"What bad man?" Chelsea asked. "Come down from there."

"Okay."

Tag descended the staircase, Stacey in front of him in case he fell, though he moved pretty nimbly.

Chelsea embraced him. He looked past her at the wheelchair lying on its side in the hall like a wounded animal. "Where did she go?"

"She disappeared," I said, still shaken from my dangerous encounter with the skull-faced lady. "Was she scaring you?"

"No, she's nice. She tells stories when I can't sleep."

"Do you go up in the attic to see her?" I asked.

"Sometimes she comes to my room. Then she told me I could go up there."

"Did you take the attic key, Tag?" Chelsea touched the key in the lock.

"I just wanted to see her."

"It's locked because nobody is allowed up there. It's not safe."

"But she didn't come down tonight, and I wanted a story. And you're always too cranky or tired when I ask."

Chelsea looked hurt by this.

"She comes down in her wheelchair?" I asked. "Down the stairs?"

"I don't know…" Tag rubbed his head. "Wouldn't that be hard? I don't know how she does it."

We returned to the hallway to find Arden arriving, looking crankier than ever, coming to check out the source of the crashing and screaming.

"What's going on around here?" Arden asked me. "I'm not paying you to keep us up all hours."

"We're still figuring out what happened," I said. "But everyone's fine."

"You can go back to bed, Arden," Chelsea said. "It's over."

"I'm not going back without an explanation."

"What was the big ruckus?" Georgette arrived after Arden, wearing a puffy peach nightgown and a long brunette wig. She was applying lip gloss in a compact mirror. "Taggart, what are you doing up so late, honey?"

"I think Tag pushed the wheelchair down the attic stairs," Arden said.

"Why would you go and do a thing like that?" Georgette asked.

"I didn't! The bad man did it!" Tag said.

"What bad man?" Arden asked.

"I think we all need to calm down," Chelsea said.

"Goodness, do you suppose that was the same wheelchair Rhea Heusinkveld got killed in?" Georgette asked.

"Who got killed?" Tag asked.

"What is happening up here?" Spencer arrived from the direction of the elevator, wearing a long silk robe and soft slippers. "I told the other gentlemen I would investigate. Consider me an emissary from the first floor."

"This is getting too chaotic," Chelsea said. "Spencer, tell everyone downstairs we're fine. Something fell in the attic."

"Or got pushed, by the sound of it," Arden said. "By some man Taggart saw."

"What did the man look like, Tag?" I asked.

"A big shadow," Tag said. That was a common form for ghosts to take, requiring less energy than a full apparition. "Mrs. Hoosie told me to watch out for him. He's mean. He hates her, and he'll hate me if he finds out we're friends."

"Friends?" Chelsea scowled up the attic stairs.

"How many times have you encountered her?" I asked, feeling very concerned about this new development.

"I don't know exactly. Sometimes when I can't sleep, she comes and tells a story."

"Is she always in the wheelchair?"

He nodded. I didn't want to push him too much when he'd just had a big scare, so I said, "Okay, maybe everyone can try getting back to bed."

"Yes, we should all do that." Chelsea locked the

attic door. "We have a busy day tomorrow. Like school."

"What if the bad man comes back?" Tag asked. "Mrs. Hoosie says he's coming around more, and he's getting stronger."

"We're going to stand guard all night," I told him. "So you don't have to worry. You saw how fast we showed up this time."

The boy frowned but nodded a little.

Chelsea cast a look my way, and I couldn't tell what she was thinking, but she was obviously unhappy. They weren't exactly happy circumstances.

"I'll be heading back down, then," Spencer said. "But I doubt I'll be sleeping again."

"It's almost time to wake up, anyway." Arden tested the locked attic door, then gave the antique wheelchair a nudge. "The old family ghosts are still here, huh?"

"That's how it looks," I said. "If that's Rhea Heusinkveld's chair, she must be the 'Mrs. Hoosie' making contact with Taggart. He probably can't say her full name."

"Well, she's probably lonely up there, the poor thing," Georgette said.

"She needs to leave that poor child alone," Arden said. "It ain't natural. I knew this place was a bad deal. I ought to get at least a twenty-five percent discount, with all the unnatural things going on here."

Soon, Arden and Georgette returned to their room, Spencer walked to the elevator, and Chelsea and Tag returned to the manager's apartment.

Stacey and I lingered, looking at the wheelchair that had clobbered me.

"That thing is so eerie," Stacey said.

"Want to see how fast you can push me down the hall in it?"

"Kind of, yeah."

"I'm just kidding." I walked back to our borrowed room instead and closed the door. "What exactly did you see up in the attic?" I asked Stacey.

"Just the kid at the top of the stairs, petrified, gaping down after the crashed wheelchair like he couldn't believe what he'd seen. He's lucky the entity didn't push him, too, because he was right at the edge of the top stair. Oh, and it was really cold up there, like ice-fishing level coldness."

"Did you see any sign of the 'bad man' he talked about? Maybe a shadow figure?"

She was quiet for a moment, as if reflecting back on her attic visit, then shook her head. "Nope. I definitely looked around, but my light might have chased it away."

"Let's see what the cameras caught."

"Ooh, good idea."

We watched again the unnerving footage of Taggart sitting and talking with the invisible entity in the wheelchair. Even though I knew it was coming, I felt a little jolt again when the wheelchair turned toward him. Then the empty chair charged, and the boy looked terrified as he managed to push himself out of the way just before it would have struck him.

On the replay of thermal video from the staircase area, a patch of deep blue surrounded the wheelchair as it crashed down the stairs and out the door. The ghosts were possibly caught in a trauma loop, the murderer pushing his mother down the stairs again and again, while she suffered death again and again, endlessly. I hated to imagine what an awful existence that would be.

If the ghosts were in a loop, it must not have involved the actual, physical wheelchair every time, or surely that would have been noticed long ago.

Once again, I thought of the importance of talking to Harold Heusinkveld. I needed to reach out to him again.

We continued watching and listening to the occasional coughs, bedspring creaks, footsteps, and faucets of the residents until the earliest hint of daylight. My side throbbed where the wheelchair's arm had rammed it.

Exhausted by the long night and long day before it, Stacey and I shut down our monitors and headed downstairs, doing our best to keep quiet so we wouldn't wake anyone.

As it turned out, this wasn't as big a concern as we thought. The lights for the kitchen and dining room were on, and Wallace and Karl were already there, drinking coffee and reading different sections of the morning paper. Spencer emerged from the kitchen with two bowls, each containing half a grapefruit. He placed one in front of Wallace and kept the other for himself as he sat down.

"Good morning!" Spencer said to Stacey and me. Karl nodded at us, while Wallace, wearing reading glasses and absorbed in his newspaper, waved a single finger in greeting. "That was certainly a wild night," Spencer continued. "And it's been quite a long time since I've had an opportunity to say that."

"Is it true the old Heusinkvelds are still haunting the house?" Karl asked.

"It does seem that way," I replied. "I can't see any reason the shapeshifting entity would pretend to be Rhea Heusinkveld when interacting with Taggart."

"She's been bothering Taggart?" Wallace lowered his paper, looking concerned.

"Telling him bedtime stories, mostly," Stacey said.

"That could be worse, but still sounds disturbing," Wallace said.

"What kind of stories?" Spencer asked.

"It sounded like fairy tales," I said. "Talking wolves trying to eat talking sheep, that kind of thing."

"Your basic Warner Brothers cartoon ecosystem," Stacey said.

"Are those ghost ladies still here?" Coach Joe trudged into the room, stooped over and rubbing his back like it was bothering him.

"We're on our way out, actually," I said.

Pablo, apparently already at work, brought Karl and Coach Joe breakfast in the form of melon cubes and whole wheat toast.

"How about sausage and pancakes instead?" Coach Joe asked.

"Those aren't on your diet plan. Sorry," Pablo said.

"Wow, dinner last night and breakfast this morning," Stacey said to Pablo. "You're working all the time. You must be exhausted."

"I'm happy to make the overtime pay. I'll miss it next week with the new staff. So I'm just racking up hours while it lasts."

"Could I get some juice, there, Pablo?" Coach Joe asked. "Orange or grape would be fine."

"Your plan says cranberry."

"You can get away with overlooking the rules

sometimes, kid."

Pablo chuckled with his usual easygoing smile and returned to the kitchen, avoiding conflict by pretending the grumpy older man had made a joke instead of a serious request.

"I sure hope I'm not too late for breakfast," Georgette said as she and Arden joined us.

"You're right on time, madam." Coach Joe pulled out a chair with a smile at Georgette, but Arden plopped into it instead.

"They'd better have honeydew this time." Arden looked at the orange cantaloupe cubes on Joe's plate and tutted her disappointment. "Of course not."

"No sausage and pancakes, either. Maybe we ought to sneak out to a Waffle House one morning." Joe raised his eyebrows at Georgette, but she wasn't looking his way at all.

"We'll catch up with y'all later," I said. "Have a nice—"

"Wait, I have questions," Arden said. "The top one being, what are you going to do about the murderer haunting the attic?"

Everyone at the table turned toward us, some subtly, others less so. Spencer raised an eyebrow. Karl cleared his throat loudly.

"That's our top priority right now," I said. "We'll develop a plan to remove Bartel from the house based on the information we've collected so far."

"And what about the shape-changing ghost?" Karl asked. "Or is Bartel the shape-changer?"

"We're still hoping Harold Heusinkveld can give us insight into that," I said. "But he doesn't seem eager to speak with us. In the meantime, we'll keep watching and studying the entity and helping you guard against it."

"I guess it's better than nothing," Arden said as Pablo brought her breakfast. "Just like this cantaloupe."

Stacey and I extricated ourselves from the conversation as quickly as we politely could, then slogged out to the van for the drive home.

Chapter Twenty-One

We returned to the house in the afternoon and headed up to the attic, closing the door firmly behind us.

At the top of the stairs, we faced decades of accumulated clutter, all sorts of boxes, bags, and bits of furniture stashed away in the abandoned attic bedroom.

"It looks like all the family's remaining possessions are crammed up here," I said. "Let's divide and conquer. You start in that corner, I'll start in this one."

"How will we know which things might have been significant to Bartel?" Stacey asked.

"We won't, so make a big 'maybe' pile."

"It's so dusty." Stacey unzipped her backpack to draw out a pair of gloves, and I did the same. There could have been sharp or rusty objects hidden within the clutter, and I didn't want to risk cutting myself. I'd put the gloves through the washing machine to make sure all the owl-pellet residue was gone.

After digging through boxes of clothes, dishes, linens, and paperwork, I pulled out a couple of photo albums, handling them gently because the pages were crumbling like dry biscuits.

"Hey, we can finally put some more faces with names here." I showed Stacey the oldest photo, a sepia-toned image of a rotund, ruddy-faced man in an apron next to a handsome, dark-eyed young man with thick sideburns, under a sign that read Morgan's Grocery & Sundries. "That younger guy is Andries when he was still a recent immigrant working as a grocery clerk," I said. "Before he became the wealthiest man in town."

"Do you suppose he murdered the grocer and took over his store?" Stacey asked. "Something like that could have really gotten a haunted ball rolling around here."

"Possibly." I turned to a family photo where an older, scarier-looking Andries glared up at me from the picture with a feral look over his ascot. Beside him stood his wife Gerda, pale and wire-thin, blonde and big-eyed like a Disney princess, wearing a stiff, high-necked dress. Their two elementary-age boys, Pieter and Isaak, wore flat, formal expressions and dark suits like they were en route to work at a stodgy law firm. They were in the foyer of the Heusinkveld House, in front of a towering, ribbon-decked Christmas tree by the winding front stairs.

"It's the happy family, kind of," Stacey said. "But Gerda doesn't look too healthy. Like she's ill. Or being slowly poisoned, maybe. She doesn't have that look in her younger pictures, before they moved into this house."

"She died less than a year after moving in."

"And it was all tragedy after that, right?"

"The family seemed to make it along fine for a while. The two boys grew up, Pieter went off to war…" I found a picture of the younger son, Pieter, as a cocky-looking eighteen-year-old in an army uniform. In later photographs, he had a sad, haunted look. These included all of his pictures with his bride Rhea, who had bright, intelligent eyes that made me think of a watchful cat. She wore a generous smile as if trying to look exceedingly happy to make up for her morose husband.

A series of wedding photographs included Pieter's aging father Andries, who still had his ferocious animal glare even though his long sideburns were going gray, as well as Pieter's ill-fated older brother Isaak, who looked like he was having a much better time at Pieter's wedding than Pieter was. Photographs showed Isaak dancing with assorted women throughout the reception, including his pretty sister-in-law Rhea, and beaming at each one. In a couple of pictures, he was in the background with a few male friends, drinking from hip flasks.

"Looks like Isaak was the wild one," Stacey said. "Didn't he get drunk and fall off a balcony at a party?"

"That's what Spencer said." The last picture we found of doomed, wild Isaak showed him a couple of years later, dressed in coat and tie, his arm around a tall, curly-haired girl in a long black dress dripping with black lace. A hand-scrawled caption indicated the photograph was to commemorate their engagement.

"Wow, imagine having just one engagement picture

instead of a whole social-media collage of them,"
Stacey said.

"It looks like Isaak was engaged to this girl here,
Agnes Donaldson, before he died." I jotted the name
down in my notepad.

"Maybe Isaak broke it off, and Agnes pushed him
from the balcony," Stacey said. "Or she caught him
canoodling around at this party, and, well, same
outcome."

"Or he just accidentally fell from that dangerous
attic balcony where you wanted us to climb."

We moved on to pictures of the next generation.
Pieter, like his father, had two sons, Gerrit and Bartel.
The younger one, Bartel, was born nearly a year after
his hard-partying uncle Isaak died. In one picture of
them as children, Bartel had an impish look, while his
older, taller brother Gerrit tried to look solemn.

Gerrit and Bartel grew up during the Great
Depression, and everyone in the family had a grim,
anxious look during that period, as if the family
businesses were feeling the pinch and causing strain.

By the 1940s, the deaths of patriarch Andries and
his son Pieter had shrunk the family down to just
Pieter's widow, Rhea, and their two children. I looked
at pictures of Bartel in particular, who often seemed to
be in his brother's shadow, always shorter and with a
hint of malice on his face—or maybe I was reading too
much into it, knowing he was a convicted murderer.

Photographs from Gerrit's wedding in the 1950s
showed Gerrit dancing with his statuesque bride Dottie.
Others showed Bartel dancing with Dottie, and also
with his mother, who he'd later be convicted of
murdering. Bartel looked right at the camera for these

pictures, with a smile that bordered on a smirk, and his dark gaze made me feel uneasy.

Gerrit and Dottie eventually had their son Harold. Harold's childhood was mostly depicted in color photographs that had faded and taken on a reddish tone, giving them an almost blood-soaked appearance, a long-term effect of a paste commonly used in picture albums of the 1960s and 70s.

"Four generations," Stacey said. "Where do you think the haunting begins? And who's the shapeshifter?"

"It could be one of the Heusinkvelds, or an older entity that was here before the family arrived."

"And it's been feeding on them the whole time," Stacey said. "Starting with Gerda. Remember how the diner guy said Harold always looked pale, even as a school-age kid?"

I nodded, and we kept digging.

In time, I discovered a box of medical records, which revealed how and when Rhea ended up in a wheelchair.

"Listen to this, Stacey," I said, and she looked up from a box of old toys she'd found. "Rhea fell down those attic stairs."

"Right. Bartel pushed her down in her wheelchair. Do you think maybe they arrested the wrong person for it? Ooh, or maybe a *ghost* did it? Like the shapeshifter?"

"No, I mean that's how Rhea ended up in the wheelchair in the first place, from injuries caused by falling down those stairs."

"Wait, the same stairs where she would later die? That's where she became disabled in the first place?"

"Exactly. And you'll never guess *when* it happened."

"At the stroke of midnight on Friday the thirteenth?"

"The night of Gerrit's wedding," I said. "She fell down the attic stairs while her son's wedding reception was happening here at the house."

"And she never walked again? And later they made her live up here in the attic until she went down the stairs *again*, and died that time? This is so weird."

I tapped the black and white picture of Bartel dancing with his mother at the wedding. "Do you think it was him?"

"Like…maybe Bartel first tried to kill her the night of Gerrit's wedding? Then succeeded years later?"

"That would kind of parallel Isaak's death, falling from the balcony during the party, after he got engaged. It might even have been an engagement party."

"So, Isaak cheated on Agnes at their *engagement* party?" Stacey asked. "That's even worse!"

"Actually, you made up the cheating idea."

"Oh, right. Juicy if true, though, huh?"

"Anyway, people should avoid heights around this house, especially at parties," I said. "And stay out of the attic altogether."

"Good thing Chelsea keeps it locked. Hey, do you think this might have been Bartel's?" Stacey held up a short wooden sword—a toy, but it looked like it could leave splinters in someone's eye—with a word painted on it in childish, uneven letters: BaRteL. "Because to me, subtle clues indicate it was."

"Yeah, good find. Let's hang on to that whole box of toys, actually."

"It could all be sentimental ghost bait, huh?"

"I don't know how strong it'll be, if Bartel's already haunting the house where these objects are located, but we might get lucky."

"It was boxed up for a long time, so maybe he'll be happy to see it." Stacey made a few swipes and stabs with the sword before putting it down.

Thankful for the elevator, we brought ghost traps and stampers up from the van. Unfortunately, we still had to lug them up those steep attic stairs.

"Not fun," Stacey breathed when that long and grueling chore was complete.

"We should probably haul the wheelchair back up the attic stairs, too," I said.

"Ha, you're funny, Ellie."

"If we want him to come back, we should re-create last night's conditions as much as possible."

"But we're not sending the kid back into the attic."

"Of course not. Remember to lift with your legs and not your back."

"Ugh. This is going to be terrible."

As we rolled the heavy wheelchair from our borrowed bedroom toward the attic door, Pablo was making his way back from the office. He slowed to watch as we stood on the bottom stair, each of us taking one handle of the wheelchair, preparing to drag it up together.

"You need one person supporting it from the bottom," he told us.

"I'll do it." I attempted to squeeze around the high-backed wheelchair, but failed, so started to roll it back into the hall instead.

"Let me," he said. "This is heavy."

"You don't have to do that."

"It's no problem. Tilt it back…"

Stacey and I tilted it back, and he grabbed the lower part of the frame.

Pablo counted to three, and we all lifted together. I grunted as we moved it up to the first step and set it back down.

"Great," Stacey said. "Just the whole rest of the staircase to go. This type of wheelchair should be illegal."

It wasn't a fast process, but it was definitely faster than if Pablo hadn't been there.

"Thanks!" I said, when we finally reached the top, which felt like hours later. "We really did need your help."

"Definitely," Stacey added.

"It's payback for helping me with dinner." He shrugged.

"We could do that again today," I said.

"I'm not working dinner, but you can help Chelsea. I'd better go." He started down the stairs.

"Wait," I said, and he stopped, but he was looking understandably impatient, because he had a lot of work to do. Still, I hesitated, because what I needed to ask him wasn't easy. I started by tiptoeing into it. "Have you…ever seen anything strange or scary up here in the attic? Tag was really frightened by something last night."

"I don't come up here much," Pablo said. "I brought up some boxes once for Chelsea. Her ex-husband's things. I didn't see anything then."

"A lot of the residents have seen strange sights that remind them of memories, maybe bad memories, things they regret. I know it may not be easy to talk about, but are you sure you've never seen anything like that in the house? A person from your past? Someone associated with regrets?"

"No, nothing," he said. "My grandmother has a saying about regrets. I used to help her in the garden behind her house. We collected everything in these straw baskets. She said, we each carry our own basket through life, and it can fit only a few things. So you have to choose what you will carry. You can carry good things, like fruit, or flowers, or vegetables. Or you can put in stones that do nothing but weigh you down. Regrets, fears, the grudges you carry—those are just heavy stones, not useful. I was still a kid, so I said vegetables are bad, too, and candy would be better."

I laughed. "Your grandmother sounds very wise."

"She is. And I need to hurry."

"Sorry! Thanks!" I said to his back as he jogged down the steep stairs.

"That was a nice story," Stacey said. "The grandma thing. He seems sweet."

"His lack of major regrets in life, or his weirdly healthy way of dealing with them, might help protect him against the shapeshifter," I said.

"Lucky him."

We baited the traps with some of the kids' toys and photographs of Bartel that we'd found, as well as soil from his grave.

"At least one of us will have to be up here when the trap candles are lit," I said. "A ghost that can push a wheelchair could knock over a trap and start a fire. I think we're done up here for now."

"Good. I keep expecting some dead person or other

to jump out and try to shove us down the stairs."

"They really need to replace these right away." I climbed down the stairs carefully, not wanting to end up with permanent damage like Rhea Heusinkveld after her son's wedding reception, or even dead like when her other son had killed her.

A little later, the house filled with the sounds of Taggart's hesitant attempts at "Puff the Magic Dragon" under Georgette's patient tutelage.

Stacey and I ended up volunteering at dinner, where I tried to milk some extra local history knowledge from the group.

"Did you know Rhea Heusinkveld suffered her spinal injury on the night of her son Gerrit's wedding?" I asked the residents while refilling their glasses of iced tea.

"I did," Wallace said.

"That must have really thrown a damper on the party," Coach Joe said.

"Does anyone know any details about how it happened?" I asked.

The group looked among each other.

"Whatever it was, they kept it real hush-hush," Karl said. "Like they wanted to keep the truth under wraps. I bet you won't find much in the official newspapers."

"If you ask me, it must have been her son who pushed her down," Arden said. "The same one who ended up killing her. Seems like a pretty clear indicator to me."

"Bartel pushed her down the same stairs twice?" Georgette asked. "My word."

"That's what we're trying to find out," I said. "Whether it was Bartel, or a genuine accident, or something else."

"Something…supernatural, perhaps?" Spencer asked, raising his eyebrows.

"That's possible, too," I said. "We just don't know."

"If Bartel tried to kill Rhea, why wouldn't she report it to the police the first time?" Coach Joe asked.

"Because he was her son," Georgette said. "Maybe she couldn't bear the thought of him going to prison, even after he did that to her."

"Heck, I would have blowed his head off with a shotgun if he tried to kill me, son or not," Arden said. "When your kid tries to kill you, it's time to disown 'em, I'd say."

"But humans aren't always quite so rational," Wallace said. "Especially where strong sentiment is involved. Desperate people make desperate choices."

"We're also trying to learn more about Rhea's brother-in-law, Isaak, who died young at a party," I said. "We think it may have been his engagement party."

"It was," Wallace said. "He was engaged to my aunt Agnes, on the Donaldson side. It all happened before I was born, of course. By the time I came along, Isaak Heusinkveld was a distant memory long buried, and Aunt Agnes had instead married a doctor from Dublin. Georgia, not Ireland."

"And your family was locally prominent," I said.

"Well, the town is a small pond, but I suppose that's accurate, or was at the time."

"That was very different from Rhea's background before she married Gerrit, right?"

"Yes, I imagine it was wonderfully scandalous, the proud and civic-minded McMurtry clan uniting with the hard-scrabble Loundes, moonshiners and general ne'er-do-wells from back in the woods around Possum Creek," Spencer said. "That wedding must have been a colorful affair. Worlds colliding."

"Rhea was clever enough to make her way into the Heusinkveld family," Wallace said.

"Maybe she was just in love with Pieter," Georgette said. "He was a handsome war hero."

"A *rich*, handsome war hero," Spencer amended.

"They say Rhea was a hot little thing in her day, too," Coach Joe said. "She'd have to be, with all the other young ladies in town flashing their petticoats at Pieter and Isaak, chasing a Heusinkveld husband."

"Rhea *was* a clever woman, regardless," Wallace said. "She kept the business running for many years after her husband succumbed to the family disease." He made a drinking motion with his hand. "Liver failure, as they say. Odds are she was running things for quite a while before that, while he caroused."

"I'm sure Pieter had post-traumatic stress from the war," Spencer said. "Though it couldn't have been easy for his wife or for his sons, either, their father dying while they were still young."

"Bartel sure didn't turn out all that well," Karl said.

"And from what y'all told us last time, his brother Gerrit was intending to move his family to Chicago before he grew sick and died?" I asked.

"That's right," Wallace said.

"And instead of that fine plan, Gerrit's widow and son kept on living here, for decades," Spencer said. "Poor Dottie died here, and Harold only recently moved away. It's as though the house wouldn't let any of them escape."

The room fell silent. Chelsea walked in from the kitchen, looking pale, and she'd clearly overheard everything. She didn't say a word as she began clearing the plates. Stacey and I jumped up to help.

The mood in the room remained muted, as if everyone who lived in the house was considering the dark history, and the scary implication that the house might have trapped them, and might not allow any of them to ever leave the place alive.

Chapter Twenty-Two

Fortunately, the house didn't try to kill Stacey or me as we left through the front door after we finished helping with the dishes. We'd declined Chelsea's offer of a dinner share for our labor, partly because we weren't in the mood for salmon patties with snow peas, but also because we wanted to hit Topsy's downtown.

We reached the diner as the dinner rush was falling off. Two tables and a lone old guy in a camouflage jacket at the counter were finishing up. I eyeballed a syrupy, crusty slice of blueberry pie under a glass dome on the diner's counter.

Vernon stood at the register, selling a vial of CBD oil to a young county trooper whose car we'd seen parked outside. The cop nodded as he passed us on the way out.

"Back for more chicken-fried steak?" Vernon asked

us. "Or today's special, the barbecued country ribs? If that's not *too* country for you. These aren't St. Louis or baby back ribs, now—"

"Excuse me?" Stacey looked mildly outraged. "We can only hope they'll be country *enough*. What's your sauce base?"

"Molasses."

"I'm intrigued." She took an empty booth. A middle-aged couple in clashing plaid shirts were just getting up from the one beside it.

"And for you?" Vernon asked me.

"Green salad, blue cheese dressing," I said. "And maybe a square of cornbread. Not too big. Or too small."

"One Goldilocks-sized piece of cornbread." He returned to the cash register to ring up the departing customers. I had a few questions for him, but it was best to wait until his other customers dribbled away.

"I was thinking," Stacey said to me, "maybe the pattern really is that the ghost tries to kill people when they want to move out. Like back in the 1920s, Isaak was engaged, so maybe he was planning to move out. And in the 1950s, maybe Rhea was unhappy and thinking of leaving when she took that first spill down the stairs. Or maybe Rhea wanted her husband to move the family out, the same way her son Gerrit would later try to move his family to Chicago in the 60s, just before he suddenly got sick and died."

"And Rhea died around then, too," I said.

"Maybe she was trying again to move out. It was so cruel of her family to trap her in the attic like that, especially when you realize it was the scene of her original accident that put her in the wheelchair. The house is like a pitcher plant. Once you're inside, you get stuck, and you can't crawl out again."

"One order of country ribs, one salad with a side of extra-medium-sized cornbread. There's butter, too." Vernon set the plates in front of us. Stacey's ribs were indeed slathered in dark, heavy, molasses-hued sauce. I was glad I'd ordered the salad.

"It looks great." I broke off a piece of cornbread. It was crumbly, but not too crumbly. Just the right amount of crumbly. "We were hoping you might help us out with something."

"I can't give you any money, but my opinion's free."

"You said you knew Harold Heusinkveld back in school, right?"

"We went to the same school, and he ate here a few times over the years, but we didn't really know each other. He kept to himself when he did come in. Always alone, looking tired."

"We came across something he might have left by accident when he moved." I carefully removed a crumbling photo album from my laptop bag. "It includes a lot of his family pictures." I pointed to a reddened image of a small child in overalls. "That's him as a kid. And here's his grandmother, in the wheelchair. We were hoping to get in touch with him so we could give it to him."

"If he left it behind, he must not want it." Vernon started clearing another table nearby, grunting as he collected the small pile of dimes and pennies that had been left as a tip.

"It was deep in the attic, though," I said. "He may not have known it existed."

"How did you end up in the attic? I thought you were just taking pictures of falling-apart buildings."

"We ended up meeting the owner and she allowed us up in the attic, where it's just storage. Anyway, since you knew Harold, we were wondering if you might reach out to him for us, so he knows we're not just random crazies."

"How can I be sure you're not crazy?"

"You'll have to trust us on that part."

"I wouldn't mind helping y'all, but I don't know how to get in touch with Harold."

"We actually have his number, but he doesn't answer."

"Then you leave a message. You kids these days with your texting. In my day, you left a message on the voice mail."

"I just feel like it'll be hard to explain who we are and how we found his old stuff in a quick voice message. And maybe he'll be more likely to answer a phone call from a familiar place in his hometown. We really need your help." I slumped my shoulders and tried to look especially unhappy. Stacey pouted and gave the old chef some big puppy-dog eyes.

"Hey, it's okay, I'll give it a try." Vernon pulled an ancient landline phone with a spiraling cord from under the counter and raised it to his ear. I gave him Harold's number. "Hey there, uh, Hal. This is—yep, Topsy's Diner. It's Vernon. How are ya doing these days? Haven't seen you in here lately...Your number? Well, it's an unusual story, but the upshot is these ladies— they're historians or vloggers or some such—they have got something that may be of value to you. Here, I'll put 'em on." He waved the phone at us, and I took it.

"Hi, Mr. Heusinkveld?" I said, while Vernon got back to work. "My name's Ellie, and I've been trying to get in touch with you."

"And I've been avoiding you," said a man's voice. "I'm not interested in any town history project. The town's not worth it. One day it'll be forgotten, and that's for the best."

"Why do you say that?"

"Because the past belongs in the past," he said. "I'm already forgetting as fast as I can, myself. And I like it that way."

"We need to learn about problems people are having in the house. The past isn't staying in the past for them. They encounter people from their past, people who have already died, in some cases. The encounters leave them weak and drained. Would you know anything about that?"

Vernon looked up from scrubbing the grill and gave me a puzzled look.

"I moved away for a reason," Harold said. "That place isn't my responsibility anymore. I put in my time, I did my duty long enough, and I'm never coming back."

"Nobody's expecting you to come back—"

"Don't call me again. I'm blocking this number. I already blocked yours." Harold hung up.

I sighed and leaned over the counter, searching for the cradle to replace the phone.

"What was all that?" Vernon snapped.

"You did kind of charge right to the point there, Ellie," Stacey said. "Maybe a little more honey would have helped you catch that fly."

"He knows something," I said, "And he let all those

people living in the house get stuck with it. He owes them an explanation. And we represent them."

"Represent them how?" Vernon asked. "What did you say about dead people in the house? Is it haunted?"

"Sorry," I said. "We thought the truth might be hard to believe."

"That the Heusinkveld house is haunted?" He grabbed a mop and started wiping up the floor around the grill. "Nah, that ain't hard to believe at all."

Chapter Twenty-Three

The night began as previous nights had, with the residents making their way to bed fairly early, and the house falling quiet. Our microphones picked up everything from Coach Joe's buzzsaw snore to the low murmur of the television in Chelsea's room, where we could see only the closet door and the armchair where the specter of her father had appeared.

"Temperature's dropping in the attic," Stacey whispered, around eleven-thirty. "Too bad the traps aren't lit."

"I'll head up there," I said.

"We should probably buddy-system this one, though."

"You know predatory entities are less likely to manifest in front of two or more people."

"That's a good point, but there is word *predatory*,

and let's remember that at least one of the entities in the house is a murderer. All this points to no, you should not go alone, Ellie."

"I won't be alone. You'll be with me in spirit, or at least in radio-wave form." I pulled on my headset and adjusted the little antenna and microphone. "Ready?"

"No, I'm not ready. I'm sulking in angry protest of your choice here."

"But you'll watch over me."

"Of course." She sighed. "Be careful on the Stairway of Death."

"Thanks."

Out in the hall, I tried to tread as lightly as I could.

Footsteps thumped at high speed down another hall. It had to be Chelsea or Taggart, and the kid had a record of finding his way to the ghosts in the house.

"Slight detour to see who's running around," I whispered to Stacey over the headset as I followed the footsteps to the curving front staircase. I discovered I was pursuing Chelsea, dressed in flannel kitten-print pajamas, as she ran down to the first floor

"What's happening?" I asked.

"Spencer pressed the emergency call button," Chelsea said. "Something's wrong with Wallace."

"Oh, no." I followed her down a branch of hallway to Wallace and Spencer's spacious room along the side of the first floor.

"I'll be right there," Stacey said over the headset, and I didn't argue with her.

In the room, Wallace's wheelchair was overturned by the bed. Wallace lay crumpled in one corner, gasping between cries of fear, holding up his hands defensively against Spencer, who stood over the helpless older man, yelling at him.

"Wallace, I am not trying to hurt you!" Spencer turned toward us. "Chelsea, thank goodness. Maybe he'll listen to you." Spencer took a step back, but Wallace still cringed away as though Spencer had instead advanced on him, wielding a knife in one hand.

"What happened?" Chelsea knelt beside Wallace. "Are you injured?"

Stacey arrived, looking shocked, and stayed near the doorway since the room was getting crowded.

Wallace was pale and shivering, breathing in panicked gasps, but no longer crying out.

"I was only away for a few minutes," Spencer said. "I couldn't sleep, so I made valerian tea in the kitchen. When I returned, I found him like this."

"I'm sorry," Wallace finally said, his voice hoarse. "I am sorry, Spencer."

"For what?" Spencer asked. "You don't have anything to be sorry about. Maybe you had a bad dream? Or did you encounter the ghostly being who takes on a role from your memories?"

"Is that what happened?" Chelsea asked. "Remember, Wallace, it's not real, whatever you saw. It takes the forms of loved ones, people you've lost—"

"No, it was him," Wallace said, staring at Spencer. "I've known him all my life. And he knows me completely, more than I ever knew. He confronted me with the truth."

"I did that?" Spencer asked. "While I was away at the teapot? I have to say, I'm impressed with my multi-tasking."

Wallace closed his eyes and let his head drop back against the wall.

"Let's move you to the bed," Chelsea said to Wallace, after carefully checking him for signs of injury.

"I can help." I picked up Wallace's overturned wheelchair to demonstrate, then moved to his other side to help Chelsea lift him.

Wallace wasn't interested in moving, though. "You never left, Spencer. You were there." He pointed to the gap in the heavy, theatrically red curtain drawn most of the way across their room. Spencer's side of the divide lay on the other side. It was dark beyond the curtain, the lamp switched off. "You threw everything in my face, all at once. You may as well tell them."

"What does 'everything' mean?" I asked.

"Erskine," Wallace breathed.

"Erskine? The acting program in New York?" Spencer's brows knitted.

"I've heard of that!" Stacey said. "Some really major actors went there. It closed down a few years ago, though."

"You spent your last dollar traveling to New York to audition," Wallace said.

"Decades ago," Spencer said. "When we were kids."

"You were. Barely twenty, and determined to learn acting, once you saved up for the tuition. Working every hour I would give you, and every odd job."

"But Erskine rejected me. And rightly so. I'm hardly the Brando of my generation."

"But they didn't," Wallace said. "As you know. As you were just screaming at me. The pretense has ended. The masquerade has reached its conclusion. How long have you known?"

"What are you saying? I'm not following you, Wallace."

"You were living in my carriage house at the time," Wallace said as Chelsea and I lifted him onto his bed. "I saw the acceptance letter first. You may recall the envelope was already open."

"I don't remember that."

"I'm having trouble following what y'all are talking about," Chelsea said.

"I substituted a false letter," Wallace told her. "A rejection. And on a few occasions when he auditioned for the stage and was offered a role, I had Sarah June— my assistant in those days—decline them on his behalf. Then I would pass on a message that he'd been rejected —"

"Are you sure this happened, Wallace?" Spencer sounded skeptical. "This isn't a dream you were having just now?"

"Don't toy with me." Wallace looked smaller and frailer than usual. I noticed how thin his legs were from disuse, and the age-spotted skin along the side of his face next to his carefully styled, very thin silver hair.

"Why would you do that to me, Wallace?" Spencer asked.

"I was afraid," Wallace said. "Afraid you'd leave me alone in this desolate little town."

"But you could have come. To New York, or anywhere. You wanted to leave. We talked about it."

Wallace chuckled. "My family wouldn't have stood for it. My mother might have disinherited me."

"You were already an attorney. You could have made it independently."

"It did not seem that way at the time."

Spencer stared at him, and something inside him began to simmer, his jaw flexing. "That rejection letter was so harsh that I stopped auditioning for even the most community of theaters. They said I lacked the basic semblance of acting instinct, and what I lacked could never be learned. That was false?"

"Of course. I wrote it myself. Reputable institutions don't generally write overly harsh rejection letters like that."

"But why?" Spencer's hands balled into fists. He was clearly years younger than Wallace, possibly the youngest of the home's retired residents. "You pretended to support my acting."

"I have always supported your creative side. It's why I left you in charge of merchandising and decorating the store—"

"My creative side? The store was only meant to be a temporary job."

"And living rent-free in my carriage house was going to be temporary, too, if you recall," Wallace said. "But you never moved out."

"You trapped me," Spencer said. "With your lies. You wanted me as your servant, so you…stole my life from me?"

"Yes," Wallace said weakly. His eyes closed. "I was afraid to leave, and afraid to let you go. Caught on the horns of a wretched dilemma. Nobody else in this wretched town understood me."

"Maybe I didn't, either." Spencer turned away from him and looked at himself in a mirror, making slight adjustments. "Now, all these years later, here I am, still fetching your comb and your socks. For what? Why did I sacrifice my existence this way? What do I have to show for it now?"

Wallace said nothing, keeping his eyes closed.

The curtain concealing half the room shifted, as if a cold winter breeze had blown through.

I stepped around the edge of the curtain to see the room's dark side.

A shape stood near the foot of Spencer's bed, its back to me. I recognized the pinstriped silk pajamas.

"Spencer?" I asked, because it looked just like him.

He turned slowly to face me. It looked like Spencer on the surface, but his face was drawn up in a malevolent smile like I'd never seen him wear, like an evil twin.

"Yes?" The real Spencer approached me from the other direction, thinking I'd called for him. It was bizarre to stand there at the curtain, looking at the real Spencer on the well-lit side and the false one on the dark side.

Spencer took in a sharp gasp when he saw his smirking double.

"Don't get any closer, Spencer," I said, and I meant it for both of them, really—I didn't want Spencer getting closer to the entity, nor did I want the entity drawing closer to us.

The false Spencer kept glaring at us. Just like when it had taken the temporary form of the child on the tricycle, it began to decay, the skin going pale and rotting. The fine pajamas faded and grew frayed, buttons falling loose, slippers rotting to reveal skeletal feet beneath.

The real Spencer drew in a sharp breath, eyes widening in terror at this preview of his own death.

"We know what you are." I advanced on the entity.

"You steal people's memories and prey on their guilt."

The entity continued to decay, watching me with eyes like black marbles, cold and distant.

"Leave this house," I said. "Leave these people alone. No one will be tricked by you again."

If my words had any effect, I didn't see it. The entity became ever more corpse-like, dressed in filthy rags clinging to its crumbling flesh and exposed bone.

"What's happening over here?" Stacey popped up beside me, looking concerned, then joined Spencer in gaping at the entity.

The decaying Spencer image was shrinking away, though, becoming murky and indistinct, as if this were far more attention than it wanted, or maybe it had completed its errand of feeding on Wallace.

A moment later, the manifestation was gone, melted away like a bad dream.

"That…was it, wasn't it?" Spencer whispered. "The spirit that changes itself like an actor?"

"Taking the form of Wallace's guilt, in this case." I drew out my EMF meter and walked to the spot where the apparition had been. "I'm not detecting any sign that it's still here."

Spencer turned and looked at Wallace lying in bed, listless and exhausted. Chelsea was checking his blood pressure.

"I'm going to need more tea," Spencer said. "How can I ever sleep in here again after seeing that?"

"Stacey, you stay and help out here, then head back to the nerve center when you're done," I said.

"Where are you going?" Stacey asked.

"I'm searching for the entity in its lair while it's still active." I headed for the bedroom door.

"Not the attic?" She started to follow me. "After all this?"

"Especially after all this. We don't want it trying to feed on anyone else."

"But feeding on you is fine?"

"Whatever gets it closer to the trap. I'll stay in touch." I left the room and hurried up the hall, passing Spencer on his way to the kitchen. He looked like he was in shock, still coping with all he'd seen and learned.

Chapter Twenty-Four

I unlocked the door to the attic, then closed it behind me as I stepped into the cool, dusty darkness.

I crawled up the stairs on my hands and feet so I wouldn't be an easy kill if a ghost decided to shove me. I listened closely for any hint of the clattering sound of the antique wheelchair crossing the attic floorboards, in case it came barreling my way again.

At the top, the chair remained where we'd left it. Nobody shoved it toward me as I arrived, fortunately, because it could have knocked me down like a bowling pin. It was hard not to picture the frightening skull-faced woman who'd occupied it when it had crashed down the stairs and slammed into me.

I walked around the attic, watching and listening, taking EMF and temperature readings. Our cameras and microphones were still up and running fine. The

room had more than one cold spot, but nothing
materialized or threw any furniture at me.

Finally, I lit one candle in each trap, then sat on the
same spot on the floor where Tag had been the night
before, not far from the wheelchair's foot supports. I
positioned a small trunk as a barrier to block the
wheelchair if it suddenly rolled my way.

Then I waited.

"I'm back," Stacey eventually whispered over my
headset. "Wallace seems fine, but an ambulance is
taking him for observation at the hospital just in case.
Spencer didn't go with him. I think Spencer's still pretty
broken up about Wallace secretly ruining his life a long
time ago and all that."

"It's been quiet up here."

"I see that."

"I'll try to stir things up." I played a recording,
amplified by the speaker on my belt.

"Hello?" It was Tag's voice from the previous
night's recording. "Are you there?"

Something shifted in the room, the air becoming
chillier and more electric. The EMF meter noticed the
changes.

I played it again. "Hello? Are you there?"

With a slight creak, one wheel of the chair
advanced just a little, the empty seat angling toward me
as if someone were now sitting there, watching me.

"Rhea," I said. "Rhea Loundes Heusinkveld. Is that
you?"

Gradually, an indistinct form appeared in the
wheelchair, the kind of still, silent human shape one
might imagine seeing late at night, usually formed from
nothing more malevolent than a coat or a blanket tossed

casually over a chair. I was pretty sure this was real, though, and not my mind playing tricks.

"I'm here to help you move on," I said. "You have been trapped here a long time, but the door to the other side is always open. You just have to look for it. Do you understand?"

The chilly apparition in the chair grew more distinct. Her face wasn't so horrifying this time. She had pale skin and paler eyes that still reminded me of a watchful cat, perhaps a frightened one right then. Her silver hair was swept up and back, set away from her face with jeweled pins.

"Can you hear me?" I asked.

She whispered something, her full, badly cracked lips barely moving, her voice like a scratching claw in the dark.

"I'm sorry, what did you say?"

Just a little louder, she said, *"He's coming."*

"Who?"

A floorboard creaked somewhere deep in the attic, back where the roof sloped down to the floor.

A second creak sounded, then a third. They were coming closer, but I still couldn't see anyone.

"He'll kill me," she whispered.

The footsteps reached the traps, which I'd placed near the center of the attic, in the most open space available.

After a long pause, the footsteps resumed, growing closer.

"Show yourself, Bartel," I said, slowly rising to my feet. "Or whoever you are." It was kind of hard to add that in the most confident of voices, but I did my best.

"Bartel," the old woman's ghost whispered. *"My*

loyal son."

The entity surged forward, a tall, vaguely man-shaped thing made of shadows, his face showing no features except grinning white teeth. He had appeared behind her wheelchair and seemed to take some glee in seizing the handles.

"Get back!" I quick-drew my flashlight like some kind of paranormal gunfighter and let him have a few thousand lumens of full-spectrum white light.

He recoiled, his grin bending into a grimace, but the wheelchair came launching forward anyway. Rhea's fragile, barely visible face took on the form I'd seen the night before, the bare-skull, hollow-eyed visage of death, the way she might look in her grave.

The wheelchair struck the wooden chest I'd set up as a barrier, so it didn't crash into me this time.

Instead, the chair rose off the floor, its forward momentum transferred upward. I expected it to immediately slam back down to the floorboards with a heavy thud, but instead it kept rising, losing momentum only gradually. It floated up until its wheels were level with my head, then levitated there.

The skull-faced woman looked down at me from the levitating wheelchair. I realized I was in a potentially fatal situation here, if the chair came falling my way.

But instead, it slowly rotated away from me, toward the entity that had pushed her.

My narrowed, concentrated flashlight beam still pointed at the spot where the shadowy, grinning entity had stood. The entity had already fled halfway across the attic, moving into the dim, distant low space like an errant shadow escaping back to its own lightless realm.

Rhea's wheels spun as she pursued the shadow-man like an avenging angel, rolling through empty air, her silver hair streaking back from her skeletal face like when she'd come flying out at me from the attic door.

I ran with her, staying to one side to reduce the odds of getting brained by the chair. I kept my beam thin and narrowly focused on the guy, and she was able to avoid the brunt of the light as she traveled overhead as if riding an invisible road.

"Ellie, uh, things look crazy up there—" Stacey's voice began.

"No time to chat!" I replied.

Ahead, the attacker ghost stumbled and swayed as if caught in a hurricane when Rhea approached him from above. The attic had grown cold fast, like a bad storm was approaching, heralded by rapid changes in temperature, pressure, and light.

The shutters enclosing the balcony windows blew open. The tall, narrow balcony door, nearly identical to the tall, narrow balcony windows flanking it, opened with a cracking sound as its latch broke.

The same cold blast of stormy air swept the dark figure off his feet and out the door, where he faded fast in the late-summer heat and moonlight.

For a moment, I saw his face, youthful and good-looking in an unkempt, unshaven way.

Then he dropped over the balcony railing and out of sight.

I ran out to the balcony and looked over, but he'd vanished.

The weathered balcony floorboards groaned and sagged under my weight. As treacherous as the balcony had looked from the ground, it looked worse up close, the railing too low and spindly, with open holes in the floor where boards had rotted away. The balcony was only decorative now, and not that great of a decoration, either.

"Ellie, what's going on?" Stacey appeared in the doorway and began to step out.

"Stay inside!" I told her as a spongy floorboard bent under her toe.

"What are you doing out there?" she asked, skittering back from potential disaster.

"Just verifying this balcony's a death trap, and that it's good we never climbed the tree up to it." I made my way back to the door, pausing at the crumbling threshold to inspect the broken latch. "And it was locked from the inside. Is Rhea gone?"

"Well, the wheelchair's not flying around anymore, if that's what you mean. Who knew it had a hover option?"

I looked past Stacey. The heavy old wheelchair was indeed resting on the floor again, looking vacant, though Rhea's ghost might still have occupied it invisibly.

The seemingly empty chair was pointed in our direction, and I was still standing in the balcony doorway, where I could be bulldozed out and fall to my death like Isaak Heusinkveld had done from this very spot about a century earlier.

I pulled the door closed and nudged Stacey away from it. The attic was dimmer than before, because the candle on one ghost trap had gone out. That trap had closed, too, its automatic sensors apparently triggered by a sufficient combination of falling temperature and spiking electromagnetic energy.

The wheelchair was parked just beside the closed trap.

"Looks like you might have trapped her," Stacey said. "Maybe she was drawn to her kids' old toys. Plenty of room for emotional attachment there."

"I told her I could help her escape this house," I said. "We'll have to find a nice graveyard to release her. Somewhere with plenty of trees and wildflowers."

"Statues are a plus, too," Stacey said. "And you gotta have walls."

I blew out the remaining candle on the other ghost trap. The attic became darker, but the darkness was softened by the moonlight from the windows now that the shutters were open, and the cold spots had been replaced by warm, fresh summer air.

Chapter Twenty-Five

"What happened?" Chelsea asked from below, drawn to the attic stairs by all the noise. "Is everyone okay?"

I stepped over to the top of the staircase and looked down at Chelsea on the bottom step.

"We're fine," I replied. "The balcony door latch had a rough night, though."

Stacey and I descended the stairs carefully. I kept watching over my shoulder for attack wheelchairs, but none came after us.

Safely down in the hall, with the attic door closed again, we caught Chelsea up on what had happened. Arden and Georgette arrived from their room and listened.

"It sounds like Rhea was finally able to turn the tables and chase off her attacker," Arden said.

"With y'all's help," Georgette said to Stacey and me.

"I didn't do much," I said.

"Maybe she didn't need much," Chelsea said. "Just a little push."

"Does this mean Bartel's gone for good?" Stacey asked.

I shook my head. "It wasn't Bartel. I'll double-check the photo album, but I'm pretty sure it was Isaak. His fall from the balcony fits that, too."

"Which one was Isaak, again?" Chelsea asked.

"The one who died at his engagement party back in the 1920s," Georgette said. "On that very balcony."

"I guess the twenties got a little too roaring for him," Arden said.

"There's a chance Isaak isn't gone for good," I said. "If he's been stuck re-enacting the circumstances of his death all these years, he'll probably pull himself back together sooner or later and do it again. But it's also possible that removing Rhea from the house will shake him out of it by breaking the pattern."

"Wait, does that mean Isaak killed Rhea?" Stacey asked. "But Isaak died decades before her."

"Being dead didn't stop him from pushing the chair tonight," I said. "Or clobbering me with it last night."

"You're telling us Isaak's *ghost* murdered Rhea?" Arden asked. "Not Bartel? And he's still running loose around here?"

"We'll keep watch in case he comes back," I said.

"Hopefully he doesn't tonight," Stacey said. "I'm exhausted."

"We all are," Chelsea said. "Ladies, we should get to bed."

"With ghosts loose in the house?" Arden asked. "Fat chance. I'm going to the sitting room." She and Georgette left down the hall. I'd glimpsed the upstairs sitting room before, a place of retreat for the ladies, with a bookcase full of novels, doilies on the couch arms, and a television in one corner.

"I'd better check on Tag." Chelsea yawned and made sure the attic door was closed. "Good thing he's a heavy sleeper."

When everyone had gone their separate ways, Stacey and I returned to our borrowed bedroom, watching the monitors again in case more activity disturbed the house that night.

For the moment, the attic lay still and quiet. So did Arden and Georgette's room, with both residents gone. Chelsea tossed and turned in her bed, sighing unhappily. Coach Joe snored.

Stacey and I had snack time—strawberry yogurt for her, turkey sandwich for me.

"I feel like we should go check on the Golden Girls," Stacey said after a few minutes. "And maybe Spencer. Why can't these people stay near the cameras where we can see them?"

"I could use a walk," I said. "Let's grab the trap from the attic. Then you go visit Arden and Georgette, while I take the trap down to the van and check on Spencer."

"And we'll sneakily add small cameras to the rooms they're in so we can keep watch?"

"You're reading my mind. Maybe spending all that time with Jacob is making you psychic."

"He says he can come Saturday night, by the way," Stacey said. "Family thing on Friday."

"That would be great." I stood and stretched.

"We're definitely going buddy system on the attic, right?" Stacey asked.

"Of course. I don't want to be up there alone with what's-his-name."

"Or the other what's-his-name."

"Exactly. Even if Bartel was innocent in life, he could be an angry ghost after decades of being unjustly locked away in the state's harshest prison, only to end up nameless and forgotten in the prison cemetery."

We cautiously made our way up into the attic, wary of angry ghosts flinging wheelchairs, but the wheelchair remained where we'd last seen it, sitting completely still next to the sealed trap holding the "BaRteL" sword, painted blocks, and other small toys along with a sample of Bartel's burial earth.

"Let's get you moved out of here." I lifted the trap free while Stacey watched the shadows nervously, her hand on her flashlight, though we could see by moonlight well enough.

We climbed down the steep staircase, then locked the attic behind us.

Music floated down the hallway, faint and scratchy.

Stacey and I looked at each other, then followed it, wary of another trick by the deceptive shape-changing ghost.

In the sitting room, a record played on a large wooden slab of an antique turntable. Georgette drank a plastic cup of bubbly ginger ale and swayed along with Loretta Lynn's *Fist City* album. Arden sat at a coffee table and dealt herself a hand of solitaire.

"Well, hello there, ladies," Georgette said. "Will you be joining us?"

"I could hang out a minute. This room is so neat." Stacey checked out a bookshelf where the content skewed heavily toward romance, biographies, and mysteries. She poked among the paperbacks, no doubt looking for a spot to hide a small camera.

"Could be bigger," Arden muttered. "And it's only got one window. They keep the balcony locked at night, how do you like that?"

"How's the view?" I moved to the locked balcony doors to distract Arden and Georgette while Stacey slid the little camera between a couple of books.

"Great, if you like looking at the old hardware store and the empty pharmacy where they used to sell ice cream," Arden said.

"Y'all come dance," Georgette said. "Show me some of them TikTok moves the kids are doing."

"Sounds fun!" She brought out her phone. "I actually prefer this site called LookyLoon…"

"I'm heading downstairs, but y'all enjoy." I stepped out and picked up the ghost trap from where I'd left it in the hallway.

"Send the gentlemen up if they're awake," Georgette said. "We could have a dance party."

"At this hour?" Arden looked offended.

"All the best parties happen late at night, Arden."

"I wouldn't know. I was always too busy working for a living." Arden snorted and resumed laying out cards.

I took the lazy way downstairs, riding the closet-sized elevator. I wished I had one of those at my building for when I needed to move heavy stuff in or out of my upstairs apartment.

Gripping the ghost trap with one hand, I leaned

against the wood-paneled back wall of the elevator and took a deep breath, letting myself relax for a second.

A low whine sounded from somewhere above, through the little rectangle of the air vent. The walls and floor shuddered.

Then the elevator stopped, lost somewhere in the twilight land between floors. Overhead, the lights in the round glass fixture blinked a couple of times, then went out completely, leaving me in total darkness.

I tried the door, but it was locked, the safety mechanism engaged for the trip.

A cold spot struck my insides hard and fast, entering my guts and my heart, turning my blood into an icy slush. My lungs seized up as the air inside them plummeted toward freezing.

I thought I would die right there, but the cold moved onward, gradually sliding through me like an icicle emerging through my stomach. The cold presence moved somewhere in front of me in the dark.

Recently, a powerful ghost had managed to rip a trap free from my grip and break it open, releasing the spirits inside, though only for the purpose of recapturing them.

If the entity in the Heusinkveld house had a habit of not permitting others to leave, then perhaps it wanted to block me from carrying Rhea's spirit out the door and on to greener pastures.

I reached for my flashlight, but I was still recovering from the cold spot's profoundly painful contact with my insides. My fingers were numb, and I moved sluggishly, like a cold-blooded creature in winter.

"Ellie," a voice said. It was soft, female, and so

familiar it hurt.

"Mom?" I whispered. Some part of me certainly felt stupid, just hearing myself saying it, knowing all I knew about this case. But that was the rational part of my brain, somewhere in a back room of my head trying to restart like a slow-running computer, the screen solid black. Up front, I was all pain, ripped open from the inside, making me vulnerable to this emotional attack. "This isn't real," I managed to whisper, clutching my aching guts with my hands, my flashlight forgotten in its holster.

Or maybe some part of me was reluctant to use the light, reluctant to end this encounter, however false it might have been.

"You left us there, Ellie," she said.

"I know," I said.

"You could have come back for us."

"I *know.*" She was stirring up thoughts I'd long suppressed, after sort of discussing them with the therapist my Aunt Clarice had found for me after I moved to Virginia to finish high school after my parents' death.

"You could have tried," my mother said. "You could have saved one of us. Me, or your father. He didn't deserve to die like that, Ellie. And neither did I. Do you have any idea how much it hurt us, how much pain we suffered?"

I shivered, unable to speak, my insides torn open and laid bare.

Her hand touched my face.

It felt like I remembered from when I was a child, just a little colder. I still couldn't see anything.

My cheek grew colder where her fingers pressed

against it, and I began to feel very tired.

"You said you hated us," she said. "And then you left us to die."

"Yes," I whispered. I had said that, because they'd forbidden me to go on a concert date with a boy when I was fifteen. Probably a typical parent-teen fight, but it had been our final conversation.

"You summoned the fire ghost that night," my mother whispered. "Your hatred for your father and me roused him from below, gave him the spark, the starting flame he needed to rise. You may as well have lit it yourself."

I shuddered, freezing. My legs went soft and weak, and I slid down the wall, slowly falling into a sitting position on the floor.

Her hand never left my face, and I felt her presence over me in the dark.

"Please," I whispered. "I'm sorry. I'm so sorry."

Some final barrier seemed to give inside me, and I slouched over the trap, faintly remembering that keeping it sealed had once been very important to me, for reasons I'd momentarily forgotten.

Then the darkness took over.

Chapter Twenty-Six

"Hey, kid, are you okay?" a man's voice asked. Thick fingers probed around my throat, then down along my collarbone, and then unfastened the top button of my shirt.

I pushed open my heavy eyelids. Coach Joe knelt over me, checking me out as I lay on the floor. I'd apparently passed out.

"Huh?" I turned my head to try to get a better view of where I was. It turned out I was on the worn carpet of the elevator floor, the ghost trap lying beside me.

"Can you breathe? Take a deep breath for me." He undid the next button on my shirt.

"I can breathe fine." I nudged him away and sat up quickly.

"What are you doing there, Joe?" Karl hobbled on his cane along the first-floor hallway, approaching us.

"I found her lying in the elevator. Just checking her vitals." He gave me a wink and touched my wrist. "Pulse could be a little stronger."

"We'd better call Chelsea," Karl said.

"Go push the button in our room," Joe told him.

"You should run and do it," Karl said. "You're much faster than me, Joe."

Joe sighed. "All right. Let me help you up, honey."

"No, thanks." I shook off his reaching hands. "I'll be fine. Go call Chelsea."

He grunted but stood and walked away.

"Give you a hand?" Karl reached one hand down, but he was leaning heavily on his cane with the other.

"No, but thank you." I pushed myself to my feet, grabbing up the sealed trap. "What are y'all doing up this late? Isn't it past your bedtime?"

He chuckled. "We were going to see why there's music on the second floor."

"Georgette and Arden decided to have a late night. They wanted to invite you up there, actually." I checked the elevator with my EMF meter. Conditions looked normal again. The entity wasn't invisibly hanging around, as far as I could tell. "Maybe you should go."

"You sure you don't need any help?" he asked.

"Nah. I'll ride up with you, though." I didn't want to be responsible for Karl getting trapped alone like I'd been. "It's fun."

Karl shook his head and joined me in the elevator. We made it safely to the second floor, and he headed down the hall, off to join the party, while I headed for the stairs, not wanting to take the elevator alone again.

Downstairs, I hurried to Spencer and Wallace's

room and peeked through the open door. The room was dark and silent. Wallace's bed was empty, of course, since he'd been carted off to the hospital. The dividing curtain still blocked off most of Spencer's side of the room as if concealing a backstage area.

Reluctantly, I tiptoed toward the curtain, remembering how the entity had been waiting on the other side after it fed on Wallace, as if eavesdropping, learning about those who now shared its house.

I approached the curtain, steeled myself, and pulled it aside.

Spencer's bed was empty, too, and the sheets were neatly made, but the pillow and blanket were missing.

I eventually found Spencer in the sunroom, lying on the sofa with his bedding, and he looked startled when I arrived.

"Oh, it's just you," he said.

"Sorry to disappoint."

"I'm relieved, not disappointed."

"Are you all right?"

"Not especially. I keep thinking of the dying image of myself by my bed. A very personal and highly dramatized *memento mori*, a reminder of my own death I'll surely never forget. I don't know whether I'll ever be able to sleep in that room. That's aside from the matter of sharing it with Wallace after learning how he betrayed me. I see now that so much of my life has been a fool's charade, but I can never reclaim all the lost years."

"I'm sorry," I said, more sincerely this time, but I didn't know what else to say.

"I'm only here because he is," Spencer continued. "I'm only sixty-one, many years younger than him.

Younger than anyone else here. I could still be a working actor at my age. Look at Ian McKellen."

"If you're not sleeping, the ladies are having a late-night party upstairs. They're coping with their discomfort with the house, too. Maybe you could join them."

"I can't recall the last time I attended a party this late at night." He sat up and adjusted his pinstriped silk pajamas. "I'm not properly dressed."

"Oh, it's a pajama party," I said. "You wouldn't want to be off-theme."

"I certainly wouldn't. Thank you for the tip." He drew his soft slippers over his feet. "Perhaps I should bring tea and crackers from the kitchen. One wouldn't want to show up empty-handed."

"Good thinking."

We parted ways as he walked to the kitchen and I headed for the back door.

I hesitated at the back-door threshold and checked the trap I was carrying. If the house, or one of the entities within it, was resistant to people moving out, it might also try to stop me from relocating Rhea to safer grounds.

Extra wary, I headed down the brick steps and into the garden. Wind rustled the leaves above. The birdhouses creaked and swung on their ropes. A dark shape fluttered from one, startling me, giving me barn-owl flashbacks, but in the gloom under the trees I couldn't see what kind of creature it was.

Beside me was the long covered porch outside Spencer and Wallace's room, with all the window curtains drawn across the darkness inside. One window above it glowed with the light of the room where

Stacey and I had set up our monitors.

I walked to the van, then stopped and held the ghost trap up to the moonlight. The wooden blocks inside were painted with letters, numbers, and animal shapes. A brown teddy bear depicted on the side of one block grinned at me, grimy with damp red earth from Bartel's grave, its eyes solid black.

A pale mist floated in the center of the trap, shapeless, but I felt it regarding me, an unnatural being who no longer belonged in our world. I shivered and quickly packed the trap out of sight inside the van until we could dispose of it.

Then I stood in the moonlight for a minute, thinking over the case. We'd removed one active ghost from the house, but not the one causing all the problems. Surely the worst was still ahead.

Chapter Twenty-Seven

The late-night party on the second floor went on for almost an hour before the participants went to bed, finally calm and tired enough to sleep. Spencer eventually returned to the sunroom rather than his own room. Stacey kept watch until dawn while I slept in my sleeping bag on Louise's old bed, recovering from my draining encounter with the entity.

Stacey eventually woke me, yawning herself. "Do you think you can drive us home since you napped? I'm beat."

"Sure," I said, though I felt weary, my body heavy as I pushed myself up. "I'll just need some coffee. And possibly breakfast."

"Maybe there's some spare grapefruit for you downstairs."

"That sounds…weirdly appealing."

"You *are* in a strange mood."

"Yep." I sat up and stretched. "I'd rather hit the road, though. It's almost four hours to Tallahassee."

"Right. Wait, what? We're driving to Florida?"

"You can sleep on the way down."

"Does that mean we're going to see what's-his-name? Harold, the last living Heusinkveld?"

"He can't hang up on us in person."

"He can run away, though."

"He can try."

Downstairs, I got myself a grapefruit from the kitchen, nodding at Pablo, who was busy reviewing everyone's morning medication schedule. Medicine and meals seemed to form the underlying rhythm of life in the house.

Only Coach Joe was awake, having missed the party and gone back to sleep instead. He smiled as I sat at the other end of the table from him.

"You really do look just like my first wife," he told me with a wink. His gaze shifted to Stacey beside me. "And this one looks like my first girlfriend. The years sure have gone by. Time was, I'd have asked you out dancing."

"Aw," Stacey said, peeling her orange a little faster.

"You meet a lot of ladies, playing ball, coaching ball," he said. "Being prominent in the community. I miss that."

"Being prominent?" Stacey asked. "Or the ladies?"

He chuckled and raised his eyebrows. "It's all one big ballgame, isn't it?"

"Well, we have to hit the road." I stood and took my grapefruit with me, finishing it by the kitchen trash. I put the spoon in the dishwasher and rinsed the tart juice from my fingers in the big steel sink.

"How's the ghost business?" Pablo asked me.

"One down, one or two to go," I said.

"Sounds like progress."

"I wish it felt like it. Have a good day, Pablo."

When we reached the van, Stacey climbed into a drop-down cot in the back with a camping pillow beneath her head.

"Try to not take any sharp turns at high speed," Stacey called as I started up the engine. "I don't want to get thrown out of bed."

"As if the van is capable of high speed," I said. "Too bad we don't have my car."

"Or my car," Stacey grumbled. "It's way more comfortable. Literally the worst of three options here."

I put on a playlist of gentle classical music at low volume, just enough to make my drive more pleasant while letting her sleep. A drive this long would be perfect for an audiobook; maybe I'd download one later, after we got going. For the moment, I just couldn't wait to get on the road again, like the song says.

We traveled southwest on a single-lane highway through pines and open green fields, a land of dirt roads and occasional sleepy small towns. A train full of rust-splotched box cars crawled alongside us for a stretch where the tracks ran parallel to the highway. Most likely the railroad tracks predated the paved road. Occasionally we'd pass a ritzy rural compound with an imposing house or two, usually painted white, with matching stables and fences. I was still yawning despite sipping a giant barrel of strong gas-station coffee.

I kept thinking about my false encounter with my

mother, something I'd been doing my best to forget about. I'd seen my parents' ghosts during my final confrontation with Anton Clay, and they were free now, like his other victims. They had to be. I needed to believe that, and I completely understood why Chelsea had reversed her stance on this investigation—because she needed to believe her father was free, too, that his apparition was only a lie, a manipulative mirage of suffering.

Georgette, on the other hand, had embraced the recurring visions of her son, had allowed the entity to feed on her in exchange for those bittersweet illusions. I could sympathize completely with her desire to believe in something that couldn't be true, if it meant reconnecting with someone lost long ago, someone still loved but forever unreachable.

I grew resentful of the shapeshifting entity, thinking how it passed through me, freezing my insides, no doubt gathering memories to use against me. The way it abused its victims angered me, and I found myself gripping the steering wheel with whitened knuckles. That was why I was making the eight-hour round trip to Florida. I was up against the wall, and the only person who might be able to shed light on the situation was deliberately avoiding us.

We didn't have long to go once we crossed into Florida. He couldn't avoid us much longer.

The map app guided us to Harold Heusinkveld's new digs, Pineapple Grove Apartments off Interstate 10 in northern Tallahassee, a somewhat rundown complex of two-story, faded-lime buildings with wooden stairs, landings, and balconies, everything ready to burn like kindling if conditions grew dry and hot enough. I was always wary of fire risk, considering how my parents had died, and glad to live in a brick building back home. However old, grungy, and cramped my apartment might have been, it had been built fireproof because of the glassblowing operation.

"There's his apartment block. He's in F2." I pointed to a crooked letter F on one building. "Stacey? Stacey, wake up! We're here!"

"We're home?" she asked groggily.

"Far from it. Let's go give Harold a big hello." I hopped out of the van.

"Okey-doke." Stacey climbed out, put on her sunglasses, and took her time stretching and yawning. "What are we going to say, exactly?"

"Just let me talk."

"So you're not really sure." Stacey trudged behind me across the parking lot, utterly failing to keep pace.

Her delay wasn't such a problem, though, because nobody answered when I knocked at apartment 2F.

"He's home," I said on the way back to the van. "I saw a window curtain move."

"What do we do?"

"Play the waiting game." I sat in the driver's seat and opened my window for fresh air. "He has to come out sooner or later."

"Sounds great. I was waiting game champion in third grade." Stacey slouched low on the passenger side and watched the apartment door with me.

Nearly an hour later, the door finally opened and a gray-haired man jogged out, wearing khakis and a white button-up shirt. He carried a bright orange apron and a matching cap with what looked like goat horns growing out of its brim.

"There he is!" I said. "Let's go."

Stacey and I hopped out of the van and hurried across the parking lot.

"Excuse me, Mr. Heusinkveld?" I said. He looked at us warily. He had the ruddy nose and cheeks of a heavy drinker, a habit rumored to run in his family. "Could we speak to you for a second?"

"Who are you?" He slowed but kept approaching his brown Buick sedan.

"I'm Ellie Jordan, a private investigator. I've been trying to get in touch with you about some research into your family's old house—"

"You're the one from the phone last night? You drove all the way down here?"

"We did, yes."

"If you don't quit stalking me, I'll get a restraining order." He unlocked his car and threw his orange garments inside. "I have to get to work or I'll be late. I'm shift manager, have to set a good example."

"If you could just spare one minute—"

"I can't." He sat down and slammed the car door shut.

I sprinted toward the van. "Let's follow him," I told Stacey as I passed her. She let out an annoyed sigh as she had to reverse course and to run back to the van with me.

We followed him a few miles to an area with strip malls lined with bushy trees. He parked near a large establishment called KIDBURGERS. Pulling on his cap and apron, he hurried inside through a door featuring a logo of a cartoon goat kid riding a skateboard. The goat kid wore his cap turned backward for added personality and wackiness.

We parked and went in after him.

The inside was a cacophony of video games, rumbling Skee-Ball lanes, and an animatronic band onstage, featuring a backward-hat goat kid playing an electric guitar, a lamb with a keyboard, and a piglet with a drum set. A row of machines sold plastic debit cards to swipe in the video games. The crowd was small and scattered, mostly preschool kids and their moms, but it wasn't hard to imagine the place swarming when school got out later, especially on a Friday afternoon. It was probably quite the hangout for the third-grade set.

"Are you here for Breighton's birthday party?" asked a young woman at the counter, while indicating a distant, kid-crowded table in front of the stage festooned with balloons and a big paper sign that said BREIGHTON.

"No, we're just having lunch," I said.

"Really? Here?" The employee looked skeptical under her orange goat-horn hat.

"Yep. Spur of the moment."

"Okay…" She looked at us like we were crazy as she handed us the menus, which were also coloring pages, along with a pack of crayons. "Sit anywhere you like. The band gets pretty loud, though, so I wouldn't sit too close."

"Thanks." I picked a table in a back corner with a sweeping view of the flashing, chiming, ringing arcade restaurant.

"What do you think?" Stacey asked as she sat on the bright plastic bench. She pointed to the menu portion of the coloring page, which offered hot dogs, hamburgers, and grilled cheese sandwiches, each with a choice of fries or a fruit cocktail cup. "I'm leaning toward grilled cheese and fries, personally."

A server in an orange apron and matching goat-horn hat started toward us, but Harold Heusinkveld emerged from the back and redirected her elsewhere. Then he approached our table himself, smiling brightly until he could turn his back on the rest of the customers.

"You followed me to work?" His smile quickly became a scowl.

"We drove four hours to talk to you," I said. "And we'd like to get home today."

"That's not my fault. I never told you to come here. I told you to leave me alone."

"Unfortunately, we can't. Because whatever is in your house—"

"It's not my house anymore."

"—it's endangering the people who live there now. It's stalking them, it's preying on them, and we need to understand what's happening in order to protect them."

"I'm not going back there."

"Nobody's asking you to. We are just trying to help some innocent people who desperately need it. Something in that house is endangering them. Threatening their lives, possibly." He looked torn, like maybe I was getting through to him, so I pressed onward. "Why are you so eager to stay away? Maybe we can help them if we understand."

He sighed. "I spent my life intending to move, but I kept getting sucked back in there. Do you know I wasn't even supposed to grow up in that house? My dad was going to move us to Chicago. Talked about it all the time. He'd get this glow when he talked about it.

Instead he died, and my mom got trapped. Then she died, and I was trapped."

"Trapped how?"

"Well, there were residents who needed my help, and I was always just about to move out, you know, in my mind. Next thing you know, I'm in my thirties, running the place while Mom was sick. She died only a few months after Uncle Bartel died in prison, not that we missed him, but it was weird timing. Anyway, after she died, I felt like she was still there."

"Did you ever see her in the house afterward?"

"After she died?"

I nodded, very gently.

He looked around, then sat on the purple bench of the table beside us. "Why would you ask that?"

"Because that's what people see in the house," I said.

"They see my mother?"

"No," I said, thinking of my encounter with the apparition pretending to be my mother, but I shoved that memory down fast. "People from their own past. That's what I was talking about on the phone."

"But why would that happen?"

"That's what we're trying to figure out. We have reports of people seeing their own family members who have passed away. And these encounters are usually negative and draining."

"Is that right?"

"Did you ever notice residents saying things like that when you ran the place?" I asked.

"Well, maybe. But their memories start to slip. And sometimes they just start talking about the past with no context, because it's what they've been thinking about. I don't know. I'll tell you, though…sometimes I did see my mother, just as if she was alive, walking around the house. And sometimes she'd speak to me."

"What did she say?"

"I'd rather not talk about it."

"It would really help us." Stacey took his hand and squeezed it, encouraging him to go on. "It would help a lot of people."

Finally, he continued.

"She said…she was disappointed in me, because I couldn't do more for her when she was sick, and for other reasons. No wife, no grandkids. But I felt like… when you're from a family that unlucky, and that crazy, sometimes it's better not to keep the crazy rolling forward to future generations. Sometimes it's better to just turn out the lights and close the door behind you."

"And she didn't like your choice?" I asked.

"No, but at the same time, she'd never wanted me to leave the house, so how was I going to meet anyone? Whenever I really tried to put together an effort to move out, to sell the place and pack my things, she would show up and accuse me of trying to abandon her. *After* she died, you understand. She'd lost a lot of the kindness she had in life. But I was still always glad to see her, even if it did leave me feeling bad."

"Would you say your encounters left you feeling drained?"

"Sure. I'd sleep for hours afterward. Feeling depressed."

I could relate, thinking of the entity that had stolen all my energy. "Did you ever encounter anyone else in the house?" I asked. "Other family members who had passed, maybe?"

"You mean like Grandma?"

"Sure."

"I remember when I was kid, four or five, and they moved her up to the attic bedroom. She lived up there less than a year before she died, but my mother said I kept going up to the attic to 'visit Grandma' for years after. They'd lock the attic door, but I'd find the key and sneak up there. Grandma was like my imaginary friend, acting like she had in life. Telling fairy tales. I can sort of remember it now that we're talking about it."

"Did you feel drained after those encounters?"

"Maybe. A lot of times it would be at night. It's hard to remember back that far, honestly. And most days, I try not to look back. That's why I work here now."

"It does seem like a big shift from a lifetime of caring for old folks," Stacey said.

"There's more similarities than you might think," he said. "There's food service, entertainment, complaining family members, customers getting sick. But it's cheerful here. Loud, but cheerful. As different from the old job as I could find. The kids are just happy. They don't have all of life's mistakes and disappointments weighing them down yet." The animals on the stage came to life, singing a loud rendition of "Happy Birthday" to a blond, cake-smeared four-year-old at the table who shrieked in either joy or terror, as did his four or five pint-sized party guests. "Getting out of that house was the best thing I ever did. I only regret I didn't leave a long time ago. I just felt stuck for so long. Most of my life. But I'm determined to make the most of the remaining years."

"That's great!" Stacey said.

"Did you ever see anyone else in your house?" I asked. "Maybe a male figure?"

"Not that I can remember. But sometimes I'd get an unsettling feeling, like I was being watched. More than once I'd hear someone, or glimpse someone, who turned out not to be there. Maybe those were other family members. It was like the weight of my whole family was always there, even though they'd passed away."

"We think the entity who appeared as your mother was likely not her at all," I said. "Focusing you on guilt and regret, then draining you once you're open and vulnerable, maybe even begging for its forgiveness—that's how this entity preys on the living. It's possible your mother never haunted that house, and that you were trapped by a lie."

Stacey winced, as if I'd put it a little too bluntly. I really needed to work on those basic social skills.

Harold sat quietly until a scream made him glance back at the crowd. It was a toddler, howling as he whooshed down a long yellow slide from a plastic treehouse. The kid laughed as his mother, who looked years younger than me, maybe eighteen or nineteen, tried to collect him at the bottom. He ran past her, giggling, and started climbing back up into the treehouse.

"It wasn't really her?" Harold asked, looking deflated, and I definitely felt for him.

"I'm sorry."

He was quiet for a minute, watching all the kids with their mothers. "So, I didn't really leave her behind."

"No, you didn't," I said. "She'd already moved on. But I'm sure she appreciated the extra adornments you put on her grave."

"You saw that? The little angels?"

"We did."

"They reminded me of a painting she hung in her bathroom. Well, a framed print. It's probably still in the house somewhere. If that wasn't really her, then there's no reason to feel guilty about leaving." A commotion erupted at the Skee-Ball machine, where a kid was running up the ramp to shove the ball into the tiny 100-point hole in the upper corner. Harold heaved himself to his feet and started over there. "No climbing on the games!" he shouted.

The waitress returned, approaching our table this time.

"Sorry, we actually have to go," I told the waitress, standing up.

"Yeah, I probably wouldn't eat here, either," the waitress said. "Want some free stickers? I have Billy the Kid and Laura the Lamb."

"No, thanks."

"I'll take a Laura the Lamb," Stacey said.

I thanked Harold on the way out.

He glanced at us and nodded quickly before looking away again, probably glad to be rid of us, the unwelcome strangers stalking him, trying to drag him back into the past he was trying to escape.

Chapter Twenty-Eight

"Should we find a place to drop off what's-her-name?" Stacey asked, glancing back to the cargo area of the van as I drove us away from Tallahassee. "I'll look on that abandoned old blog that lists the ghost towns."

I thought about it. "Maybe hold off."

"Really? I get weirded out riding with a trapped soul in the car. And I kind of feel bad for her. She had such a rough life. And afterlife, too, so far."

"Another day or two won't hurt," I said. "Just in case we need her help. Rhea and I kind of ran Isaak's ghost out of the attic together. She could be a good teammate."

"Wait, should I be worried about my job? Maybe a tiny bit jealous of the new girl?"

"Of course you should. Ghosts work cheap."

"And that levitating-wheelchair trick was pretty cool, once it was over and we knew it wasn't going to hurt you," Stacey said.

"If Rhea was involved with Isaak's death, her ghost could give us some leverage over him."

"So, Isaak is the shapeshifter, maybe?"

"It's possible."

"This would be a lot easier if we could unmask the shapeshifter."

We reached Savannah in the late afternoon, where we picked up some items from the office. Then we each went home to our respective apartments for a chance to shower and grab a couple hours of sleep.

In the early evening, I made a detour on my way to the office to visit some people I hadn't seen in a while.

My parents were buried at Greenwich Cemetery, adjacent to the city's much more famous Bonaventure Cemetery. They shared a simple rectangular headstone, buried in sandy gray earth near a live oak whose limbs were sheathed in dense resurrection fern restored to life by the recent rain.

"Hey," I said. "Sorry I can't stay long. And sorry I didn't bring any flowers. Sorry for a lot of things. I could have come looking for you before I left the house. Or I could have gone back in for you. But I didn't. And I couldn't even save Frank." I thought of our loyal golden retriever, who'd woken me and helped me find my way out of the smoke-filled house. He'd expired a few hours later after breathing too much smoke. "I was useless. Why should I be the only one who lived?"

A cool breeze passed through the cemetery. A few leaves swirled down from above. They were still green, but maybe they were early victims of the coming fall.

"Obviously, you already know all this," I said. "Not that you're here to listen. I hope you're not. I hope you've moved on." I thought of my last glimpse of them, vanishing along with the ghost of their murderer. "I just wish I could see you again or hear from you somehow."

A swirl of motion erupted from the nearby undergrowth. A family of chickadees hopped their way out from under a bush. The tiny birds scratched and nosed in the dirt, chirping at each other. They reached my parents' headstone and searched the small wildflowers growing around it before moving on.

My phone buzzed in my pocket. It was Michael, actually calling, not just texting.

"Hey, you," I said. "What's up?"

"Just heading home from work."

"Weird coincidence. I was just heading into work."

"I got stuck behind a hearse starting up a ghost tour. That one where the driver wears a top hat and skull makeup. It made me think of you."

"That's me, the freaky ghost girl."

"The freaky ghost girl I'm going to miss this weekend. Any chance you can fix the haunting tonight and meet me later?"

"I wish! This one's complicated. It preys on guilt, the way the one that haunted your building fed on people's fears."

"Good thing you don't have much to feel guilty about," he said.

"Are you kidding?"

"How would I be kidding?"

"What about how my parents died?"

"Why would you feel guilty about that?"

"Because, obviously…" I made a vague sweeping gesture with my hand, as if the answer was so obvious that it was hard to imagine needing to break it down into words. "I was there. I could have helped them. Saved them."

"That's not true."

"How would you know?"

"Because it's my job, Ellie. You had no way of saving your parents, believe me."

"I could have gone back in—"

"With no protection? No helmet? No oxygen? What kind of footwear are we talking about?"

"I was…" I struggled to remember, but I'd been asleep before the fire. "Barefoot."

"Did you have a hose to connect to the nearest hydrant?"

"Of course not."

"You couldn't have saved them. If you'd gone back inside, you would have died, and I'm sure your parents wouldn't have wanted that."

I looked at their headstone.

"I promise you that you made the right choice," Michael said.

"I couldn't even save my dog," I said. "Little Frank. Frankfurter, my dad called him, because he was a stray who hung around the food truck near this construction site where my dad worked. My dad fed him a hot dog, and he followed my dad for the rest of the day. That's where he came from."

"And he couldn't leave the house without you opening the door for him."

"Actually, he had a dog door to the back yard. He

could have escaped."

"Then he would have been the lone survivor. But he woke you up instead. Frank made his choice, and he was a good dog."

"Yeah." I tried not to think of the dog's fuzzy yellow face and big, kind, dark eyes. I tried to keep my voice steady. "Anyway, Stacey's waiting, and these particular clients like to go to bed early, so I'd better run."

"Sounds like you could use some company," he said. "I don't have another shift until Sunday morning."

"Thanks, but I wouldn't bother. We'll be busy all night."

"I could check out the sights around town while you work."

"There aren't any, unless you're into abandoned canneries."

"Who's haunting that? The ghost of Chef Boyardee?"

"That would explain the mysterious levitating ravioli," I said. "Seriously, I appreciate it, but I'll be fine. I just had kind of a rough experience with this case, which I will tell you about sometime later, because like I said—"

"You gotta go punch the clock. Be careful."

"I will."

By the time I reached the office, Stacey was already waiting.

"Everything okay?" she asked as I climbed into the van.

"Yeah, just overslept a little. Sorry."

"You needed it. Want me to drive?"

"Nope." I set out a pair of tall coffees from Sentient

Bean, moving them from a flimsy four-drink carrier to the van's cupholders.

"Wow, thanks!" Stacey took her coffee and sipped gently from it. As I drove us away from the building, she glanced back at the sound of large cardboard sheets shifting and sliding around in the back of the van, protecting the extra supplies we'd picked up. "What do you suppose are the odds of this working?" she asked.

I shrugged. "There's no way to know. If it fails, at least we'll learn something from it."

"Hey, keeping a positive attitude in the face of adversity," Stacey said. "I like it."

"I guess I'm turning over a new leaf."

"Just in time for autumn, too."

I turned up the music and pressed down on the gas, hoping to find the country highway wide open tonight.

Chapter Twenty-Nine

Night had fallen across the cloudy sky like a black curtain by the time we reached Burdener's Hill and parked at the towering house. Scattered windows were still lit inside.

"I would rather have set up during the day," I said as Stacey and I approached the front door. "We're way behind the ideal schedule here."

"Then I guess we'd better make like a couple of squished tomatoes and ketchup," Stacey said. Fortunately, she got this terrible joke out of her system before the front door opened. A tired-looking Chelsea let us inside. The sound of the piano hesitantly plonking out "Puff the Magic Dragon" drifted up from the back of house again.

"I thought you'd arrive earlier," Chelsea said. "Arden's irritated. Maybe you can have a turn listening to her about it."

"Sorry," I said. "We met with Harold Heusinkveld but didn't learn as much as we'd hoped. Apparently, the entity fed on him for years and used guilt to keep him from moving out. He really ended up serving as its unwitting accomplice, too, by keeping this house open as a retirement home and bringing in new residents to replace those who, uh, left." I stumbled over my word choice because Arden had entered the room, listening intently.

"You mean kicked the bucket," Arden said. "Bringing us in to die here while that thing sucked the life out of us. Are you sure it was unwitting? Because if it was witting, we ought to sue him."

"I think it was unwitting," I said. "And we apologize, but we need to set up in the attic, and it might get noisy."

"As long as you drown out Coach Joe's constant jabbering," Arden said. "You think you'll catch that sucker tonight?"

"I can't promise anything, but we'll do our best."

"Your best better include ending these problems, or Chelsea ain't paying your bill," Arden said. "Ain't that right, Chelsea?"

"I…" Chelsea left her mouth open as if unsure what to say.

"You gotta play hardball, honey," Arden said, "or folks'll walk all over you. Believe me, I've got the footprints to prove it." She turned and shuffled away.

"How's Wallace?" I asked Chelsea.

"The hospital found nothing wrong. They gave him fluids and sent him back home this afternoon. But Spencer moved to the vacant room on the men's floor.

My dad's old room. Spencer's the first one to occupy it
since…anyway, I don't think Wallace and Spencer will
be getting along anytime soon."

Stacey and I took our gear upstairs, still warily
taking advantage of the elevator but never riding it
alone.

In the attic, we tried to bait a trap for Isaak, though
we didn't have much to use. We placed in assorted
photographs of him at different ages, which meant
doing some irreparable damage to the family photo
albums. We also found a flask that resembled one he
surreptitiously held in a photograph at a party, though it
may not have been the same one. We put it in the trap
anyway.

Then we moved on to the more experimental side
of things.

We'd brought several mirrors with us in the van,
insulating them with cardboard so they'd be less likely
to move and crack on the way over. We mounted them
around the attic, affixing them to heavy furniture with
zip ties, and sometimes nailing them right into the wall.

The sound of hammering drew Chelsea to the attic.

"What are y'all doing up here?" she asked, looking
a little startled to see herself in so many mirrors.

"We want to try to see the shapeshifter's true face,"
I said. "Sometimes mirrors can reveal that. And
sometimes mirrors can force a delusional entity to
confront its real self, to remember who it really was."

"And then what?"

"That moment of awareness can dislodge the entity
from its pattern of behavior and help it move on. And if
it doesn't, at least we may know exactly what we're
dealing with and what its motives might be."

By the time we finished, mirrors were spaced around the attic, mounted high and low, so it was hard to go anywhere without seeing one.

To stop the wheelchair from clobbering anyone again, I tied it to the heavy bedframe with a short length of rope.

Stacey and I moved down to our borrowed room on the second floor to watch and listen. We'd made enough noise to keep the house's residents up late, but things were finally settling down and getting quiet. The light went off in Chelsea's room as she went to bed.

Georgette and Arden's closet lay quiet for a long while, as did the bathroom where the apparition of Karl's wife had emerged to haunt him. A camera now monitored Spencer's side of the room, watching the spot where we'd seen the shapeshifter, though the drawn curtain kept us from seeing Wallace himself.

A couple of hours passed before we saw the first hints of paranormal activity. Wisps of cold moved in the attic, which really seemed to be the center of the haunting, the place where entities emerged and then returned when moving around the house. The traps up there were open, but I hadn't lit the candles yet.

"I should go up to the attic," I said.

"You mean *we* should go up there," Stacey said.

"It's still more likely to approach one person than two. Even when it emerges into the residents' bedrooms, it waits until one is asleep. Remember the fearfeeder in Michael's building?"

"The boogeywoman?"

"She had much more control in one-on-one encounters, because she could only take the form of one person's fear at a time."

"And we hid in the big booth trap and all jumped out at her," Stacey said. "She couldn't decide which form to take and got all confuzzled."

"Don't come up unless I tell you to." I grabbed my leather jacket in case I got attacked, then checked my portable headset and headed for the door. "I'll stay in touch."

"Wait," Stacey said. "Something's happening in Karl's room."

"Is his wife back?" I looked at the monitor. The thermal camera watching the open bathroom door showed a rapidly forming cold spot.

"Do you think that's the shapeshifter?" Stacey asked.

"We'd better head down and check it out."

"I get to come? Sweet!" Stacey jumped to her feet, grabbing her own jacket and following me out into the hall.

Chapter Thirty

We were in a hurry, but for obvious reasons we took the stairs and avoided the elevator.

Downstairs, we raced through the hall to Karl and Joe's door. I motioned for Stacey to stay silent, since we didn't want to panic the old men ourselves by suddenly barging in. We leaned against the door, listening.

"It can't be you," a man's voice said, barely loud enough to be heard.

"I think that's Coach Joe," Stacey said.

"I can't tell." I eased the door open into the darkened bedroom.

Karl snored on his narrow single bed, one arm hanging out almost to the floor. The bathroom door stood open. The air in the room was ice cold.

Coach Joe grunted and gasped somewhere out of

sight, behind the privacy curtain drawn across the middle of the room. "No," he said in a strained, crushed voice. "The past…stays…past…"

"Not always," another voice whispered, low and sharp, feminine. "You knew I'd come back. You've been waiting for me."

Stacey and I shuddered at the unnatural voice in the freezing room. It had the flat pitch I usually associated with the voices of the dead.

We stepped around the curtain and into Coach Joe's area.

On the bed, Joe lay on his back in his frayed, stained pajamas, pinned in place.

The entity straddled his chest and gripped his thr oat with two hands. It had taken the form of a cheerleader with long blonde braids, and apparently it was crushing the air out of him.

Stacey reached for her flashlight to blast the entity, but I grabbed her arm and shook my head. She gave me a questioning look, but she obeyed.

I stepped forward, careful to leave the curtain in place, blocking most of the light from the hallway.

The cheerleader turned to look at me, neck twisting unnaturally far. Her eyes were like pools of blood, full of ruptured vessels. A chain of bruises encircled her neck. Stacey, who'd tiptoed in beside me, gasped at the sight.

"Get rid of her," Coach Joe croaked. Apparently, his attacker's grip on his throat had loosened because of my interruption, letting him breathe. "Make her go away."

I again stopped Stacey from grabbing her flashlight. "Turn the camera to record this," I told her.

She looked puzzled but stepped over to the tripod by the closet and rotated the camera toward Joe.

"Who is she, Joe?" I asked. "Who's haunting you?"

"Nothing," he said, trying to get free, but the entity had him pinned. "She's nothing."

"Her name," I said. "Or we leave you alone with her."

"No…" Joe moaned, and the cheerleader gave a vicious grin and clamped down on his throat again.

"The only way to weaken her hold is to release some of the guilt," I said. "That's where she draws her strength. Tell me her name or I can't help. Or I won't help, would be more accurate."

He whispered something, and I leaned closer, wary of the shape-changing entity atop him.

"Louder," I said.

"Tiffany," he gasped.

"Last name?"

He closed his eyes, as if considering just letting the entity strangle him to death. "Dunlap," he finally whispered.

"Stacey, search that name." I scurried back to stay out of the entity's reach, though no doubt it could pounce on me in an eyeblink if it wanted. "Add 'missing person.' Or 'murder.'"

"No," Coach Joe whispered. He'd almost ceased struggling against the entity.

Stacey worked quickly at her phone. The cheerleader was starting to decay, her skin sagging and rotting, stains spreading across her uniform as it unraveled into filthy rags like Cinderella's dress at midnight. The small hands and slender legs pinning the coach down became skeletal.

"Holy cow," Stacey said. "You were right. Tiffany Dunlap, high school junior, missing since 1985—"

"Did you kill her, Coach Joe? She'll only release you if you confess." I really had no idea whether this was true, but I wanted to record him saying it.

"Yes," he whispered, barely able to breathe. "I killed her."

"You killed who?"

"I killed Tiffany Dunlap."

"It says she was never found," Stacey read, the glow of the phone lighting her face from below, like the flashlight of someone telling a scary story at a campfire.

"Where's Tiffany's body, Coach Joe?" I asked.

"The…the old Stedman farm back home," he said. "In the barn. Nobody would ever buy that land. Too rocky."

The entity crumbled into a black fog. It drew back from Coach Joe and retreated into the bathroom.

With that off his chest, Coach Joe could finally take a deep, ragged breath through his recently crushed throat. I'd been trying to extract his confession, not help him, but they say confession is good for the soul. It might have loosened the shapeshifter's grip on him for the moment.

"Wow," Stacey said, eyeing the coach warily. "That was a lot."

I looked at the old man wheezing for air, the puffy waistband of his adult diaper visible above the saggy waistband of his food-stained pajamas. "Now what do we do about you?"

Coach Joe looked back at me, then at the camera Stacey had brought over. He closed his eyes, as if that would make his troubles end. "Oh, leave me alone," he moaned.

"We can't do that," I said. "You're a risk to everyone else. The other residents. Chelsea."

"Come on," he said. "That wasn't...none of that was..."

"Tiffany Dunlap went missing after her school, Culver High, won the regional football playoffs in 1985." Stacey did a quick search. "They defeated reigning triple-A champions, the Mortimer County Bears."

We both looked at the AAA championship pennants on the wall. The fabric was faded, but the words *Mortimer County* were plainly visible, as was the hairy, smiling bear logo.

"Is it true, Joe?" Karl pulled the curtain aside. He stood next to his bed, leaning on his cane.

"Of course not." Joe still hadn't opened his eyes.

"It's pretty true," Stacey said, showing Karl her phone. He squinted at the screen, then took his reading glasses off his nightstand.

"What were you, angry about losing?" I asked Joe.

"No," Joe said. Then he opened his eyes. "Maybe that got it started, but it went beyond that. But it was also *her*. Her fault, a little bit."

"Who? Tiffany?"

"Yeah. She saw me looking at her across the field, and she teased me on purpose. Mocking me while we lost. When it was over, her running back boyfriend, the lousy kid who'd killed my three-season winning streak, went and pawed at her. She had everything. You could see it. Young, pretty, all her life ahead. And what did I have?" He coughed, as if all the talking pained him. He pushed himself up to a sitting position. "I'd better get some water."

"Don't move. Stacey, get the water."

"Uh, okay." Stacey grabbed a plastic cup from his dresser and hurried to the bathroom.

"Were there others, Joe?" I stood over him, ready to shove him back down if he tried to stand.

"Others?" He rubbed his injured throat.

"Who else did you kill?"

He looked down at the floor. "Nobody."

"That's what you said about her at first. You said she was nothing. Here's your water. Maybe it'll help you talk."

Stacey handed it to him, and he drank slowly, prolonging this break in his interrogation as long as possible.

I shrugged off my backpack, opened it, and drew out some rope left over from tying the wheelchair to the bed upstairs.

I tied one end around Coach Joe's free hand.

"What are you doing?" Joe asked, trying to pull away, but Stacey took his water and shoved him onto his back, then planted her knee on his chest. "Hey!"

"You can't be allowed to roam free, Joe." I threaded the rope under the narrow bed and picked it up on the other side. Then I tied his other hand in place so neither hand could reach the other, and he was pretty well stuck there.

"Yeah, there's women and children in this house." Karl hobbled over to his nightstand and picked up his phone. "Mind if I do the honors of calling the police?"

"Please," I said.

Karl nodded. "I always did think there was

something off about you, Joe, but I never would have suspected this. Not in a million years." After a pause, he added, "Well, you know, maybe in a million."

I hurried to the bathroom, but the entity had already fled, not lingering like before.

"Stacey, I need to get moving before the shapeshifter goes into hiding," I said. "Keep your headset on."

"You can't go to the attic without me!" Stacey said. "Not now."

"We're here to keep our clients safe. I need you to help Karl keep an eye on Joe until the police arrive. Get in touch with Chelsea, too." I handed her the call button mounted on a cable near Joe's bed.

"But—"

"Keep your headset on." I dashed out of the room, not wanting to lose any time.

Running down the hallway and up the front staircase seemed to take forever.

Upstairs, I stopped by our borrowed room to check the monitors, seeing whether the entity was menacing any of other residents.

The only place I saw activity was up in the attic, which was abnormally cold.

As quietly as I could, I walked over to the attic door and up the stairs, using both my hands and feet on the stairs to minimize my risk of getting thrown down them by an aggressive ghost.

When I climbed high enough to see the attic, I froze, because something waited for me by the top of the stairs. Shrouded by the room's darkness, it reeked of fire and burnt hair. Soot and ash darkened its golden coat.

"Frank?" I whispered.

My childhood dog moved closer, and the burning smell intensified. He coughed, wheezing, as he had while slowly dying on my front lawn. I could see his smoke-damaged eyes, blind and rimming with red. He shuddered and collapsed.

"Nobody took you to the vet," I said, reaching out to touch his face. "If I could have gotten you to one, like an emergency one, open late—"

"Ellie, who are you talking to?" Stacey asked, thankfully, breaking my train of thought.

I jerked my hand back and reached for my flashlight.

Frank whined pitifully, as if in terrible pain, then rolled to his feet and skulked away, charred tail hanging limp behind him.

"You're evil," I said. "Whoever you are, you're evil for that."

The dog looked back at me. In life, he'd sometimes had what I could swear was a mischievous grin, usually after dropping a drool-soaked chew toy in my lap.

The expression it wore was similar, but with a malevolent edge, the lips pulled back too far, the sharp teeth exposed and threatening, his eyes solid black.

He loped on, deep into the distant, low part of the attic.

I followed warily, looking at my dim reflection in the mirrors we'd set up. The entity had slipped away into the attic's deeper recesses, but I wasn't going to be drawn over there.

Instead, I stopped between the traps and lit the small candles atop each. The mirrors reflected the little flames, creating a constellation of tiny burning lights around the attic.

"Is this yours, Isaak?" I pulled the flask out of the trap and waved it around. "Come show yourself to me. Your real self. It'll be a relief, I promise. Dropping all the pretense will feel great."

I thought I heard something move back there, out of sight among the shadows and bric-a-brac, but I wasn't sure. The air was getting even colder, like the ghost was drawing up the energy needed to make an appearance.

"You killed Rhea, didn't you?" I asked. "You pushed her down those stairs."

My mother emerged from the darkness, dressed in the old grass-stained white t-shirt of my dad's that she liked to wear when gardening. Her hands and nails were covered in dirt like she'd been digging in the earth. Her blue eyes stared at me with a coldness that nearly broke my heart. She looked beyond disappointed. Hateful, even.

"There's no hope for you, Ellie," she said. "We did our best, but you were such a problem. Ruined our lives."

"Shut up," I said, resisting every urge to blast the entity with two flashlights' worth of white light. "I hate you."

"Your famous last words to us. You would know all about hate, wouldn't you, Ellie?" She smirked as she moved closer to me. "There never was anything good in you. Not one thing." She reached out and tucked a loose strand of my hair back behind my ear. Her icy touch numbed the side of my head.

"Stop it!" I pulled away and slapped at her hand, but it was like marble. This entity was dangerously strong and dangerously present.

"Hate, Ellie. That's why you let us die. Because, deep down, you wanted us gone so you could live in your natural state, alone and without love—"

"It's not my fault," I said, feeling tears well up in my eyes. Then I reminded myself of everything Michael had said. "I couldn't have saved you. Them. You are not my mother. You are Isaak Heusinkveld," I said, still not altogether sure, even after all this time, that I was pronouncing the last name correctly. I repeated it a couple of times for emphasis, trying to verbally pry my way beneath the entity's mask.

As I said his name, I looked from mirror to mirror, looking for any crack in the illusion, any sign of what lay beneath the painful illusion of my mother.

Her image didn't change, but something moved behind the mirrors, scuttling from one dark nook of the attic to another like a spider on the wall. It was dark, shaped like a man, its teeth visible in an otherwise featureless shadow of a face, exactly the way Isaak Heusinkveld had appeared until he went over the balcony.

Outnumbered, I prepared to hit them with light and holy music, but then he spoke.

"Rhea," he said. "I'm marrying Agnes. Aren't you happy for us?"

My mother turned toward him...and she was starting to look less like my mother, changing into someone else. As she did, the apparition of Isaak grew clearer, though still thin and colorless, resembling his image in the black and white photographs. His shadowy body suggested a dark suit with the necktie loosened. He staggered toward the balcony doors.

The entity wearing the form of my mother morphed into a youthful version of Rhea, younger than me, clad in a short, shimmering party dress with large, showy jewels at her ears, throat, and fingers. She watched her brother-in-law Isaak with her big, catlike eyes.

"You need some air." Rhea opened the balcony door for him.

While Rhea momentarily turned away from him to focus on the door, the apparition of Isaak winked at me, as if we shared some joke. When she looked back at him, he swayed drunkenly again.

"What's in my drink, Rhea?" He squinted into a flask he held—identical to the one I held, actually—and then dropped it to the floor, where its content dribbled out into a puddle on the attic floorboards. The burning, stinging scent of alcohol filled the air.

"My brothers' strongest 'shine," Rhea said. "Make you blind if you drink too much."

Isaak drew his sister-in-law close, as if trying to plant a drunken kiss on her, but she pushed him out onto the balcony.

"I thought we were coming up here to…you know…" Isaak stumbled against the railing, swaying over the long drop below.

"Don't you wish. You remember my brothers, don't you?" Rhea asked. "From up the creek? I invited them to the party, of course."

"Brothers?" Isaac gaped as massive shadows loomed over him, as if cast by heavy clouds rising to block out the moonlight.

"Sorry, Isaak," Rhea said. "I can't have you getting married and making children. Everything'll go to my kids and my kin. Throw him over."

"Rhea, no!" Isaak said as he rose over the balcony railing and then plummeted out of sight, repeating what I'd seen the other night, yet another re-enactment of his death. The looming shadows indicating Rhea's brothers vanished the instant he did, as if they weren't really there as anything but extensions of Isaak's memory.

Rhea smiled, a cat who'd successfully chomped down on the canary, ruthlessly securing resources for her offspring by murdering her husband's brother.

"We better get back to the party," Rhea said. "Remember, we were never up here. Never."

She stalked toward where I stood, next to the trap baited for Isaak, in the center of so many mirrors. She stopped suddenly at the sight of me, and her victory smile faded. White streaks spread like a Bride of Frankenstein dye job through her cutely bobbed chestnut hair. Her skin aged and wrinkled, and she dropped into the antique wheelchair by the bed. Her party dress became a faded nightgown, her dancing shoes a pair of thin slippers.

"It was you, Rhea," I said. "You had your brother-in-law Isaak killed. Then, years later, his ghost pushed you down the stairs on the night of your son's wedding. That's how you ended up in the chair. Am I right? Did Isaak's ghost lure you up here for that? Or were you sneaking someone up here for a little added celebration, and Isaak's ghost saw an opportunity for revenge?"

Rhea glared at me from her chair. I hoped she wouldn't go all skull-faced on me like before, because that was a really disturbing look.

"You're the shapeshifter," I said. "Deceiving, manipulating, using guilt and regret as weapons. Is that how you acted in life? Using others, preying on them, draining them?"

"Ellie, sounds like major stuff is happening up there," Stacey said over my headset. "Should I come?"

"Grab the trap from the van first," I replied.

"The one with Rhea inside?"

"That's not Rhea in the trap." I stared at the apparition of Rhea in the chair, expecting her to move against me at any moment. "Bring it up the stairs and then hurry back down to safety."

"How dare you enter my home," Rhea said, "and interfere with my family?"

"Your family's gone," I said. "And if they're here, I'm sure they want revenge."

"I've done everything to protect them," she said.

"By murdering them? Who else did you kill, Rhea?" I thought of the various deaths we'd learned about in the Heusinkveld family. "Your father-in-law, maybe? Your husband, Pieter, who also died of the family tendency toward fatal liver problems? Those can result from heavy drinking, which they were known for, but also from arsenic—"

"My husband drank and gambled and fooled around," Rhea said, her countenance growing stormy, her eyes darkening. "I had to protect the children."

"Got it, El!" Stacey said when she burst through the attic door below. I stepped to the top of the stairs, the dangerous place where Rhea had fallen twice and died once.

"Thanks." I accepted the trap from Stacey. "We should get away from these stairs...Stacey?" I snapped my fingers, because she was gazing past me as if in a trance.

I turned around, reaching for my flashlight,

expecting that Rhea had crept up behind me.

The entity was indeed much closer, and she had taken the form of a young teenage boy with short-cropped dirty blond hair and braces, wearing a filth-darkened tank top.

"Why did you leave me there, Stacey?" he asked.

"Kevin?" Stacey whispered. I knew the name right away—it was Stacey's older brother who'd died when he was thirteen and she was eleven. They'd gone exploring an overgrown, badly decrepit house rumored to be haunted, where they'd encountered an aggressive entity in a veiled bridal dress. Her brother had fallen through a rotten-out floor and landed in the cellar, breaking his neck.

"It's not really him." I took Stacey's arm and steered her away from the stairs and deeper into the attic, away from the danger zone. I wasn't going to let her die the same way her brother had, a steep fall at the hands of a dead thing.

"You abandoned me, Stacey," he said, stalking after us. He might have only been thirteen, but he was as tall as me.

"I'm sorry," Stacey whispered, her eyes shiny as she looked at him. "I'm so sorry. I didn't know what to do—"

"You could have come down into the cellar," the apparition said. "You could have stayed with me, instead of letting me die alone with that dead lady touching me." He began to weep. "I'm still trapped down there with her, Stacey."

"Oh." Stacey paled, covering her face. She moved closer to him, out of my grasp. Surely, she knew this wasn't really him. But I remembered my own encounter in the elevator, when the logical part of my brain knew it couldn't possibly have been my mother, but that part of the brain had been drowned by grief, guilt, and regret, like electrical wiring destroyed by a flood.

"It's your fault," Kevin said.

"I know," she said and embraced him, crying. She sighed and sagged as the entity began to drain her.

"Stacey, don't!" I said. "It's not really your brother. There was nothing you could do about Kevin. He died instantly. You have to try to forgive yourself. It'll weaken her hold over you."

Stacey ignored me, clutching the illusion of her brother closer. If she wasn't going to be able to shake it off, then I was going to have to shake things up and distract the entity.

"I know you're Rhea Heusinkveld," I said. "But I can only guess who we captured in this trap. Why don't we open it and see?"

I popped the lid, and the cold attic grew colder.

In front of me, close enough to grab me, stood a shadowy form I'd seen before—the shaggy haircut, the small, dark eyes that had stared at me over the anonymous numbered headstone at the prison cemetery.

"Bartel?" The apparition of Kevin began to slip, the face becoming wrinkled, the hair growing from close-cropped dirty blond to longer, messier, chestnut streaked with white. The entity staggered back toward the wheelchair, and I gently drew Stacey away in another direction, toward the attic closet.

"I won't do it," Bartel said, his voice thin and sharp, like a harsh winter wind across a windowpane. "I won't kill her."

"You'll do whatever I need." Rhea looked like her old self again, by which I mean like an aging lady in a wheelchair, and not her youthful self from the Roaring Twenties. "You're my good son, my loyal son. You won't let me down."

"I can't, Mother," Bartel said. "We already poisoned Gerrit. My own brother." His voice choked up.

"Gerrit was trying to leave me," Rhea said. "To leave *us*. Chicago! Renting my home to strangers! Trapping me in this attic. He knew how I hated this attic. And so did Dottie, you can bet. They put me up here to torture me."

"They wanted you to have privacy. A whole floor of the house to yourself."

Rhea let out a derisive laugh. "They turned against us, Bartel."

"I won't kill Dottie. The little boy will have no mother or father."

"I will be his mother. And you will be his father." Rhea smiled. "We'll raise Harold together, as if he were our child." Rhea rolled closer to Bartel's apparition, almost to the full extent of the rope I'd used to anchor the heavy wheelchair to the bedframe. She took his hand and looked up at him with an expression of long, deep suffering. "Do this, Bartel. I've sacrificed everything for you, and now I want the boy for my own. For ours. We'll be a happy family together."

"No." Bartel shook his head and walked toward the stairs, beginning to fade away.

Rhea watched him go with an expression of shock, but it slowly changed to fury, her eyes hardening, her lips turning down in a hideous grimace.

She pushed forward the wheels of her chair, charging toward her son, plainly intending to push him down the stairs, to punish his defiance with violence, dealing him a severe and possibly fatal injury.

The rope drew taut, reaching its full extent, and the old wheelchair abruptly ceased its advance and shuddered. It rolled back a little, recoiling on the tightened rope.

Rhea transformed instantly, her angry old lady form changing into the horrifying, skull-faced monster that had crashed into me the other night.

She kept traveling forward, riding in a ghostly mirage of a wheelchair made of spindly bones, the wheel rims insulated in dry, leathery hide.

The ghost of Bartel turned at the sound, his foot hovering in the air over the top stair, his jaw dropping at the sight of his mother on her way to shove him down. He began to lose his balance even before she reached him.

Then another shape scurried out of the shadows, a big grin visible on its shadowy, otherwise featureless face.

It collided with Bartel, knocking him away from the staircase and sprawling across the attic floor.

Rhea let out a horrified shriek as she passed through the empty space where Bartel had been. She rolled out over the stairs and dropped out of sight. We heard her crashing and screaming all the way down, and then she went abruptly silent.

Bartel, still on the floor, turned his head to see who'd pushed him aside.

"Uncle Isaak?" Bartel whispered, sounding frightened as he saw a dead relative whose face he would have known only through family photographs. "How?"

"Now you're free, kid," Isaak said, becoming just a little clearer before vanishing completely. Ironically, this hadn't been true at all, because Bartel had ended up in prison over these events.

"Is that what happened?" I asked the fading apparition of Bartel lying motionless as a corpse on the floor. "Rhea killed herself trying to attack you? And you got blamed?"

"Hey, Bartel *did* help kill his brother," Stacey said. "He's not blameless. Brother-killer!" She kicked at Bartel's apparition, and he dissolved away into the floorboards, leaving no trace behind. Stacey was upset, her face red and wet from crying.

"It's okay." I touched her shoulder. "I know it's hard. That's how she preys on the living."

Stacey turned and embraced me, clutching me tight, and I wished I'd taken a deep breath first because I started to run out of air.

I watched the stairs to see if Rhea returned, perhaps by levitating up from the stairwell. She didn't appear at all, though, which made me worried about the safety of everyone else in the house.

Over by the bed, the physical wheelchair remained tied in place, abandoned like a snake's skin.

"We'd better get moving, Stacey," I said. "Rhea could be anywhere, going after anyone."

"So, we captured Bartel and not Rhea?" Stacey pulled away and wiped her face on her sleeve. "And now they're both running around free?"

"Now we understand the real history here, I think," I said. "But I'm not sure freeing Bartel was worth it."

We cautiously approached the stairs and looked down, ready to blast Rhea with light and holy music if she attacked.

The steep stairs lay quiet and empty, though, leading down to the open door to the second-floor hall.

"Did you leave that door open?" I asked.

"Definitely not."

"Then she's loose in the house." I blew out the candles in the traps before we headed down. I also grabbed Bartel's wooden sword from one trap and Isaak's flask from the other. I wasn't sure what I might do with them, but those two entities were my best chance of getting some supernatural aid around here.

Shoving the relics in my jacket pockets, I started downstairs along with Stacey.

A woman screamed somewhere around the corner and down the hall, and Stacey and I took off running toward it.

The hallway lights were out, lit only by moonlight from a window. Arden was backed up against a wall, wearing her beige housecoat, her face bleached with terror.

The sour smell of cheap bourbon was thick in the air. It was her father, and he was slipping off his decayed, cracked-leather belt.

"You gotta pay for what you done to me," he said. "Leaving me alone like that."

"He's wrong, Arden," I said. I was ready to attack the entity with lights and such, but I thought I understood a new way she could defend herself against it, a more permanent and solid defense. "You did the right thing. You had to protect yourself, and you didn't have anyone to help you. You have nothing to feel guilty about."

"You shut up, little girl!" Arden's father turned on me, raising the doubled-over belt like a whip, ready to strike me.

"He's the one who should feel guilty," I said. "For how he treated you. For being a terrible father. That kind of thing. You know it's the truth."

"Yeah." Arden eased forward from the wall. "Yeah, it is."

"Tell him," I said.

"You should feel guilty, not me," Arden said. "I done the best I could, which is more than can be said for you."

Arden's father shrank back, recoiling from her as though burned by acid, lowering his belt-whip and finally slipping away down the hall, its appearance decaying quickly, like a cadaver in a time-lapse video.

"He's headed toward my room. Georgette's alone in there!" Arden shuffled after the entity at her top speed, which unfortunately wasn't very fast.

"I'll go after it. Stacey, stay here with Arden."

"I'm going the same place you are," Arden said. "Just on a different schedule. You ladies run ahead and check on her, though."

I did run ahead, while Stacey walked alongside Arden in case the entity doubled back.

Before reaching Georgette's room, I heard her soft voice through the open door.

"But you aren't really here, Dex," she was saying. "I know it now."

"It *is* me, Mommy." The child's voice was sobbing. "Please don't leave me alone again."

In the room, Georgette sat in her vanity-table chair,

turned so she could face the apparition of her son as a young child sat on his tricycle, holding out a hand to her.

"Come with me, Mommy," he said. "Come with me to the attic, and we can be together forever. There are toys in the attic, and we can play all the time, and I'll never grow up. I promise. You can make it all up to me."

Georgette let out a pained sound. She began reaching out a hand to accept his.

"Georgette, you can't," I said. "That's not him. That's Rhea Heusinkveld. She's the shapeshifter, and it sounds like she's trying to kill you."

"Also, Coach Joe murdered a cheerleader and buried her in a barn," Stacey said.

"What?" This bizarre, unexpected fact seemed to jolt Georgette more than my reminder about the shapeshifter. She took a fresh look at the image of her son, then scowled. "How dare you? I may owe my son a world of apologies, but you ain't him." She grabbed a hairbrush off a table and threw it at him, striking the shiny red tricycle's handlebars. "You're nothing to me!"

The brush's impact created an immediate change, a total shift in the entity's appearance. The tricycle took on the same nightmarish look as Rhea's spectral wheelchair, bones and joints fitted together with dried tendons and ligaments.

The entity shifted, too, its eyes sinking away into darkness, its skin decaying from its bones until it looked like the child wraith I'd pursued near the beginning of the case.

The dead-child apparition drove through the wall and out into the hallway, where Stacey and Arden were approaching. They recoiled from the shadowy blur that quickly vanished from sight.

"Stacey, take Arden and Georgette to our room and keep watch over the house," I said, running past them. "I'm going after the Creepy Toddler."

"Should you really do that alone?" Stacey asked, but I continued out of sight, worried who the entity might go after next. We'd shaken Rhea loose from her usual routine and unmasked her, and it seemed she was going on a rampage as a result.

My worst fears were confirmed as I once again pursued the Creepy Toddler to the closed door to Chelsea's office. I called Chelsea, cradling my phone to my face with my shoulder, and dropped to my knees to pick the lock.

"I was fixing to call you," Chelsea said. "I'm down here in Karl and Joe's room. I can't have my residents tied up like this, regardless of what you may suspect, and Karl's sitting here in a chair threatening to crack Joe's skull with his cane if he tries to get loose. What is going on?"

"Did Karl explain?"

"I explained!" Karl said in the background.

"He told a pretty wild story, all right," Chelsea replied.

"We have Joe's murder confession on video and the location of the victim's body," I said. "Forget about Joe for now, because the entity just went into your apartment. Is Tag alone in there?"

She drew a sharp breath. "I'll be right up."

By then I'd opened the lock to her office, so I hurried through into the cold living room beyond. Voices spoke from the little dead-end hallway with the bedrooms. I listened as I approached the open door to the boy's room.

"You mean the divorce was my fault?" Tag sat cross-legged on his bed, lit by the gentle blue hue of a Smurf nightlight. A man stood over him in the shadows. "But Mom said—"

"Mom lies, all the time," the man said. "It was you. The fights. The problems you caused. The hate between us. All because of you."

"Dad, no." The boy grabbed the shadowy man's hand. "Please don't leave us again, Dad. I promise I'll be good."

"It's too late, Taggart. You're no good. You're too much like your mother."

"Tag, this isn't your father." I stepped in through the doorway. "This is the old lady ghost from the attic, playing a cruel trick on you. She played it on me, too. She pretended to be my mother." I tried to keep my voice steady as I said that last part, fighting against both rage and grief.

"A trick?" Taggart asked.

"Like the wolf putting flour on his fur to disguise himself as a sheep," I said, glad I'd actually looked up that story. "So the lambs will believe it's their mother. Only this time the wolf is pretending to be your father."

"This is between me and my son." Taggart's father emerged from the shadows. He was hardly the most threatening of men, a balding guy with a weak chin, not much taller than me, but his eyes were black as skull sockets, and I knew a dangerous entity looked out at me from within. "Leave now."

"Dan?" Chelsea arrived, and I had to scoot over to make room for her, almost tripping over some baseball shoes. "What are you doing here?"

"It's not really him," I said.

"He says I made you and Dad hate each other," Tag said. "I already knew that, kind of, but—"

"It's not true," Chelsea said. "This is not your father, Tag, and nothing he says is true."

"Stop it, Rhea!" I used the most commanding voice I could summon. "You did this to your grandson, pretending to be the ghost of his mother. You're not going to turn Taggart into a substitute for Harold."

"How dare you say his name!" The man in the shadows hissed, his voice changing into Rhea's. He squatted, and a wheelchair formed around him.

He didn't become Rhea, though, and the wheelchair was light and modern. The man aged and slumped, becoming elderly and haggard, his eyes glazed and empty.

"Dad?" Chelsea whispered.

"How did Dad turn into Grandpa?" Tag asked.

"It's not really either one," I said. "The ghost's name is Rhea Heusinkveld, and she used to live here."

"Mrs. Hoosie's the bad ghost? But she acted so nice."

"The bad ones often act that way at first," I said. "Ghosts and otherwise."

"You really fouled it all up good, didn't you, sweetheart?" the old man rasped, looking in Chelsea's general direction. "Your marriage, your career, if you can call it that. Now this. Now your kid, a complete screw-up. I always said you were the hopeless one. Worse than your mother, even. Your sister, she was the only one in that house worth a dime."

"You only liked Cindy because she was the pretty

and popular one," Chelsea said. "She was a hood ornament to you. But where is she now? Where was she, in those last years when you needed all the help? I didn't see her flying home to help. She managed to squeeze in trips to Cabot and Provence in that last year of your life, while I was taking care of you. I guess that all worked out the way you would have wanted it, though."

The man in the chair seemed to wither under this barrage, and then he finally disappeared.

"Whoa," Taggart said after a long silence. "You really gave Grandpa the business, Mom."

Chelsea gaped at him, perplexed, then burst into laughter. "Where do you get these random sayings?"

"The internet."

"Y'all should join Stacey and the other ladies in our room until this blows over," I said. "I'll walk you there."

"What about the Karl and Joe situation downstairs?" Chelsea asked.

"I'm heading down to the first floor now. I'll check on Spencer and Wallace, too."

"I should go with you," Chelsea said. "They're my residents."

"These aren't normal circumstances. You should help watch over the house. We have a lot of monitors going now, with a lot of video feeds."

"I can watch, too," Tag said. "I'm good at watching videos."

We grabbed a couple of extra chairs along the way and carried them to the nerve center bedroom, where Georgette and Arden sat with Stacey.

"I'll do a quick walk-through downstairs," I told

Stacey. "Let me know if you see any activity."

"Be sure to check on Spencer," Stacey reminded me. "We don't have anything set up in his new room."

I hurried out, once again foregoing the elevator for the stairs.

Downstairs, it took me a minute to actually find the door to Spencer's new room, since I hadn't been there before. Chelsea gave me directions via Stacey over my headset.

Then a few voices rose there in the nerve center all at once.

"What's happening?" I asked.

"Major cold-spot action over in Karl and Joe's bathroom," Stacey replied. "We can all see it."

"Karl's already alone with a murderer there," I said. "When will the police show up? They're sure taking their time."

"I guess they figure looking into a decades-old murder isn't that urgent," Stacey said, and I sighed.

Sprinting across the first floor, twisting from one hallway to the next, I found my way back to the room where Karl watched over the prisoner.

Approaching Karl's slightly ajar door, I was overwhelmed by the smell of gasoline and fire.

"Karl?" I pushed the door open.

Coach Joe lay still and limp in the bed, liked he'd slipped into unconsciousness. That seemed believable, since the entity had probably sucked out all his energy.

Karl had been sitting in a chair beside the bed, ready to whack the old murderer with his cane if necessary, but now he rose unsteadily to his feet, using the cane to support himself.

All the lights and lamps were out. A flickering red

glow illuminated the room from the open bathroom door, where the apparition of Wendy stood in her mini dress. Flames surrounded her, slowly charring her skin. The sight of so much fire, and the heat and gasoline smell, terrified me.

"Ellie, major activity at Karl's—" Stacey began over my headset.

"I'm here." I stepped through the door.

"Karl," the burning woman whispered. "You did this to me."

"Remember she's not real, Karl," I said. "It's the shapeshifter. We've discovered her real identity, and it's Rhea—"

"My wife's death was my fault," Karl said, his gaze fixed on the apparition. "I was driving. There's nobody else to blame."

"Come with me, Karl." She held out a burning hand, the flesh sizzling and dripping from the bone. "I need you, baby."

"Stay back," I said. "She might be in a killing mood tonight."

Karl didn't even acknowledge that I'd spoken. He kept staring at his long-lost wife, the love of his life. "I hear you feed on people's regrets, Rhea," he said, and his wife flinched at the name. "But I'll tell you what. I've been drinking my own grief like a bitter ale for years, and I haven't got any left to share with you. Do I blame myself? Am I guilty? Yes. But I'm happier now than I've ever been, and getting happier by the second. Because with every second that passes, I'm closer to being with Wendy again. Not even you can put a stop to that. All you can do is bring me closer to the end, and it's an end I'm ready for."

The fiery glow faded from the bathroom, along with the illusion of his wife.

"Wow," I said. "Great job there, Karl."

He gave me a slight smile, though his gaze was still focused on the empty place where his wife had been. "I've had plenty of time to think it over, and you told us how the thing operates. I've got no end of guilt and regret…but that's mine to carry."

I checked the bathroom, confirming the entity had fled. "How's the prisoner?"

"I wouldn't mind the police showing up, but they didn't sound like they were rushing over," Karl said. "He looks helpless for now, but he could be playing possum. I'll keep my eye on him."

"Thanks. You have my phone number if you need me." I stepped back into the hall. "Stacey, any sign of where the entity went?"

"Not so far," she replied over the headset. "And we've got almost as many people watching as we have monitors. Team Sunshine House is on the case."

"Keep me posted. I'll check on Spencer." When I reached Spencer's newly assigned room, I knocked on the closed door. "Hey, sorry, I know it's late. You okay in there, Spencer?"

I knocked again, but he didn't respond, so I pushed the door open.

A low, wide figure stood over Spencer's bed. He lay there in the dark, weeping. His downgrade of a room only had two small windows, and they were on a side of the house without much moonlight tonight.

"…you selfish, strange, evil boy," the figure said in a high, squeaky voice that made me think of balloons rubbing together. "A bad seed like your father. Soft and weak like your father. He left us because he was so weak. I'll make you a good, strong boy. I'll toughen up that hide." She raised a long, flat wooden yardstick. "Get on your knees, Spencer."

Weeping, he slid down from his bed to the carpet, until he knelt at his bedside like a child saying prayers, as if begging angels to protect him through the night.

"Don't listen to her, Spencer," I said. "You know you're not evil. If anything, you've done too much for others, and too little for yourself."

The short, bulky woman lined up the stick across Spencer's back as if trying to decide where to strike him. She seemed to relish the anticipation of striking him. A stout woman with a wide mouth, she made me think of a frog preparing to eat a fly.

"That isn't who it appears to be, Spencer." I advanced. "It's the shapeshifter, who is actually Rhea —"

"Tell your naughty friend to leave, Spencer." The apparition's squeaky voice grating on me. "This is private family time."

"My mother," Spencer whispered. "Dead thirty years and haunting me still."

"You humiliated our family," his mother said. "I could hardly show my face in town. I told you that you'd fail. You needed to quit dreaming and man up. But you never did." She raised the yardstick, ready to swat it down on him, her smile sickening. "You haven't got enough man in you for that."

"Say what you're feeling, Spencer," I said. "Don't give this illusion power over you. She only has what you let her take. Remember, it's not your mother—"

"Quiet, hussy!" Spencer's mother snapped, but

Spencer was looking at me and nodding.

"Rhea is the shapeshifter?" he asked, rising to his feet. "Interesting. I've seen your pictures from the olden days, Rhea. You were quite the vivacious bon vivant in your day."

"I am your mother!" the apparition said, but the squeaky voice was slipping.

"If you were," Spencer said, drawing himself up so he could look down on her from the greatest possible height, "I would tell you that I've had years to develop my own thick hide, years of lashes from the world. I was a fool to trust Wallace, but not to believe in myself. Nor to *be* myself, regardless of what you may have preferred."

The short, wide shape began to change form, becoming narrower and taller, face dissolving like she was a wax doll next to a space heater.

Moments later, Spencer faced a dim reflection of himself.

Then the entity vanished.

"I wish it wouldn't wear my face," Spencer said.

"It's probably jealous of your acting talent," I said, and Spencer chuckled a little, shaking his head.

"An underdeveloped resource is nothing to be jealous of," he said. "Especially at my advanced age. You said it's actually been Rhea Heusinkveld this whole time?"

"Yes. And since she's taken your form, I'm guessing she's on her way to visit Wallace. I'd better check on him."

"I suppose I'll come with you."

"It would be safer if you didn't."

"Sad as it may be, I'm still in the habit of looking

out for the old dog." Spencer left the room with me, walking quite briskly. He was in good shape, like he exercised regularly. I arrived at Wallace's room before him, but not by much.

Wallace lay in his bed while the Spencer apparition stood beside him, a hand on his shoulder. The lights were out, but moonlight poured in from the windows lining his private porch.

"I'm sorry, Spencer," Wallace whispered. "What I did, I did out of fear of losing you. I wish there were some way to give back what I took, but…" His voice grew increasingly weak. The entity was feeding on him.

"You'll never make it up to me," the apparition said. "All the lost years. You deserve to suffer."

"I know." Wallace's eyes began to drift closed.

"Stop it." Spencer stepped forward. "You don't speak for me, Rhea. My relationship with Wallace is my problem, and it may be a major one, but it's nothing to do with you. Go on. Hop in your wheelchair and slink away."

"Leave us," the apparition snarled. "You hate him. Leave him to me."

"Wallace," Spencer said. "I don't know if I can ever forgive you, but maybe I can begin to understand you. You hurt me out of fear and desperation."

"Because I didn't want to be alone," Wallace said, opening his eyes to look at the real Spencer. "I didn't want to be without you."

"But I wasn't yours to take in that way. Not through deception. It's the deception I may never get past, Wallace. If you had been truthful with me, given me a choice…"

"You would have left."

Spencer though it over. "Probably. But we are all time's captors now. Just as I have been yours."

Wallace closed his eyes. "But now you've eaten of the tree of knowledge, and so you're free."

"Free for my remaining years, at least. The third act of my life, the final one." Spencer watched the apparition of himself seem to decay and rot into a corpse, seemingly less frightened of this stark reminder of his mortality than before. "I wish you wouldn't do that, Rhea. It's unnerving."

The apparition hissed and blew past us, out of the room and into the hall.

"Looks like I'm chasing her again," I said. "Y'all stay here."

"Everything good, Ellie?" Stacey asked over the headset.

"Stay put with your eyes open. I'm following our girl." I ran down the hall after the decaying apparition, which was already well ahead of me even though it walked with a limp that seemed to grow worse with each step. It reached the sunroom and turned out of sight.

I arrived a few seconds later and quickly scanned the place. It looked quiet and empty. Moonlight from the tall sunroom windows landed on the closed piano and the empty sofas and armchairs, where all the little throw pillows had been arranged and straightened for the night.

"Eleanor." My mother emerged from the shadows, wearing a simple blue dress she'd sometimes worn on date nights with my dad. It matched her eyes, and mine. "I couldn't be more disappointed in you."

"Rhea, we all see through you now," I said. Watching how the elderly residents had stood up to her had emboldened me, as if I'd learned something from the wisdom and hard experience of each of them. "The show's over. You're just a sad clown in bad makeup. And guess what?" I stepped closer to her, boldly doing my best to ignore my swirling, conflicting feelings about seeing my mother along with my fear of the shapeshifter. "I hate clowns."

She glared at me, her eyes sinking away into blackness, and I advanced.

"Surely, if you regret anything at all, you regret trying to kill Bartel, your favorite son, the one you called loyal," I said. "Or maybe you have no heart, and your biggest regret is that fatal, stupid mistake, because when you tried to kill him, you killed yourself instead. Either way, this seems appropriate."

From my jacket pocket, I drew out the little wooden sword with BaRteL painted on it in childish, uneven letters. I grunted in anguish as I forced myself to slam the blade into my mother's chest like a wooden stake through a vampire's heart. She screamed.

Not my mother, I reminded myself. *It only looks like her. And sounds like her, that scream—*

The apparition shuddered, streaks of white appearing in her hair, her face changing.

"Isaak's ghost saved Bartel, while you threw yourself down the stairs. Your plans failed then, and they've failed now," I said, twisting the knife both figuratively and literally.

Rhea fell away from the wooden sword, her old self again, dressed in a black funeral dress, perhaps her own. There was no physical injury from the toy sword, but it was meant to be an emotional blow, hopefully turning her regrets into weapons against her, as she did to others.

She landed on the gruesome wheelchair of bone and hide, formed as part of her apparition. The chair looked about as comfortable as a medieval torture device.

"Harold is never coming back," I said. "You had a pretty good carrot-and-stick act going with him, acting as a sweet grandma ghost and then pretending to be his mom's ghost when you wanted to control him with guilt. But you've lost all that now. You won't be able to fool Chelsea and Taggart into taking the place of Dottie and Harold. You have no victims left to prey on in this house. This is the end for you. Do you understand?"

Rhea glanced around, frowning, looking confused. She didn't have her skull face on, but she looked very old, and very small, her limbs like sticks.

"Where am I?" Rhea whispered. "What's happening?" She looked helpless and panicky, almost pitiable, seeming to shrink in her chair, slumping to the side, too weak to rise. "Where is my son, the good one? I need to see my son." She almost reminded me of Georgette, eager for the upcoming visit of her own son, addicted to the illusion Rhea had provided her.

"I'm here." Bartel's ghost was faintly visible, as if made of spiderwebs catching the moonlight in the air beside her, his voice dead flat like when we'd recorded it at his grave. "Mother, it's time to go to your new home now. We can't wait any longer."

"Who else is here? Gerrit? Is it Gerrit? I miss that boy." She sounded wistful, as if she hadn't murdered that particular son.

"It's Uncle Isaak." As Bartel's ghost said it, a faint partial apparition of Isaak formed beside Rhea, arriving in a dim, misty form.

"No!" Rhea twitched helplessly in her chair of bones. "He'll kill me."

"You killed yourself." Isaak reached beneath the ligamented cluster of bones that formed the wheelchair's arm and drew out a long, dried-leather strap. He looped this over Rhea's left forearm and cinched it down tight. Then he did the same to her upper arm, lashing her to the chair.

"What are you doing to me?" Rhea whispered.

"It's time to go, Mother." Bartel joined in and strapped her other arm into place.

While Rhea gasped and weakly protested, they tied her down, even cuffing her neck to the central spine of the chair's back, made of sharp vertebrae.

"No..." she whispered. "This wasn't the plan..."

"You'll be fine." I opened the back door onto the brick steps outside, leading down to the moonlit back yard. "Just focus on the light. Follow it."

The faint apparitions of Bartel and Isaak rolled Rhea to the open door. I hurried to step out of their way. I still gripped the wooden sword in case she tried to stage a comeback.

The three of them moved out of the door and into the moonlight outside.

Just when Rhea's chair should have fallen and crashed down the outdoor steps, all of them were abruptly gone. The ancient tree limbs outside creaked and swayed in a strong breeze and then fell still, shedding dry leaves that drifted down toward the earth.

Chapter Thirty-One

The county police did arrive, eventually, and acted puzzled, but we showed them Joe's confession, and he agreed to make a statement at police headquarters. Joe didn't say anything about that, just trudged off to the police car in the gray predawn light. A gathering of early birds twittered and chattered excitedly around the hanging feeders as if gossiping over breakfast about the murder and mayhem in the house.

The residents of the house were left to do the same, gathering for breakfast and discussing the events. At least, Arden, Georgette, and Karl gathered, eating bran cereal, and Taggart joined them with a bowl of Honey Nut Cheerios. His presence kept the conversation fairly moderate.

Spencer and Wallace sat at opposite ends of the table, avoiding each other and eating silently.

Stacey and I said our exhausted goodbyes before we returned home. Chelsea walked us to the front porch, and Arden followed us out.

"This has been quite a night," Chelsea said. "Do you think the worst is over?"

"My impression is that Rhea, Isaak, and Bartel may have finally moved on," I said. "But we'll come back tonight and do a walk-through of the house with our psychic consultant, Jacob, and see if they're really gone. If they are, we can remove our equipment soon and close the case."

"And Chelsea's picking up the tab, since she sold me a pig in a poke with this haunted house," Arden said.

"Obviously, I didn't know it was haunted, but yes." Chelsea sighed. "Good thing I haven't had much staff to pay this week, anyway."

"You say it's a good thing, but we've had the same hand towels in our bathroom since Wednesday," Arden said.

"I'll get you fresh hand towels today," Chelsea said wearily. "And when Pablo comes back, I'll have him pack up Coach Joe's possessions."

"I'd recommend getting all of the Heusinkveld family's possessions out of the attic, too," I said. "Obviously, Harold doesn't want them, so you can sell, donate, or toss it all with a clear conscience. Have the house blessed, especially the attic."

"And replace those crazy stairs!" Stacey said. "Sheesh."

"I will," Chelsea said. "We were going to do the stairs before everything else. That was top on the list before things got wildly off track."

"Attic renovations should go much more easily with the entities gone," I said.

"I'm starting to feel some genuine relief here. Thank you so much." Chelsea hugged me tight, then Stacey. A real hugger, that Chelsea. I supposed it helped in her line of work, caring for people in need.

"Took long enough," Arden muttered as she and Chelsea returned inside. "We ought to get a discount. You notice everything finally got fixed once people started listening to me. I'd say there's a lesson in there somewhere, don't you think, Chelsea?"

Stacey and I ambled out to the driveway.

"I feel like we did some good work here," Stacey said. "And it was a positive journey. Like when you reach the end of a solid river run, or hike up to a peak and see the whole world spread out below you."

"Or when you make popcorn and binge-watch a true crime series until five in the morning."

"Maybe? Hey, nice sunrise."

The dawn colors soaked the old house in soft, pastel hues of pink and gold. It looked less spooky than before, certainly, as if a darkness had gone out of it, leaving only the antique balusters and high windows, the thick drapes drawn snugly against the hot daylight rising in the east.

Even the little town looked almost charming in the sunrise, as we drove down the sleepy main street, watching a few lights come on, a few old cars and trucks at the local diner where people gathered for coffee and grits and conversation.

We left town, heading home.

Chapter Thirty-Two

Jacob's walk-through confirmed that we'd cleared the entities from the house, and within a couple of days, we'd removed all our gear.

That wasn't our last visit to The Sunshine House, though.

A couple of weeks later, we received, on crisp white linen stationery, a formal invitation to attend the First Annual Sunshine House Talent Show, to be staged at four-thirty p.m. on a Saturday, reception to follow. I RSVP'd right away.

The driveway was full when we arrived, so we parked on the street, near several other vehicles that weren't normally there. Stacey, Jacob, Michael, and I had all ridden in Stacey's Escape since it was large enough to seat everyone comfortably. She'd brought a camera and other gear to record the show, since

Spencer had asked her to actually follow through on that idea. She'd agreed cheerfully.

Chelsea met us at the door and took us through the foyer, where an easel offered a fanned-out stack of talent-show programs and directed visitors to the sunroom for the show. We set down the camera gear and took the grand front staircase upstairs, then continued down and around the hallway to the attic door.

"We've already begun renovation." Chelsea unlocked the door and revealed an amazing new, not-so-steep staircase with wide, safe steps and a right-hand turn with winders halfway up, which would give their apartment a little more privacy. There were even handrails on both sides. "Want to see?"

"Of course," I said.

"Ellie loves attics," Michael said. "Especially if they're full of cobwebs and strange noises."

"Yeah, right. Some of my worst experiences have been in attics. This one looks great, though," I added as I followed Chelsea up the solid new stairs, which smelled like fresh lumber and recently dried wood stain.

"We're just getting started," Chelsea said as we emerged at the top. New flooring had been installed around the staircase. Most of the attic clutter had disappeared, leaving a cavernous empty space. The air was tinged with the purifying pine scent of Murphy's Oil Soap.

"Wow, clearing out the junk really opens the place up," Stacey said. "I didn't even know there was a whole other room over on that side."

"There's a lot of potential." Michael took a slow lap

around the attic, checking it out and seeming to visualize the possibility. He'd helped his landlord fix up portions of the house where his apartment was, so he had some experience. "Make those low spaces into storage, obviously…"

"Are we still ghost-free up here, Jacob?" Stacey asked.

"Still ghost-free," Jacob replied, looking around. "And now dust-free, which is a major improvement."

"Tag will have a nice, big room for a change," Chelsea said. "And I'll have a walk-in closet. We're making a full kitchen up here, too."

"Yeah, this is like a whole extra house," I said. "I think y'all will enjoy it. What about the balcony, though? That's in bad shape."

"We're removing it and replacing the balcony door with a solid window," Chelsea said. "The balcony's too rotten to restore without building a whole new one."

"That's probably for the best," I said.

"Ellie never liked that balcony," Stacey said.

"I heard the Mortimer County prosecutor's office is charging Coach Joe with murder," Chelsea said. "They found that cheerleader's remains. It was in the *Journal Sentinel*, so everyone here read about it. It's hard to believe a monster like that lived here in our house."

"Sometimes, you just don't know who people really are," I said.

"Any luck with hiring new staff members?" Stacey asked, probably hoping to lighten up the conversation.

"Yes, thank goodness," Chelsea said. "Hopefully there won't be any more disturbances to run them off. Honestly, solving the staff retention issue alone was worth the cost of hiring you, never mind ending the nightmare of living here with Rhea's ghost. We've got a couple of prospective new residents, too. I'll need them to replace the rent from Coach Joe and Spencer."

"Spencer's leaving?" I asked.

"Yep." Her phone beeped. "That's Pablo. He's getting a promotion next week. Don't tell him I said that. Anyway, I should go back downstairs before the show."

"Yikes," Stacey said. "I'm the camera crew. I'd better check the sound situation."

In the sunroom, extra seating had been brought in from around the house to accommodate the twenty or so visitors attending the show. All the furniture was in rows facing the piano area. Georgette sat at the piano, whispering intensely with Spencer, and Stacey scurried over to join their confab.

The other residents and assorted guests had already seated, leaving Michael, Jacob, and me to sit near the back.

"I knew we should have checked Ticketmaster first," Michael whispered. "We could have gotten one of those nice couch seats up front."

"But then you have to pay all those fees," I said.

At the appointed time, Stacey closed the window curtains, turned down the overhead lights, and gave Spencer a spotlight cooled with a blue lens. Dressed in a solid black suit, Spencer seemed to feed off the light and the attention.

"Hello, everyone!" Spencer said. "What a fantastic crowd. Give yourselves a hand for coming!" After some clapping, and some whistling by Georgette, who sat in a chair near the piano, Spencer continued. "For our first act, we're proud to introduce, for the first time on a major stage, the musical stylings of Taggart Bridger."

The crowd cheered as Tag walked up and sat at the piano, wearing a baseball hat with construction-paper dragon teeth for his performance of "Puff the Magic Dragon." He sang haltingly but played well, and ultimately the tale of the boy growing out of childhood brought a few tears to a few eyes in the mostly elderly crowd, who gave him an enthusiastic applause when he finished. Tag bowed and took off, not deigning to stick around and watch the other performances.

Next, Spencer returned to the stage wearing a tunic and cape. After praising Tag's performance, he explained that he'd be performing a selection of famous monologues from *Macbeth*, but would "skip over the great majority of the play due to time constraints and insufficient cast members."

As Spencer became Macbeth and spoke of killing King Duncan, and later wiping out Macduff's family line, Spencer's performance seemed to strike Wallace more than one painful blow, making him shudder in his wheelchair as if assaulted by a sort of dagger of the mind like the one seen by Macbeth. Wallace seemed physically weakened by the time Spencer delivered the final monologue.

"Tomorrow, and tomorrow, and tomorrow," Spencer said, his voice soft and sorrowful, "creeps in this petty pace from day to day, to the last syllable of recorded time, and all our yesterdays have lighted fools the way to dusty death..."

Wallace closed his eyes and bowed his head, as if the excerpts of the play had managed to stir up all his guilt.

When Spencer concluded, the spotlight went out and the audience applauded and cheered. When the spotlight returned, Spencer was all smiles, and he took a little bow. Georgette had moved to the piano bench, wearing an enormous golden-blond wig and glittering gold dress.

"Thank you so much for your kind applause, and I appreciate your indulgence in listening to me stand up here talking to myself," Spencer said. "For the grand finale of our little show, I am pleased to present the star of the Sunshine House retirement community, Ms. Georgette Chambers."

The spotlight moved to Georgette, and Spencer took the armchair she'd been using.

"Hey, y'all," Georgette said, playing a few notes on the piano. "Before we wrap things up, I'd just like to say..." She trailed off as Wallace approached, rolling out of the audience area and up next to the piano. He whispered to Georgette, who smiled and nodded, patting his shoulder. Spencer scowled at the interruption.

"Listen up, y'all," Georgette said. "It looks like we have a surprise third act. Mr. Wallace McMurtry, attorney at law, is gonna do a staged reading for us, of an original poem." She turned the microphone Stacey had set up on the piano toward him.

A few people clapped. Spencer looked ready to strangle Wallace, but he didn't move from where he sat.

"Sorry to interrupt," Wallace said to the audience. He drew on his reading glasses, took out a folded yellow page from a legal pad. He hesitated a moment then began to read, never lifting his gaze from the paper.

To my departing companion
Your need to leave is understood
I will not try to hold you here.
The road will take you now
Wherever you wish to be.
At my side these many years,
You were a constant source of strength,
From you I took
What can never be replaced
Because you had all that I lacked
All that I could not provide for myself
My gratitude and affection for you are great
As is my regret and sorrow for my betrayal.
I am and will be forever sorry.

Spencer sat with a stony face as he listened, and Wallace left the room to a smattering of applause as people realized he had finished.

"Thank you for adding a little high-brow culture, Wallace, and Spencer, too," Georgette said, playing a few notes on the piano to liven things up. "Shakespeare and poetry, my goodness, those are tough acts for a simple honky-tonk gal like me to follow. But first, I've got a special treat for y'all. My son Dexter is a big-time magician out in Las Vegas, and he drove all the way here with his very lovely new wife Terra!"

The crowd cheered as the spotlight found Dex, who I recognized from the picture in his mother's room, next to a woman with short purple hair and matching lipstick. Dex waved a hand enthusiastically. Terra nodded and smiled, looking nervous.

"Dex, why don't you do a trick or two for us tonight?" Georgette asked. "Everybody loves magic."

"I don't know," he said. "I'm actually out of practice, after that heavy run of the catering gigs this summer, and I don't have anything with me—"

"I have your old Blackstone junior magic kit upstairs," Georgette told him. To the audience, she said, "Don't y'all want to see some magic happen tonight, folks? Let's hear it for my son!"

Everyone applauded to encourage the magic act. Georgette certainly knew how to work a crowd.

"You could do some card tricks," Terra said.

"Yeah, if I had some cards—" Dex fumbled around, searching his pockets like he expected to find a forgotten deck somewhere.

"Can someone check the game cabinet?" Georgette asked.

When the deck of cards was found, Dex pulled off a few card tricks before bowing and returning to his chair. Georgette at the piano regained the spotlight.

"I'd like to dedicate this song to my son and his wife, and all of you for coming out to watch your friends and family make fools of themselves tonight," Georgette said, then wrapped up the show with a cheerful performance of "Here You Come Again" that was a definite mood-brightener after Spencer's and Wallace's dramatics.

The performers participated in a final bow, except for Taggart and Wallace, who'd each left after their performances.

For the reception, Chelsea and Pablo brought out sparkling grape juice and plates of fruit and cheese.

"Are you really moving out?" I asked Spencer at

one point.

"Yes, the rumors are true," he said. "I've decided to choose boldness over brooding. I'll start with a small move to Atlanta, where there's something of a little theater scene and a tremendous film and television industry. I'll be auditioning for the first time in years. I may only find work as a background player, but perhaps, in time, I can work my way up to faintly recognizable character actor. Perhaps those Hollywood directors will have use for a quaint Southern gentleman every now and again."

"I'm sure they will!" Stacey said. "Break a leg out there."

"I may as well roll the dice. It's not as if I have anything to lose." He noticed Wallace return to the room. "If you'll excuse me," Spencer said, then hurried to exit in another direction.

"Wow, look at you," Stacey said to Karl, who wore an old tuxedo and matching black velvet eyepatch. "That is some dapper stuff right there. Like a dangerously charming Bond villain."

"How have you been?" I asked him.

"Good. I'm still adjusting to having the room to myself, not that I would ever want to see Joe again. He wasn't a great roommate even before the dark secrets came out. But with Spencer leaving, too, it's going to be quiet on the first floor."

"Chelsea mentioned there were some new residents coming along," I said.

"Really?" He turned to Chelsea, who wasn't far away. "Is this true, Chelsea? New residents are coming?"

"No new roommates for you," she said. "But two

are moving onto the second floor next week."

"The second floor?" Karl raised an eyebrow.

"They're here tonight." Chelsea indicated a couple of ladies across the room. "I didn't have time to introduce them yet—"

"I know one of them from school," Karl said. "Andrea Miller. Ran track. Better at math than I was. I didn't know she'd moved back to town."

"Oh, good," Chelsea said. "Maybe she'd feel more at home if you talked over some shared memories."

Karl checked his bow tie in a mirror. "I'm suddenly glad Georgette talked me into wearing this old tux. If you'll excuse me…" He cruised smoothly toward his new housemates like a plane taxiing for takeoff.

"It was good to see you," Chelsea told Stacey and me. "I look forward to seeing the official talent show video."

"It'll be great," Stacey said. "Or the best I can do, at least. But the content is definitely solid."

Over at the piano, Georgette began to play again, with her daughter-in-law beside her on the piano. It was an old song I vaguely remembered hearing on the country-gold station in my dad's old car when I was a kid, "I Wouldn't Have Missed It For the World." The daughter-in-law belted out the words, drowning out Georgette's softer voice, so she must have heard the song before, too.

Arden took Pablo by the arm and made him dance with her, diverting him from his work. A visiting elderly couple joined in, too.

"Everybody's dancing!" Stacey proclaimed, then dragged Jacob toward the piano with her.

"Should we dance?" Michael asked me.

"Is this really a dancing song?"

"You can dance to any song if you try hard enough."

"Fine, but only until this one's over."

"It's almost over now."

"Perfect."

He put his arms around me, and I leaned into him, not really wanting to dance, just wanting to feel embraced and supported.

Someone drew open a curtain, letting in the dark reds and oranges of sunset through the enormous western-facing window. While we danced to a few heartfelt old songs, living while we were still alive, the light grew dimmer outside, and a gentle darkness closed in softly around us all.

FROM THE AUTHOR

I hope you enjoyed the latest haunted mystery with Ellie and Stacey! For those interested in the historical aspects of things, this story was largely inspired by the horrifying case of Janie Lou Gibbs, a woman from south Georgia who murdered her husband, sons, and grandson. It was believed there was a liver disorder running in the family until it was determined to be arsenic causing all the deaths. This happened in the 1960s and is chilling to read about.

Burdener's Hill is a fictional town, but continues my fascination with the countless small ghost towns I've seen around the countryside, where the brick and stone buildings outlived the economics behind their construction but remain like shrines in memory of the vanished people who created them. I always wonder what happened, what inspired people to settle there and why they eventually had to leave. Empty places like that always feel like they're full of unseen things.

The next book in the series delves into the history of television a little bit. It's called *The Funtime Show* and you can pre-order it now if you like. It's kind of a strange one, but I'm having fun with it and I hope you will, too.

Sign up for my newsletter at my website (www.jlbryanbooks.com) (alternate signup address: http://eepurl.com/mizJH) to hear about my new books as they come out. You'll immediately get a free ebook of short stories just for signing up.

Follow **J. L. Bryan's Books** on Facebook for more frequent updates, ghost memes, etc. @jlbryanbooks on Twitter, which I don't update as much as I should.